MALIGNANT

By

Michaelbrent Collings

Written Insomnia Press
WrittenInsomnia.com
"Stories That Keep You Up All Night"

DEDICATION

To…

The victims…

And to Laura, FTAAE.

A Warning
Introduction by Connie Kendall
PART ONE: TAINTED
CHAPTER 1 The Plan
CHAPTER 2 Students and Staff
CHAPTER 3 Students and Staff
CHAPTER 4 The Plan
CHAPTER 5 Students and Staff
CHAPTER 6 The Plan
PART TWO: WHEN I GATHERED
CHAPTER 7 Intended Response
CHAPTER 8 Intended Response
CHAPTER 9 The Plan
CHAPTER 10 Intended Response
CHAPTER 11 The Plan
CHAPTER 12 Intended Response
CHAPTER 13 Intended Response
CHAPTER 14 Intended Response
CHAPTER 15 Intended Response
CHAPTER 16 Intended Response
CHAPTER 17 The Plan
CHAPTER 18 Intended Response
CHAPTER 19 Intended Response
PART THREE: MANIACAL HORROR
CHAPTER 20 Intended Response
CHAPTER 21 The Plan
CHAPTER 22 Intended Response
CHAPTER 23 Intended Response
CHAPTER 24 Intended Response
CHAPTER 25 Intended Response
CHAPTER 26 Intended Response
CHAPTER 27 Intended Response
CHAPTER 28 Intended Response
CHAPTER 29 Intended Response
PART FOUR: IN MY OWN FLESH
CHAPTER 30 Teachable Moments
CHAPTER 31 Teachable Moments

CHAPTER 32 Intended Response
CHAPTER 33 Teachable Moments
CHAPTER 34 The Plan
CHAPTER 35 Intended Response
CHAPTER 36 Teachable Moments
CHAPTER 37 Understanding
CHAPTER 38 Understanding
CHAPTER 39 Understanding
PART FIVE: SUFFICIENCY
CHAPTER 40 Teachable Moments
CHAPTER 41 Homework
AUTHOR'S NOTE

A Warning

Michaelbrent Collings here. You know, the author of *Malignant*. The following is a book within a book – a book I've written, but under the guise/pretense of a fictional author named Connie Kendall – a local reporter and someone I think I'd enjoy meeting (so long as I stayed on her good side).

But this part isn't hers. There's nothing of Connie Kendall here, and everything of Michaelbrent Collings.

I'm not telling you my name here so you remember it (though feel free to do so), but because this is a warning, and there should be no confusion about what it is or who's giving it.

***

I once wrote a book called *Apparition*, whose subject was filicide (parents killing their children). It was the most disturbing thing I'd ever written – so much so that my dad couldn't even finish it. This was a big deal, considering who my dad is: the only academic ever awarded the Grandmaster Award by the World Horror Convention (alongside folks you may not have heard of, but of whom I predict great things: like Anne Rice, Dean Koontz, Richard Matheson, and some guy with the ridiculous name "Stephen King" who sounds like a froofy romance writer), as well as an excellent horror novelist in his own right.

Put those two things together, then ask yourself how disturbing a book would have to be to keep *him* from finishing it.

I hoped that, as I grew as an author, I'd write scarier things than *Apparition*, but doubted I'd ever write something with a more disturbing subject matter.

And then this book came along.

***

I will tell you a bit more about my reasons for taking on this story (and horrifying subject) in my Author's Note at the end, but for now, if you're easily triggered, ***please set this book aside and go find*** *something else to read.*

As for the rest of you... the brave, or perhaps the foolish... good luck. I hope to see you on the other side of "The End."

- Michaelbrent Collings

A Lesson in Blood:
An Insider's Look at the Tragedy
at Reina High School and
a World-Wide Disaster

By

Connie Kendall

Dedication:

For Karl Helmsworth,
who trusted my story would matter;
for those who died during
the Reina High School disaster;
and for those who lived to find even worse.

Introduction by Connie Kendall

When I was approached to write a book about the catastrophe at Reina High School, I resisted. It was already months into inquiries, investigations, and more than a few witch hunts, and people still seemed to be shaking their heads and shrugging, looking around for answers.

But the answers were there. They were written in the blood of teachers, staff, and students. They were in the silence of those who died quickly, in the maimed forms of those tortured to death, and in the empty spaces left by those who were just… gone.

I know from the interviews I conducted in the days and weeks following the takeover, the lockdown, and the aftermath, that more than a few people pray nightly for those poor souls who are "gone." And what do they pray for? Not that those who are gone will be found, *but that they are dead.*

I have prayed for that myself. Not much of an admission perhaps – either that someone in my line of work prays, or that the first time I did it in more than a decade was to pray for the death of children.

But, again, those who know… who *understand*… they will only have one thing to say to this admission: "Amen."

***

That brings me to an important note: A journalist is supposed to present the facts, but keep themselves out of the story. That's what many of us are told in school, and even believe early on – before idealism has faded a bit, or been covered over by dark patches of cynicism.

Some of us who still believe in that goal even believe we've done it, presenting "just the facts" and staying out of the way. Most of us, though, recognize that such a thing is impossible (even if many deny it). The reporter is present in every letter, every word, every syllable. Language is a funny thing, and different words can accurately portray "the facts," yet actually communicate vastly different things.

Given that, and given the unique part that I played in some of the story that unfolded, I hope the reader will forgive me for my insertion of myself in the story. And more than that, for the perspective and conclusions I drew during the retelling of it.

A reporter's stories will always be slanted (again, we can't help but subtly push one position or the other through our decisions of what facts to include, and where, and the word choices we make on a granular level), but in this case I'm not even trying that hard to excise that leaning.

The way the situation at RHS panned out was a strange mix of tragedy and – well, not triumph, but at least a chance to make a change. I'm still trying to work out the details in my own mind, and still trying to figure out the "goods" and "bads" of the way it all unfolded.

But some of the things were evil, and I won't try to pretend otherwise. Giving space to both sides of a story is all well and good, but at a certain point you have to just turn off the Devil's microphone, and ratings be damned.

***

In addition to my break with good reporting practice inasmuch as I participate in the story, and drive some of the events, I will also note here that the manner I've laid things out is unusual.

First, I've added a bit more flair than most true crime writers would. That is mostly because I really want you as a reader to understand the sights and sounds and smells of those early summer days. I want you to be there with us, as much as possible. If you stand outside, if you are merely a bystander, you'll never take in what I think you need to. You won't be affected, and if you aren't affected personally, can you – can any of us – ever really change?

Second, I've reported the events in a way that mirrors how it all unfolded to members of law enforcement, the media, and the viewing audience. That's the only way to have a chance at making sense of it all. It's also the only way to appreciate the genius behind its solving – or, perhaps better said, its *revealing*.

The police, both local and federal, who played their parts, did so with varied expertise. Some were great, others mediocre, and a few were downright inept. But even if every single person arrayed against those who took over RHS had been a genius, a Sherlock Holmes, an Elliot Ness... even then they wouldn't have been able to solve the case and bring things to a resolution. There *was* genius involved in the way things finally ended, but the genius wasn't theirs. It was given to them as a gift.

A very dark gift.

***

The following is taken from my own observations, from careful readings and re-readings (and re-re-readings, and re-re-*re*-readings) of news reports, court filings, police reports, and any other credible document I could find. I viewed the infamous Reina Recordings time after time, and spent hundreds of hours interviewing those who witnessed and survived the attack that played out at two speeds over that Memorial Day weekend.

Where possible I used only quotes that I could cite to first-hand sources. Occasionally I had to guess, but all of the instances I have done so are noted in the appendix, along with my reasons for believing it happened that way. I have a friend who insists that history is just fiction told in reverse, but I have endeavored to strip as much conjecture as I can, and leave only fact behind.

- C. K.

PART ONE:
TAINTED

I WAS so weary of the world
I was so sick of it
everything was tainted with myself...

- D.H. Lawrence
 "New Heaven and Earth"

CHAPTER 1
The Plan

The man took a moment to breathe in deeply, the air feeling clean in a way that it hadn't for a long time. The man didn't know if that was because of what he was about to do, or if it was, instead, a product of the idyllic surroundings.

Not many schools could manage to feel so close to nature, the way this one did. But of course, unlimited funding could purchase a great many things. All the money in the world couldn't buy a single sunrise, but – and this the man knew well – it *could* buy just about anything under that sunrise. And in the shadows, all bets were off.

So the man held the air in his lungs until it burned, until the pleasantness of the morning that he had drawn into himself had turned to something that hurt, that made his blood pulse in his ears, that seared his body from within.

That was appropriate: the joy of the breath turning to pain within him, leaving behind only struggling lungs and the foreshadowing of his own death.

It was to be a day of pain, after all. He might as well get used to it – both the pain he would feel, and the pain he would cause.

***

Though the school did appear idyllic, it was just an illusion. Closer examination revealed a place designed to be something of a fortress, a world apart from the world. If asked whether it was a fortress crafted to keep the world out, or one designed to keep things in, the man suspected no one could say.

A high brick wall enclosed the front half of the school. A thick forest blocked off the rear: technically permeable, but one had to know that forest intimately to have any assurance of going into the place and then coming back out again. There were a few rutted paths – mostly made by the deer who roamed the woods (though keeping well away from the human sounds and scents of the school outside the sheltering trees) but for most, the forest would be every bit as impassable as the wall in front.

The man knew that "most" included the school's teachers and staff, its students, and even the local police.

***

The brick wall had been designed with one way in, and one way out: a break in the wall with a (currently unmanned) guard station on the small road that passed through the gate. Other than that, visitors could wait outside. People did not enter the school uninvited.

Indeed, the school had been born with one word in mind: *exclusivity*. A place where the ins and outs could be strictly controlled. That was one of the prerequisites of power: utter control of the comings and goings of all within a person's domain.

The person in charge of entry and of release, of captivity or escape, had been the principal of the school. But the man who breathed in some of the last air he would enjoy knew that today that would change – radically and, for many, painfully.

For others, for the *lucky* ones, fatally.

***

Beyond the guard station and the gate – a lowered arm that extended from where one stretch of the wall ended to where the other began – lay the school proper. Reina High School.

The buildings were as elegant as their surroundings. Most schools – even other very rich ones – have an institutional, utilitarian feel. No matter how hard they try, they cannot quite shake the underlying knowledge that they are here for a purpose, and that purpose overrides considerations of form.

Not so Reina High. The most expensive artists and architects had been hired to ensure that visitors saw only grandeur, peace, beauty. Once past the gate, a visitor (or intruder) would see brick and ivy, rife with neo-Georgian multi-paned windows; short, covered porches; and gabled roofs. Romanesque Revival style was on parade via many round towers with conical roofs; columns and pilasters with leaf designs; and low, broad, "Roman" arches over doorways that would make those entering know they were walking Somewhere Important.

It was beautiful.

It still is, in a way. But just as other schools carry with them that underpinning of form over function, so RHS – now empty and haunted – will always carry with it the shadow of death and pain.

The property has been for sale for over a year.

To date, no one has made so much as an offer on the land. No one wants it. Perhaps no one ever will. And perhaps that is for the best.

***

Beyond the school buildings, a small soccer field and circular track lay beside a large gymnasium: the only building with the "normal" drab, functional look the man associated with most schools.

The gym was a concrete block: steel doors, the only windows mere slits almost at roof level. It had not been constructed until fifty years after the rest of the school, when the Trustees had finally decided that students could be permitted to sweat without the school's reputation suffering irreparable damage.

But even with the change in architecture, that air of exclusivity remained. No one could get in, no one could get out, save through those steel doors that made it clear the huddled masses yearning to breathe free had no place here.

***

The man arrived while fingers of morning fog still reached into the school's byways: a lovely spring day had just begun. It would be too hot later, but for now the man's black balaclava felt comfortably warm in the misty morning air.

He arrived early so that he could ready the final preparations. That was what any educator would do. And the man was an educator – one highly committed to his chosen subject matter. He had arrived early, and would stay as long as he needed to. Until his students had seen what he wanted them to see. Until they had – finally, painfully – *learned*.

The man wanted that above all else.

That was why, for this lesson, he would be called Teacher.

***

Teacher had had another name once. But that name was dead, and had been for years. "Teacher" was the only thing that he would answer to from now on, and it was the only thing that mattered on this day of instruction. This day where the world finally, he hoped, would begin to change.

Teacher stepped toward the gate. The guard station was usually manned, but not today. The digital marquee in front of the guard station – low, unassuming, and so not at all a threat to the school's overall grandeur – provided one reason for this lapse, in dignified letters that marched slowly across its face:

NO SCHOOL… MEMORIAL DAY… NO SCHOOL… MEMORIAL DAY… NO SCHOOL…

Even so, there should have been a guard for at least part of the day. Exclusivity was the watchword, secrets the result, a guard one of the necessary trappings of both.

But Teacher had ensured that none of the guards who typically staffed the place would come in. All four were home, serious food poisoning requiring them to stay close to their bathrooms at all times.

The food poisoning was no accident. Nothing about this day would be accidental. Teacher had planned for everything.

***

Teacher put a hand on the sidearm that rested comfortably on his hip. He was not as good with it as some on his team, but was more than competent in its use. Just as he was more than competent with the assault rifle slung over one shoulder.

He turned, hand still on his gun, and waved toward the nearby trees that stood tall and imposing on either side of the road that led to the guard shack and from there into the school.

Seven figures emerged from behind the trees.

Like him, they were all dressed in black, with black masks covering their heads and black guns holstered at their hips. Like him, they also carried additional weapons slung on straps over their shoulders.

Six of the people who emerged wore colored armbands: red, orange, yellow, green, blue, purple. Those colors would serve as their only names for the purposes of this mission. The colors of the rainbow – though this was no rainbow of hope, promising that the world would never again be flooded and destroyed. This rainbow promised only death, destruction, *in*struction.

All in the course and support of Teacher's lesson.

***

Red and Purple took point, fanning out with their rifles in hand, moving swiftly to either side of Teacher.

Yellow, Orange, Green, and Blue formed the points of a square, protecting and escorting the seventh person who had emerged from the treeline:

The Lady.

She was petite in figure and, like the rest of them, was dressed only in black. Like Teacher, she wore no armband, though her shorter height and feminine curves marked her clearly enough.

She wore weapons, as the rest of them did, but did not expect to need them. That was not part of the plan.

She did, however, plan to use the portable stick welder she held in one hand. Small, easily portable, but strong enough to cut through plates of steel, then weld them together in new shapes for new purposes.

Also strong enough to sear flesh, to char skin. And that, too was also part of the day's lesson plan.

***

Once The Lady and her well-armed and vicious honor guard had reached him, Teacher reached out a gloved hand and touched hers once, briefly. There was no affection in the touch – how could there be, on a day like today? – merely the silent question:

Are you ready?

Her gloved hand closed ever so slightly on his: *I'm ready.*

Teacher nodded. He gestured for the Colors to proceed.

They entered the school.

CHAPTER 2
Students and Staff

The gymnasium could hold up to four hundred people on the bleachers that, during home games, telescoped out from the walls. Now, however, they were pushed back, maximizing space on the hardwood floor. In the center of the space: the basketball court.

The court was constructed of maple hardwood, but where most courts had outlines painted to show the limits of the court, the area inside the Key, the Central Round, the three-point line, and the rest of the demarcations necessary to play, Reina High School had opted instead to show all these with flooring stained to different colors. The cost was enormous; not just to acquire the materials and to stain them to exactly the right shades, but to lay them in at the gentle curves and broken lines that were anathema to the straight, parallel lines of typical wood flooring.

No one at Reina High School cared much about the cost. One student's tuition for half the year would cover ten floors like that.

***

That kind of ostentatious spending had been a bit overwhelming when Jonas Chambers first started working at RHS. Based on the salary they offered, he knew they were working with serious cash, but even the extra zero on his check hadn't fully prepared him for the magnitude of wealth in plain view everywhere he looked.

Wealth doesn't buy happiness, though, does it?

Jonas could easily see the answer to that question in the forms of the students who stood nearby him in the gym. The troublemakers, the problems even among the generally problematical students at RHS. These were the kids who were here just about every non-school day, working off a demerit in exchange for detention time spent cleaning the grounds.

Money or not, none of these kids looked happy.

***

To Jonas' right, twelve seniors leaned against the retracted bleachers. Leather clothes (including more than a few dog collars), nose rings, harsh hair styles, and a surfeit of attitude had earned these kids the nickname "the Misfits."

To Jonas' left – standing as conspicuously far from the Misfits as possible – stood the cheerleaders. It wasn't the entire cheer team, but if you said "the cheerleaders" to anyone in the school, they would immediately know who you were talking about – the clique of a dozen girls who dressed in tight stretch pants and tighter shirts every day of the week, who walked with arrogant swaggers designed to arrest attention, and who knew that their physical appearance would *keep* that attention.

The cheerleaders carried around a raw sexuality Jonas found unnerving, but not at all attractive for a variety of reasons. The young women fancied themselves as polar opposites to the Misfits, but both groups were nearly the same at their cores: kids projecting aggressive, tough shells to protect them from the pain of lives largely broken.

***

Everyone at RHS had parents so far beyond "rich and powerful" that they were almost in a class by themselves. And people like that, Jonas had discovered, were often so wealthy and influential that no one would ever notice the child when the parent was in the room. Not even the parent him- or herself.

Jonas knew that kids needed to shine. And if you refused to let them shine, they grew dim and dark. Some turned into wraiths, shadows trailing the people whom everyone around treated as the only *real* people. Others turned to stormy skies, with jagged lightning dancing always in the clouds, ready to strike out and destroy anything they touched.

The kids at RHS were all broken, one of those ways or the other. The cheerleaders and the Misfits had simply been broken into those cloudy, fire-filled skies. They were only seen when they were hurting, or hurting others.

Still, knowing that didn't mean Jonas was immune from the kids making his life a living hell. And from the fragments of conversation he could hear, he knew that was just the kind of day he was heading into.

"… the hell are we doing?"

"… totally unfair of them to just *text* and we have to *jump*…"

"… Memorial Day means we're off limits from after school on Thursday all the way until Tuesday morning…"

"… gonna make someone pay…"

Jonas shivered at how often that last sentiment was repeated.

So why be here at all?

***

It was true that he didn't have to be here. He had come to his office to see to some work that had to be done, but then he could have simply walked away. Could have gone home instead of heading over to the gym to see if he could help with detention. None of the other teachers would have done that, he knew, just as he knew that none of the teachers he came to help would care, and none of the students would change because of the gesture.

Now, hearing the students plotting revenge in the million different ways they could, he thought about leaving.

Just go already.

Go before you get caught up in today's nonsense.

He knew his inner voice was giving good advice. But he also knew he wouldn't listen, just as he knew why: he didn't want these sad, broken kids to be alone with the men assigned to punish them today. As bad as the kids were, the teachers – these teachers, especially – could be far worse.

***

Fertetti, Slattery, Mulcahey. They had more in common than the hard "e" sound at the ends of their names. First (and most easily seen), all three of the men looked more like prison wardens than teachers.

That, Jonas supposed, wasn't necessarily inappropriate. It was no secret that RHS was essentially a continuation school for ultra-rich delinquents. A "next stop jail" kind of place.

Still, these guys looked and acted like they thought this was *already* jail. Not just a juvenile detention center, either: they acted like this was Alcatraz. Like the kids were Capone, entering as self-styled kings and needing to be shown that they were nothing but scum fit to be wiped off the wardens' feet.

Coach Fertetti was senior in age, time at RHS, and ability to be hateful. In his fifties, the gym teacher had hair so dark that Jonas knew it had to be the kind of black that came in a hair-coloring box, probably one featuring an older man with a far-too-young-to-believe woman draped across him like a cheap coat.

Fertetti added to the disconcerting look of that perfect black hair by slicking it back every day with some compound that rendered his 'do into a solid chunk of acrylic. It made him look like a mob boss, even wearing the khakis he sported every day of the week.

Now, Fertetti strode forward, taking a position roughly equidistant from both the Misfits and the cheerleaders, and shouted, "Shut the *hell UP!*" Silence slammed down hard as Fertetti glowered at each group in turn. Jonas was always kind of surprised when that look didn't evince either tears or heart attacks.

Still, Fertetti *did* manage to quiet the kids.

Heaven knows that's something I've never managed.

But, if that was the cost of retaining his soul, Jonas figured he'd take a bit of chaos in his classes and be happy at the exchange.

***

Fertetti wheeled back and forth a few more times, then shouted, "You think we wanna be here with you? We're called, so we come. End of story, and end of complaining, you all hear?"

Fertetti spun on his heel. For a moment Jonas was worried he was going to get yelled at next – and was pretty sure that, unlike the kids, he *would* have a heart attack.

But Fertetti kept pivoting until he came face to face with Mulcahey. Isaiah Mulcahey, the school's geometry and trigonometry teacher, had the face of a thirty-year-old weasel who was training to be a used-car salesman. The first time Jonas met him, the guy had grinned in a way that made him check his wallet the second the math teacher's back was turned. Weak chin, shifty eyes, and a body that could have doubled as a spaghetti noodle.

But Jonas knew Fertetti liked the guy – mostly because Mulcahey was a born beta, willing to follow any instruction Fertetti might utter.

"Where are Daxton and Paige?" Fertetti asked Mulcahey in a low, almost dangerous tone. Mulcahey shrugged, managing somehow to make even the confused gesture look vaguely sycophantic.

"Probably 'together,'" said the third member of the team left in charge of the students. Slattery was in his forties, and everything about him screamed "disappointment." Jonas got the feeling that, like the students, Slattery hid the hurt of his life behind a rough countenance and sexual innuendo calculated to put the listener off-balance.

Sure enough, when he said, "together," he pumped his hips forward and back a few times.

At any other school, Jonas would have expected that kind of gesture – especially in plain view of the students – to draw a reprimand. But Fertetti just sighed.

"Find 'em," he said to Slattery. Turning to Jonas, he added, "You look, too. It'll give you a chance to get to know the school a little better." Then, with a wag of his eyebrows, he added, "And with Daxton and Paige involved, you might even see something worth writing to Hustler about."

Jonas felt like throwing up. He didn't think Fertetti was joking – either about the possibility of discovering two students having sex, or about the enjoyment the gym teacher would take in the discovery.

He turned away, trying to think of where he would start looking, as Slattery headed toward the doors that led outside.

As he began walking, he saw Mulcahey look around. The man's weasel expression shifted to one of concern. "These kids aren't happy about being here."

Fertetti let out an angry chortle. "Get in line. Bad enough we have to babysit these little assholes on a day we all count on for barbecue and beer, you'd at least think they'd call us in personally instead of having some computer voice do it for them."

"Progress," said Mulcahey. "Computers are taking over the world."

Fertetti sighed. Eyeing the still-silent students, he said, "At least the scenery is nice."

Jonas couldn't help it this time: he gagged.

CHAPTER 3
Students and Staff

"Do it, man. Do it!"

Daxton Leigh glared at the guy who'd spoken. Unlike Daxton, Zane was…

A moron.

That was about right. Daxton was the king of Reina. His father was the most powerful of men – literally one of the most powerful in the United States, and by default therefore, one of the most powerful in the world.

Zane Kennedy, on the other hand… the hulking moron's daddy was rich, sure – you didn't get to be at the hellhole known as Reina High to the world, and Queen Bitchschool to the kids inside, without having serious flow. Beyond that, though, Zane had little in the way of redeeming qualities: just a hulk with enough muscle to fight to the top levels of the social circles of Reina High, but not enough brain to stay there on his own.

At least the eighteen-year-old – two-hundred-fifty pounds of solid muscle – was smart enough to know that Daxton was the guy in charge.

Which, frankly, is good enough for me.

***

Another voice piped up: "C'mon, man."

Daxton shifted his gaze to Konstantin Tarov, the third guy in the Holy Trinity of Queen Bitchschool. Konstantin was slim, with hair so thick it was almost unreal. Bright red, too, which Daxton viewed as a tragedy. Red hair *could* be nice – but Konstantin Tarov was the unfortunate owner of hair that Daxton could only have described as Neon Carrot.

Unlike with Zane, Daxton flashed Konstantin a smile. Konstantin was smarter than the muscle-bound Zane – *much* smarter. Which didn't make him as smart as Daxton, but then… few people were.

Still, Konstantin was smart enough to be a threat should he decide to do so. That made Daxton nervous. The fact that no one knew what Konstantin's father or mother did for a living also made Daxton nervous – impossible to know if they would be afraid of Daxton's father. They *probably* were, but there was always the chance that they'd belong to that rarified strain of people who just didn't give a fart in the wind about Daxton's dad.

So Daxton kept Konstantin in a good mood. He humored the guy. Zane: dumb enough to be a friend. Konstantin: a potential enemy. And everyone knew the saying about how close to keep friends, and how close to keep enemies.

So when Konstantin said, "C'mon, man," Daxton allowed that to be the thing that put him over the top. To do the thing they'd come here to do.

He unbuckled his belt.

***

For a moment, Daxton thought his belt would stick. And at this point in the plans, any and every hitch would be an embarrassment. But just at the point where he was worried he'd really have to work to get the thing untangled from his beltloops, it slid free.

He dropped it on the ground. Unzipped his pants enough for them to fall a few inches – just enough.

He pulled out the waistband of his underwear. The biggest studs in porn either wore Speedo-style briefs or nothing at all, and Daxton followed their lead. Those guys would never amount to much in the grand scheme of things, but there was no denying their expertise in the sex department, and he'd happily learn from the best. So Daxton often went commando. But not today. Because the two other members of the Trinity would be there.

He took his phone –

(*The latest and greatest model, with more megapixels than there are stars in the sky, thank you Daddy.*)

– made sure the flash was turned on, aimed it toward the family jewels, and clicked the shutter button.

He handed the phone to Zane, knowing the big idiot would go next without hesitation. Why? Because Daxton had done something, and Zane "As Stupid as I am Strong" Kennedy would do anything Daxton did.

Zane was wearing basketball shorts. Unlike Zane's tight underwear, this wasn't in prep for the day: Zane *always* wore basketball shorts. Except in the dorms, when he walked around in boxers. Basically the same thing.

Zane took a junk-shot of his own, then passed the phone to Konstantin.

Unlike Zane, Konstantin hesitated a fraction of an instant. But, looking quickly at the other two, he seemed to realize that if he backed out now, he'd be the only chicken among a den of foxes.

Which is just why I had you go last, numb-nuts, thought Daxton.

Konstantin undid the drawstring of his sweats. Aimed the phone down. Unlike the other two, he couldn't resist making a comment. "Do you have a wider lens?"

"Ugh," Daxton said. But he laughed.

The disgust was real. The mirth was not.

Both worked together to get the desired effect. Konstantin took his own d-pic, then handed the phone back.

Daxton appended the three pictures to a text – noting with satisfaction that his Kielbasa was much longer than Konstantin's stubby little Vienna Sausage.

Zane's? The dude had an entire horse leg hiding inside those basketball shorts. Which was no real shame to anyone else – the guy was a Goliath, so the simple proportions nature usually demanded would render him a penile deity.

"Send it," whispered Konstantin.

Daxton glared at him, showing Konstantin he didn't need to be told what to do – that wasn't the order of things around here. Konstantin smiled evenly back at him.

Some day I'm going to yank that smile off your face and shove it up your ass. See how you like the feel of it.

But not today. Today, Daxton would bind these two a bit tighter to him, and that was all. So he shifted his glare to a grin and clicked send.

***

Paige Delroy sat in a stall in the girls' bathroom in the gym, thinking about what she was doing, worrying more than a little.

She wasn't worried about Daxton, of course. But the other two were more than a little bit nerve-wracking. It wasn't that Paige was ashamed of her *body*. No way. She knew that, between the cheer outfit she wore (modified by Mom's tailor so the hem was inches higher than the other girls') and her generous boobs (also "modified," this time by Mom's plastic surgeon from Cs to generous Ds), she was something that every male in the school could only gaze upon with wonder.

Daxton had gazed on a lot more than most. And touched quite a bit of it.

But Zane? Like she'd *ever* let a big dumb donkey like that touch her. Let alone Konstantin, that greasy little cockroach.

So she was still deciding what to do, even though she'd promised Daxton that she'd go along with it. He'd hinted that if she didn't, one of the other girls would. And had straight-up threatened to show one of the other pictures in his personal collection to *everyone* if she failed to go along.

She didn't know why she was still with the guy.

"Because he's cold and calculating. He reminds you of your father, and you never had his love, so you'll do anything for the next-best thing."

That was what every shrink she'd ever been forced to endure had said. Shrinks were all idiots. She didn't know why Mom even kept trying.

The phone beeped.

The words came up first:

DAXTON: *Your turn.*

Then another beep:

DAXTON: *It's a 3-4-1 deal!*

And then a third:

DAXTON: *CUM onnnnn. You owe us now.*

She frowned.

"Easy, Dax. I'm thinking."

She knew he wouldn't hear it. But she did want to think. About Zane and his big, dumb grin. About Konstantin and his beady little eyes.

About Daxton and the other pictures he had.

Plus, he's the Big Man on Campus. And if he went with one of those other bitches on the cheer team? Disaster.

***

Outside the gym, Daxton and the others leaned closer, closer. Daxton could feel Zane's breath on his cheek. Dude smelled like fish sticks.

Truth be told, Daxton couldn't care less about the picture they were waiting for. Sure, staring at Thing One and Thing Two (his own personal pet name for her boobs, which she hated but put up with) was always fun. But he could do that any time he wanted.

But this was just one more moment that would cement Daxton's power over the other two. And no matter their value today, someday they were destined for greatness, if only because of their parents' standing.

Daxton wanted to be like his dad someday. Not as soft as his dad – old asshole was kind of a pussy, all things considered – but equal in power. No, greater. Daxton's dad could change millions of lives with a word, and that was fine and dandy… but Daxton wanted to crook his finger, and see the *world* kneel before him.

And he could tell that people like Zane and Konstantin would be useful in years to come. He wanted the shared shame of their taking pictures of their junk, and knowing that Daxton had seen it all. He wanted the shared feeling that Daxton was the guy who could get them things – in this case, a look at the most highly-desired sweater stuffers at Queenbitch High.

Daxton knew he already had more than enough dirt on Zane and Konstantin to keep any normal person permanently under his control. But these weren't normal people, were they? Zane and Konstantin were wealthy, they were powerful – or their parents were. So Daxton kept urging them to see more, say more, *do more*. When he could, he photographed or recorded it. Proof of drugs, of cars stolen for joyrides, then trashed for the hell of it. Of beat-downs given in the night, of old people they ran up to and punched and then ran from without slowing down.

Of that other thing – the biggest thing, the worst thing. The *best* thing.

For a moment, Daxton heard the screams again. He heard Zane's bellowing laughter, heard Konstantin's wheezing, the guy's weak body straining to the limit. Daxton heard himself making noises he'd never imagined as he crushed a soul beneath him.

It was terrible, frightening.

It was beautiful, wonderful.

And it was, ultimately, all in service of the same thing he was doing now: cementing his power over the people who would one day rule the world.

***

Paige's phone beeped again as the three images came through. Konstantin had about exactly the un-generous proportions she expected. That would be good for a laugh in the girls' dorm common room tonight.

Zane, though?

Might have to spend some alone time with him. Daxton can't know, but... wow.

She was tugging at the top of her outfit when her phone beeped again.

If it's Daxton again, I might just tell him to screw himself and deal's off.

(*No, you won't.*)

She sighed. Looked at the phone. It wasn't a text notification after all, but a beep to notify her of the words that flashed in bold at the top of her display: "NO SERVICE."

***

Daxton's phone beeped.

"This is it, this is *it*," said Konstantin. Dude sounded like he was close to needing new pants.

"Dude, chill," said Daxton. "It wasn't my text tone."

He swiped out of messages to look at his home screen.

He groaned as he showed the others what had just come through. No boobs. In fact, it was the one thing guaranteed to stop any and all boobage in the enlightened Internet Age: "NO SERVICE" blinking at the top of his homescreen.

"I hate this place," he said.

***

Paige, one hand still on her tube top, stared open-mouthed at the phone. "Are you kidding me?" she demanded. She swiped back to her messages. Typed. No joy.

"Are *you* kidding me?"

Paige screamed in fright, realizing as she did that the stall door had somehow swung open and she was staring at the one teacher in the school that she didn't fear. Which didn't make him less imposing. Because unlike every other man around, Paige had yet to be able to either visibly shock or overtly hornify Jonas Chambers.

He might, she thought, be gay. Gay dudes were the only ones who were able to resist her charms. And even if they didn't want to sleep with her, they still wanted to *be* her, and that was almost as good. She owned their asses either way.

But Jonas? Gay or not, she was starting to worry that he was a Truly Good Person. Both Mom and Dad had warned her against his type: they were the hardest to manipulate, the hardest to scare, and were therefore the biggest pains in the ass.

Still – "What the *hell* are you doing?" she shrieked, one hand covering her boobs as though she'd already pulled her shirt down.

Mr. Chambers grimaced. "I called three times before coming in. And again when I saw your feet under the stall. What was I doing? Worrying, to be totally honest."

Paige realized she was still holding her phone. Mr. Chambers couldn't know what she had been doing – and about to do – could he?

But he did. She saw it in his eyes. Saw something no one else in the school would dare. He was judging her. Worse, she saw *pity* in his eyes. As though an impotent turd burglar like Mr. Chambers could ever hope to have enough to be worthy of pitying someone like her.

Then why does the look in his eyes hurt so much?

Mr. Chambers held out his hand, and Paige handed over the phone without thinking. Again, she was surprised that he managed to control her this way. Any other teacher – even Principal Gersham – asked for her phone, she'd put up a fuss.

Mr. Chambers asked and she just handed it over. Actually, he hadn't even bothered asking. Just held out his hand and she complied.

I'll make him pay. I'll make him –

Oh, HELL!

She realized – too late – that she'd handed over her phone so quickly that it was still unlocked, and the messages still on the screen.

Mr. Chambers looked down at the phone. "Is this really what you want for yourself, Paige?"

Again: pity.

How dare you.

"What?" she bit back. "Pervy teachers sneaking looks at me on the toilet?" When that failed to put him on the defensive, she took the next tack: if she couldn't intimidate or turn him on, she'd try to embarrass him. That was just one more way to control a person – especially a man. So she put on her best porn star grin and inhaled deeply, leaning forward as she did. In her best baby-girl voice, she said, "Maybe that *is* what I want."

Mr. Chambers looked quickly away, his cheeks reddening. He didn't look turned on, but that was fine. She'd gotten what she wanted: to know she could pull his puppet strings and make him dance.

***

Jonas led Paige back into the gym. As he did so, he saw that Slattery had found Daxton, Zane, and Konstantin – likely the subjects of the three pictures he'd glimpsed on Paige's phone.

Not for the first time – and certainly not for the last – he wondered how people could do that kind of thing. He knew – intellectually at least – the lust for fame that drove so many of the kids, that passion to be seen as important in a world where importance was measured by clicks, views, and likes. But he had never really felt that desire himself. And he had certainly never understood why a guy would post pictures of his genitals and send them to a girl.

He did, sadly, understand why a lot of girls did it: it was simple blackmail. They'd email their boyfriend a picture of themselves in shorts and a tank top. The boy would wheedle his girlfriend into sending a picture of herself in a bikini, and then lingerie, then on to topless. If she refused, well, he had a treasure trove of images he could threaten to post on social media.

Pressure, cajole. Then blackmail.

The kids in this school had access to the entire world, and most of them managed only to think as far as the screens of their phones or tablets or computers – usually, in a place like this, several of each.

Sometimes that saddened him. Sometimes it sickened him. Usually it was both.

As he led Paige to Mr. Fertetti, who waited with arms crossed as though he was the king of the world's smallest kingdom, Jonas heard the cheerleaders whispering (intentionally) loud enough to be heard.

"Why's she wearing her uniform?" one asked, side-eyeing Paige.

"Just advertising what's for sale," said another girl.

Neither apparently noticed the irony of calling out Paige for that kind of thing while wearing stretch pants so tight that anyone could see exactly what they looked like in the nude, or their own barely-there shirts.

Jonas didn't judge the kids. Or tried not to. They operated in a tough world. Not just as kids of uber-wealthy parents, though that had to add even more layers of difficulty to their lives, but simply as teens. Jonas had been in that boat until only a few years ago, and knew that they were functioning under pressures their parents had never faced and could never understand. So he felt for them.

But occasionally, he also wanted to slap them. Less for what they were doing than for the shortsightedness of their attitudes.

***

Danila Tarov – one of the cheerleaders whose bright red mop marked her unmistakably as Konstantin's twin sister – shouted out, "Ooh, *busted!* Dad's gonna flip out when he gets back, K!"

Konstantin flipped her the bird. "Dad won't give a shit and you know –"

"Shut up, both of you!" shouted Fertetti.

Jonas and Paige reached Fertetti right as Slattery did, Daxton & Co. in tow. Slattery handed over a phone that Jonas knew was Daxton's – he'd confiscated it enough to recognize it immediately.

Fertetti glanced at the phone. Like Jonas, Slattery must have caught Daxton, Zane, and Konstantin in the act of texting and tapped the phone every few seconds to keep it from locking.

The head gym teacher glanced at the screen. "Anything good to see?" Fertetti asked.

Slattery grinned at the boys. "Not unless you like

miniatures."

Fertetti held out his hand to Jonas. Jonas hesitated. He had only been here a little while, but he already didn't like or trust his coworkers. He decided to click the button to put the phone to sleep – and lock it – before handing it over, but Fertetti seemed to sense Jonas' decision. The gym teacher's hand darted out with shocking speed, grabbing the phone out of the younger man's hand.

Fertetti stared at the messages, scrolling back a bit. Then, with a sigh, he looked at Jonas and said, "You could at least have waited until the good part."

Jonas was shocked. Not just because this was the kind of thing no adult man should ever say to a girl so much younger, but because Fertetti was a *teacher*. And the lack of response on the part of either Paige or the trio of boys Slattery had dragged in showed that this wasn't the first time they had heard something like this.

Jonas wondered for a moment whether he should quit. Just walk away right now and leave the weird vibe and terrible teachers of Reina High School behind without looking back.

And then who'd watch out for the kids?

That argument trumped everything.

He'd stay. But he'd also do his best to get Fertetti, Slattery, and Mulcahey fired.

Hopefully their attitudes didn't come as trickle-downs from the principal or vice-principal. Jonas didn't know what he'd do in that case. Probably get fired.

"Okay, people, get in line against the wall!" Fertetti blared. It was a standard command: line the kids up so that order could be imposed. Then the work of a detention, harder still since it took place during the three-day Memorial Day weekend.

Standard move. Seen it a thousand times.

So why does it look less like a beginning move for a teacher in charge of difficult students, and more like someone lining people up to be shot?

**

Two secretaries worked in the front office. Of the two, Janine Welner had been working here far longer, and was far tougher than the other. Which was why she got extra money in her account periodically, and Holden Wright never did.

The younger secretary, she knew, was not the right kind of guy for the work here. Sooner or later he'd probably be shown the door. Holden – and that new teacher, Jonas – were just too goody-goody to ever feel at home at RHS.

For the most part, Janine liked working at RHS. Unlike Holden and Jonas, she possessed the right combination of intelligence, discretion, and intestinal fortitude to do what had to be done here.

Though on days like this, she questioned whether leaving wouldn't be a better idea.

Her computer beeped. Another error message. No internet, and the school's Ethernet had been acting screwy for days. Which meant half the paperwork she'd been called in to see to couldn't be done, which meant her three-day weekend was likely going to end up short a day.

She hit a few keys in frustration. "I thought when they said the new system would be 'automated,' they meant it would take care of itself, not that it would auto-call us every two weeks to come in and fix something."

Beside her, the vice-principal, Thaddeus "Don't Call Me Thad" Ulric was also trying to carve his way into the school's network. And, she was satisfied to see, having as little luck as she was. She didn't want to stay here all day, but the idea of having Thaddeus Ulric figure out what was going on before she did was wholly unacceptable.

Ulric sighed. "Reina High: where your idiot children get the best money can buy, as long as they don't want to use a computer."

Glancing at a closed door nearby, he said in a low tone, "At least this time His Highness got called in, too."

Holden snorted at that. Maybe he wasn't wholly without merit after all. At least he knew what a jackass the principal was.

To Vice-Principal Ulric, Janine said, "Think Principal Gersham will finally change service after seeing this mess himself?"

Ulric snorted – much harder and louder than Holden had done.

Holden, who had been sifting through the new system manual printouts, trying to find something useful, suddenly stiffened. "Did you guys see that?" he asked.

"We're a little busy for Eye Spy, Holden," said Janine.

"Sorry. But –"

"What did you see?" said Ulric. The vice-principal didn't bother looking up.

Janine watched as Holden struggled to figure out what it had been. "Looked like someone was in the hall for a second."

Ulric shook his head. "Outer doors are locked. And what kind of nutcase would be here on a day off unless they had to?"

"Mr. Chambers would," said Holden without hesitation.

Vice-Principal Ulric massaged his temples as though a migraine was coming on. "It was a rhetorical question, Holden."

"Right, sir. Sorry."

Janine sighed at the *sir*.

Holden's definitely not the right kind of person for RHS. He's not going to last long here.

Then the door opened, and everything went to hell.

CHAPTER 4
The Plan

Teacher strode into the office, a silenced pistol in his hand, extended so that, hopefully, he would get a maximum of attention and a minimum of fuss in the next few moments.

Vice-Principal Thaddeus Ulric – whose name and face Teacher had memorized, as he had memorized the names and faces of every person who worked at or attended Reina High School – didn't seem to notice the gun. Just the person walking in. "Who are you?" he asked, rising a bit from his chair. "What –"

Pht.

Teacher shot him, the high-tech suppressor muffling most of the noise. It wasn't time to make a racket. Yet.

Ulric's eyes rolled back as though he was trying to see the neat hole in his forehead from the inside. Then the vice-principal slid forward onto the desk in front of the secretaries' station, exposing the gaping exit wound that had pulped the back of his head.

Janine Welner screamed. The scream brought out the bigger game.

The door with "PRINCIPAL GERSHAM" written across it in elegant gold script yanked open and the head of Reina High School strode out. Even on a non-school day, the stocky man wore a suit that cost more than most families made in a month.

Disgusting, thought Teacher.

The principal was usually the type of man who exuded power. Not in the quiet, assured way of people who had the competence and self-assurance to persuade others to follow him, though. The man was a bully. And worse.

Principal Gersham's eyes widened and his face paled as he saw what Janine was still screaming about. "What are you doing?" he asked in a hoarse voice.

Teacher smiled behind the balaclava. There was no humor in the smile. "Physician, ask thyself," he said. Then he pivoted.

"No, please," whispered Janine.

Pht.

Unlike the ex-vice-principal, the secretary didn't flop forward. Her head snapped back as the bullet entered her right eye and then turned the back of her head into a crater.

The chair she sat on, like everything at Reina High School, was expensive and built to last. So it didn't tip when her body weight was flung backward. It creaked, but stayed upright. Her head lolled backward, blood and brains streaming onto the floor behind the chair, her hands hanging limp over its arms.

***

Teacher pivoted. While he had been killing Thaddeus Ulric and Janine Welner, the remaining secretary had surreptitiously – he thought – taken the desk phone off the hook. He had punched in a "9" and a "1" when Teacher said, "I don't want to kill you, Mr. Wright, but I will."

Holden Wright, who now comprised the entire remaining office staff of Reina High School, froze. He slowly put the phone back on the hook. "How do you know my name?" he asked quietly.

Teacher was unsurprised at the man's calm reaction. Holden Wright, unlike the recently-departed man and woman whose brains now decorated various parts of the front office, was a good person. One of whom Teacher approved.

And, Teacher had found, especially in recent years, good people were less likely to react with panic than the average human.

Teacher flicked his gun upward, motioning for Holden to stand. As he did, the Colors entered. Teacher motioned for Green to bind Holden's wrists behind him. Green had been briefed ahead of time and, like Teacher and The Lady, knew the names and faces of every person at RHS. He knew who Holden Wright was, and how to treat him.

Because of that, Green moved carefully, gently, as he bound the secretary's wrists.

As Green did so, Teacher said, "I'm truly sorry about this, Holden."

Still moving with a care and concern that belied the carnage of the front office, Green ushered Holden Wright out as Teacher returned his attention to Principal Gersham.

The man had wet his pants. That would have been a hell of a cleaning bill under normal circumstances.

But Teacher knew the circumstances here were anything but normal. And, as a result, he knew that the principal was unlikely to worry about having to clean his pants ever again.

***

Teacher watched as Gersham looked from the body of his vice-principal to that of the secretary. Teacher knew that this was a man who dealt with powerful, important people. He also knew that he fancied himself as powerful and important as well.

To some extent, that was true. The man had great power, but had shirked the responsibilities that came with it.

That was why Teacher was here.

Teacher waited as Gersham stared at one body, then another. He had time. And he liked seeing the principal's terror grow.

He knew that Principal Gersham was trying to figure out what had happened, what he could do, and how to get out of it. He was also trying to avoid looking at Teacher. Eventually, though, he had to. The other man obviously knew that the man in black held his life in his hands, and could cut that thread at any moment.

Teacher chuckled at the principal's expression. Gersham blanched, as though worried the sound itself might kill him. Teacher had been planning to make Gersham speak first, to ask what was going on and no doubt plead for his worthless life.

But in that moment, Teacher realized that he had no desire to hear the man's voice. Killing Janine Welner and Thaddeus Ulric was one thing. Listening to Principal Gersham?

That was too much to handle right now.

"Wondering why you aren't dead?" said Teacher. "Wonder no more: it's because you're my attention-getter." He motioned at Blue, who shoved the principal toward the office's exit

Like Green, who had ushered Holden out, Blue had been briefed on how to behave toward his captive. Unlike Green, who had been instructed to treat Holden with care and as much gentleness as possible, Blue had been instructed to move the principal out with as much force as he felt like dealing.

The principal turned halfway toward Teacher. Blue cut that off by slapping the principal violently in the face. The strike whipped Gersham's head around and spattered flecks of blood across the nearest wall while a pair of expensively capped teeth bounced under a bookshelf.

Gersham got the message. His shoulders drooped and, meek as a lamb, he left the office.

Teacher smiled behind his balaclava. He fingered the sheath at his side. It held a very long knife that had been carefully prepared to do a very particular job.

"My attention-getter," he said to himself.

**

A few minutes later, Teacher had exited the office and entered the science building with the Colors who were not otherwise occupied. They would have to clear the building, which shouldn't take long. There were several people inside to be dealt with – some carefully, others harshly.

Then it was on to the *real* fun and games.

CHAPTER 5
Students and Staff

Jonas passed out trash bags to Daxton, Konstantin, and Zane. They took them, though the looks in their eyes promised that he would pay for being the one to make them hold something they'd probably rarely had to encounter in their lives.

The Misfits took the bags with a bit less attitude. Like everyone else at the school, they were over-privileged and under-disciplined, but at least they weren't likely to murder people in their sleep.

Jonas wouldn't be able to sleep a wink if he knew Daxton or his cronies were near.

He headed toward the gym's exit, the students in tow.

At least it's a nice day out.

***

Winona Jackson could actually *hear* her teeth grinding. She whacked the computer tower. Usually she hated when people did that, and if she saw any other member of the Computer GurlZ doing such a thing she would almost always give them a talking-to. "Think hitting a machine will make it think faster? How about I punch you in the head while asking you to do complex math! Think that would work?"

But today, none of the other members of the RHS computer club were in the computer science room. Just Win and Beatriz. And Beatriz didn't count – she was experiencing the same thing Win was, which was total lack of functionality on the computers, and was nearly as frustrated.

"Come in here on a non-school day to finish the coding assignment…" Win growled, slamming her palm down on the tower again. "What the hell's wrong with you?" she demanded of the equipment.

Beatriz slid forward and put a hand on Win's. "Easy, Winona."

Win's eyebrows bunched. "I told you," she said to her friend. "Call me *Win*."

Beatriz grinned. She had amazingly bad teeth. She wore braces, but even they seemed to have met their match. That was, though, part of what Win liked about her. Like Win, Beatriz hadn't been born wealthy. Like Win, she had acne and hair that ricocheted between "unruly" and "unkempt."

Also like Win, Beatriz had ended up at Reina by being smarter than her teachers in other schools and letting them know it so vocally that she was expelled from one place after another.

That, plus their matching Computer GurlZ t-shirts, made them sisters. The rest of the students looked down on them as freaks and low-life, springing from the loins of parents who had actually *earned* their wealth, rather than being born into some dynasty.

"Winona," said Beatriz, her grin widening as she said the magic word. "I think –"

"It's. *Win*."

Beatriz's grin just got that much bigger. She was picking at her best friend, and as much as Win pretended to mind, it was just another part of their relationship. Hassling each other was as natural as anything, and neither took it seriously.

Mostly.

"Dude," said Beatriz. "Being an online player won't make you any cooler. Even when it's just you and me. So drop the 'Win' thing already."

"It's my handle. Deal with it."

"Because you won *one* online tournament. And beating a bunch of kids at MarioKart –"

"It was Smash Bros., dude!" Win shouted.

"Whatever, Win*ona*," Beatriz said. "Again, being an online player isn't much to crow about."

"But being an online god is," Win retorted. She smacked the tower again.

"Which means you're not a god now, technically, because you can't even get online," said Beatriz. She mimed hitting a tennis ball. "Game, set, match."

Again, Win gritted her teeth. But it was for show. She was smiling inside. She hadn't had friends in a long time, but with the Computer GurlZ – especially Beatriz – she felt more at home than anywhere else.

Win sighed theatrically. "We're gonna have to go talk to Aldritch."

"Suck," said Beatriz.

"The big one," agreed Win.

Beatriz was already standing. Turning.

Screaming.

Win jerked around, following her friend's gaze. She screamed, too.

A man was standing in the doorway. At least, Win was pretty sure it was a man. Hard to be certain when the person wore an all black outfit, covered in lumpy, bulging pockets that masked the person's body shape, with the only really distinguishing feature a red band on the arm. Harder still when the person wore a ski mask that made it impossible to tell anything about their face.

Hardest of all when that person was pointing what looked like an automatic weapon at them.

***

Fertetti hated everything about his world, down to and including his own name. "Fertetti" was fine, he guessed, but the first name his parents had given him always made him feel like a pussy.

Who named their son *Valentine*?

He wanted to change it, but every time he made a noise like that was a possibility, his mother gave him one of her passive-aggressive sighs and then shared some memory about her nightmare of an episiotomy. "I thought they'd have to cut me open from my privates to my neck, your head was so big."

That, he figured, was just about the only good thing about being here today: his mother wasn't in detention. She was in a rest home – a good one, thanks to the extra money he'd pulled in the last couple years – which was similar in some respects. But at least she was far away.

Actually, there is one more good thing about today.

He faced the cheerleaders in their tight pants and tube tops, and tried not to check them out too openly. It wasn't like the principal was apt to scold him if one of the girls complained, but it *was* a hassle if they got up in his face about it.

He rolled his eyes as he looked at the girls – they'd probably interpret it as exasperation, but it allowed him to sweep across all those young bodies with ease – as he said, "What does Ms. Kertz usually have you do?"

Kertz was the cheer coach, the person who should have been here given the percentage of her team that had been sentenced to prison over the long weekend. But for whatever reason, the gods behind the school's shitty auto-dial system had decided Fertetti should come in instead.

Instead of answering him truthfully, the team just mouthed off. Several of them mimed oral sex, a few shouted out: "She makes us smoke pot!" "She has us do Daxton!"

Paige, ever needing to maintain her title as High Queen of the Bitchlets, glared at the girl who'd said that last, and Fertetti didn't envy the recipient of that look. Paige Delroy had an ability to make people miserable that was rivaled only by Fertetti's ex-wife.

"Okay," he said. "If you're not going to answer straight, then laps it is." The girls groaned. *"Shut up and start running!"* Fertetti shouted, then moved to where he could watch from behind.

Mom's not here, the cheerleaders are, and I get to watch all sorts of interesting bouncing as they run.

Okay, so there were three good things about today. Not quite enough to balance out the lost holiday, but they came close.

***

Raymond "Ray" Gunne had been Reina's entire IT department until last year, when they finally hired another person to help with the steadily increasing work load. Ray was glad when Vachnarian came along – the guy was good with computers, and more importantly he had a certain level of "moral flexibility" that Ray really appreciated.

He especially appreciated Vachnarian on days like today, when everything was going to hell – even if the other man tended to smell like garlic when he sweated, and was most definitely sweating now.

But then, so was Ray.

In all his time at Reina, he'd never had a day quite this bad. Called in to work because of computer problems the school's Ethernet was experiencing, he'd barely been at his desk five minutes before Vachnarian walked in – which was almost exactly the point Ray realized that the "computer problems" were something much more serious.

"Not a virus –" Vachnarian grunted beside him, the words punctuated by the *tick-click* of fingers pounding on plastic keys.

"Almost like a DDoS," said Ray, his own fingers moving just as fast. "It –"

"Gersham's going to fire us if –"

"What kind of hackers would target a *school*, for God's sa –"

The conversation had been like this for over an hour now:

nothing but truncated phrases as the two of them delved deeper into the problems. Every passing second made Ray Gunne realize just how deep a shitpool they were standing in. And then the following second he'd sink just a bit deeper and realize that everything had grown somehow worse.

Vachnarian was good at his job, but Ray was better. They both knew it, and neither minded it. But that also meant that their best and brightest was already on the job. And if their best and brightest was in over his head, what were they going to do?

Normal schools might call out for a specialist. But Reina wasn't a normal school. Beyond its elite status as the most exclusive of institutions (though Ray thought it functioned as more of a cross between a military academy and a toddler care center), neither Ray nor Vachnarian could afford to have outside people poking around on the school's computers.

There were things there that no one in this room wanted seen by anyone else.

Something tickled at Ray's mind as he continued working. He tried to ignore it – now wasn't the time for distractions – but his brain kept poking him, calling for attention. Finally, Ray realized what was bothering him:

Vachnarian had stopped typing.

Ray turned to face the other man, a shout on his lips.

The cognitive dissonance he'd been experiencing ramped up as he saw what Vachnarian was doing.

Why are his hands up?

He couldn't imagine a reason why. Not until he saw the two people standing in the doorway. Identically dressed save only the armbands they wore – one bright green, the other bright yellow – and the fact that they each held a different kind of weapon.

Ray knew guns pretty well. He'd never fired one in real life, but he played tons of Call of Duty. So he knew that the person wearing green held a submachine gun, maybe an Uzi. The other person, with the yellow band, held what he was pretty sure was an AK47.

"What the –"

As had been the case all day, the sentence ended unfinished. This time, though, it wasn't because he or Vachnarian were working so fast and hard that they left words behind, but because the person wearing the yellow armband strode forward and slammed the butt of the AK into Ray's face.

He heard something crack, and it felt like someone had put ground glass directly into his skull. He lurched backward, only peripherally aware that Vachnarian had tried to stand before being similarly attacked by the person in the green armband.

What the –

Even the thought was interrupted this time.

Hard to think when some maniac was beating him to death with the butt of an automatic rifle.

***

Jonas watched the Misfits picking up trash, and wondered if there was any way he could get the whole thing shut down early. Not that he didn't think the kids deserved the punishment – if there was one thing every kid at Reina shared an aptitude for, it was acting out. But he was still a young enough teacher that he had successfully fooled himself into believing he actually *liked* these kids. Plus, he had been raised by a mother who said, "You catch more bees with honey than with vinegar" at least seven times a day in her quest for never-ending smiles.

Even when Jonas was a kid, and popped off with, "Why the hell would you want to catch bees if you already have honey?" his mother didn't stop smiling. She laughed, and hugged him, and that made him want to make his bed and clean his room and get straight As until he died or graduated (both seemed equally far away at the time).

Slattery wouldn't mind any overtures Jonas made to cut detention early. He might not back Jonas directly, but he wouldn't object outright, if only because he probably had a hot date with the internet and an industrial size vat of petroleum jelly waiting at home.

Mulcahey was a bigger problem. The guy had the morals of a wet fart, and inevitably followed along with whatever Fertetti decided.

Fertetti himself was busy watching the cheerleaders run toward the track. The gym teacher had his gaze so firmly glued to Paige Delroy's gluteus maximus – which could be seen, thong and all, as her decidedly-against-school-policy-length, bespoke cheerleader skirt flipped up with every movement of her legs – that he looked like an owl zeroing in on a field mouse. Only this was a creepy, old owl.

And, Jonas reflected, Paige was no field mouse.

Paige looked in Jonas' direction and grinned. For a moment the teacher was worried she was grinning at him, misinterpreting his attention for the same kind of leering, lustful look she thrived on. But then he realized she was looking past him, at the spot where Daxton was belligerently refusing to pick up trash.

She shook her butt, and the skirt flapped, and then something like rapid burst of thunder shook the world, and the grass erupted in front of the cheerleaders' feet, the Misfits' feet.

Bullets.

***

All matter is mostly empty space, the void between neutrons and protons and the electrons orbiting them. Jonas discovered in that instant that sound was no different: as fast and as loud as the bullets were, there were still spaces between their explosions, still crevasses between each shock of sound.

Those spaces filled, though: with screams and with the sounds of bodies falling to earth.

Jonas spun automatically. He wasn't sure if he was looking for where the sound came from so he could try to stop it, or simply to find out which place to run away from. But he was one of the few who turned and saw five people standing atop a small, grass-covered berm to one side of the well-manicured field outside the gym.

All were dressed head to toe in black. Three had armbands on: red, green, and blue. The red-armbanded person and the two without armbands – one a man, one with the distinct outline of a woman – were the ones firing at the students and staff.

The men with green and blue armbands held guns trained at Principal Gersham and the only person at RHS whom Jonas was pretty sure still possessed a fully intact soul:

Holden. Not him, too!

As Jonas watched, stricken dumb and rooted to the spot by the sheer, unmitigated horror of it, the man with a red armband dropped a magazine from his weapon and then reloaded it and kept firing.

That was when Jonas finally moved. When he turned toward the students and tried to figure out if he could get any of them to safety. He wanted to run to Holden, to get the secretary away from whatever was happening, but the kids were his first priority. And he saw Holden nod at him, knew the other man agreed: *Save the kids*, the look said. *Forget about me.*

Movement caught Jonas' eye. Another person in black, coming around the corner of the gym, wearing a yellow armband. The person raised his weapon, aimed. Something about the way he held it told Jonas that he wasn't aiming to aerate the grass, the way the others had done so far.

Jonas spun and saw Slattery, miraculously far away, his slender form managing more speed than Jonas would have thought possible as he ran from the demons that had appeared at RHS.

A sharp trio of bullets punched out, filling in more of those cracks in the deafening din caused by the rest of the gunfire.

P-p-pow.

Jonas saw three bursts of red appear on Slattery: one on his left shoulder, one that tore out the right half of his neck, the final one stitching its way up to blow apart the man's skull.

***

Jonas felt something in his hand. It was the first time he realized he'd been moving; that sometime in the space between seeing the man with the yellow armband aim and the first pull of the trigger, he'd moved toward a handful of the Misfits, grabbed several, and began herding them together, away from the lines of fire that continued chewing up the thick grass.

Jonas looked around. He spotted Daxton and his crew. Could he get to them?

No. Several of the attackers had already surrounded them.

God, how many are there?

Jonas turned, not even sure how many of the Misfits he had with him, his mind falling into those silent cracks between *p-p-p-pow!* He only knew that he had to get them to safety. He had to get them away.

The gym was the only logical choice. It was a big, heavy structure. No windows, only a few doors. If he could get at least some of the kids in there and barricade them in…

Fertetti was already ahead of him – figuratively and literally. He'd apparently decided on the same course of action Jonas had, though without encumbering himself with any of the student body.

Fertetti had almost reached the gym doors. Jonas suddenly worried that the man would get in and lock them without waiting for anyone else to make it to safety. Worry morphed to certainty in an instant, and as Fertetti reached for the doors, Jonas yanked on the students he was pulling –

(Is it Evans? Collins? God, please let me save them.)

– and screamed, "Hurry!"

Fertetti's hand touched the door.

Everything around Jonas slowed down.

He's going to save himself. Shut himself in.

Leave us to die.

***

In the stress-induced time dilation Jonas was experiencing, he saw it happen with perfect clarity: Fertetti's hand touching the door. Fingers clawed to encircle the handle, to jerk the metal door open and then dart behind it to safety.

The door had other plans.

It slammed outward, and Jonas watched as it hit Fertetti's hand so hard the fingers splayed –

(cr-cr-crack went fingers and wrist,

p-p-pop went guns and bones)

– and the hand itself folded back almost to the point that it lay against the outside of Fertetti's forearm.

Fertetti opened his mouth to scream, but again the door decided otherwise. It continued rocketing out, catching Fertetti across his chest, continuing its arc into the center of his face where it flattened his nose and then slammed into the gym teacher's forehead.

Fertetti dropped bonelessly as the man behind the door came out.

Another one. Purple armband this time.

***

Just like that, it was over.

Just like that, it started.

CHAPTER 6
The Plan

The silence burned her ears.

Some of the Colors had worn hearing protection in the form of small, expensive earplugs that could be yanked out using the cords that trailed out the bottoms of their balaclavas.

The Lady hadn't done so. She didn't see much point, given what everyone expected of the day.

Now, she regretted it. She was no stranger to gunfire – thousands of hours logged shooting at targets on the range and in several national parks with plentiful wildlife and forest rangers whose blind eyes could be purchased had ensured that.

But she'd never heard so *many* guns going off at once. Her ears throbbed. Her head hurt.

Or maybe that wasn't the result of gunfire. Maybe it was just the rage she'd felt for years, finally come to a glorious head.

The gunfire petered out as the students and staff – those who were left – were rounded up.

Blue had his gun trained on Principal Gersham. He had orders not to kill him, but Gersham didn't know that. And if he did make a break… well, Blue could do a lot to the man without killing him.

Beside them, Green had his own gun trained on Holden Wright. The secretary was a bit of a wrinkle. He had not been called in by the school's robocalling service, and so was outside the plans. But The Lady was nothing if not thorough, and between her and Teacher's obsessive planning and their obsessive checking and re-checking of those plans, they had built in contingencies for him.

Just as Blue had instructions not to kill Principal Gersham, so Green had instructions not to kill Holden. But where Blue *was* authorized to do a tremendous amount of damage to his charge,

Green had also been told not to harm Holden at all if it could be managed.

If resistance proved problematic, they all held sidearms with rubber bullets, and each had a small packet with bottles of tranquilizers and a few syringes, just in case. If they had to be used on the secretary, then he would wake up with bruised ribs and a scorching headache. But given everything else that was to happen today, The Lady and Teacher both had agreed that he'd count his blessings and enjoy the hospital Jell-O.

***

The Lady continued turning, taking in the scene, making sure everyone was where they were supposed to be and doing what they were supposed to do.

As though he had heard the thought, and wanted to prove he knew his cues, Orange kicked Mulcahey's legs. The teacher tumbled to the grass. Even this far away, The Lady could hear the sound of his breath exploding from his lungs as the impact knocked the wind out of him. He managed a single, strained croaking noise before Orange brought the butt of his rifle down on the back of Mulcahey's head, knocking him out.

Almost in the same motion, Orange turned and strode to where Slattery's corpse lay. Slattery was beyond caring about what would now happen, but the others were not. They would be witnesses.

The gunfire of moments ago had ended, but The Lady's head still rang, the thunder of her pulse and the echoing recollections of the bullets' reports still nearly deafened her. Just the same, she heard the wet crack of the impact as Orange brought down the butt of his gun. She saw bright blood spray out, a cone in the outline of a red Christmas tree, startling against the deep green grass.

She saw Slattery's body give a convulsive shake. Maybe he hadn't been dead after all. Or maybe it was just the force of Orange's blow, sending ripples of kinetic energy through his corpse like a child snapping a jump rope.

The students screamed.

More screams when Orange spun his rifle in his hands, aimed, and emptied the remainder of his AK-47s magazine into Slattery's body. Then they fell silent as Orange once more reversed his grip and started beating the teacher's corpse. He was meticulous, working his way down from the man's already-wrecked head to his feet.

When he was finished, he wiped his gun against the grass. Dark red tinsel beside the bright red tree, a lumpy rug of bone and broken flesh the hearth.

***

Teacher watched, too. He watched Orange do his job, then turned to watch the students as they witnessed the intentional brutality of the moment. They had to understand the message: this could happen to you.

There would be other messages delivered later. But this one was critical. Some people had to die. Some people would receive far worse.

But they all had to fear. They all had to obey.

That was the only way anyone would learn.

His eyes lingered on certain of the students. The cheerleaders, in particular. One of them had worn her uniform – which Teacher had expected. The rest had eschewed their uniforms in favor of designer "work" clothes that probably cost more than most people made in a week.

A few saw him looking. They looked away.

He smiled. He would let them look away.

They were blind now, but they *would* see.

"They'll all see," he whispered.

Beside him, The Lady jerked to look at him, obviously surprised that he had spoken. But she wasn't surprised at the statement; he could see that in her eyes, and in the terse nod she gave.

***

The Lady hadn't expected Teacher to say the words, no, but she had expected him to be thinking them. It was what she was thinking herself.

It was the whole point, wasn't it?

When Orange was done cleaning his gun on the grass, he stood and looked at her and Teacher. Orange's arms were sopping, covered in blood and bits of flesh and bone.

Several of the students gave a small scream as Orange reached into one of his pockets, obviously terrified at what new horror he would draw forth.

It was a small square of black plastic. He unfolded it, turning it from a small square to a larger one, which he in turn shook out into a large, heavy garbage bag.

He put his gun on the ground and began sliding what was left of Slattery into the bag. They didn't want bodies on the grounds. Not yet, at least.

The blood and gobbets of flesh and shards of bone were fine, though. Maybe they'd be seen, maybe not. It didn't matter.

As Orange worked, The Lady looked at two of their captives. First, Holden Wright. He was closest to Orange, and she was worried he might see the gun on the ground as an invitation. Might try to do something heroic and end up seriously injured for his pains. Luckily for all of them, he showed no indication he would make a move.

Neither did the other one The Lady worried about. Jonas Chambers had his arms outstretched, a mother hen trying to protect several of the Misfits from harm. He wasn't going to run, not with Purple aiming his gun at them.

The Lady gestured. No words were needed – the Colors herded the staff and students into a rough line on the grass. The living and conscious ones, at least.

As they did so, a few more students were brought out of one of the buildings: Winona "Win" Jackson and Beatriz Alcivar.

When the Computer GurlZ had joined the line, Teacher stepped toward the captives. Several flinched. Win jutted her jaw out like she was considering the wisdom of saying something to him, then looked over at where Orange was still piling bits of a teacher into a bag and decided on wisdom over wit. Both Holden and Jonas extended their arms as though they had some chance of stopping Teacher from hurting the kids in their charge.

Speaking to the group in general, Teacher said, "Take out your phones and throw them on the ground. Now."

Most of the students did. The Lady gathered them, noting the makes and models of each, then brought them to Teacher and whispered into his ear. They had decided early on that his would be the primary voice the captors heard – feminist theory aside, his voice was deeper and simply more likely to send fear burrowing a bit deeper into the bones of the people they needed to keep in a state of near-panic.

Besides, The Lady worried that if she spoke to these people – to any of them – she would start screaming, then would start killing and wouldn't stop until every soul standing near her was dead.

***

Teacher nodded as The Lady whispered in his ear. She dropped the phones on a black sheet of plastic then used a hammer she had brought (for just this purpose) to smash them to pieces. The phones had been jammed earlier, to be sure – the reason why Daxton's and Paige's sext thread hadn't gone through – but there was no sense taking chances.

And besides: this, as everything, was part of the lesson. The kids had to know that their phones weren't part of the solution – if anything they were part of the problem.

As she crushed the kids' remaining lines to the outside world to bits, Teacher walked over to stand next to two of the students who were at the front and center of everything.

Even in the chaos and bloodshed, Daxton Leigh had somehow stayed close to his sad little entourage. The hulking moron Zane Kennedy; the cunning and conniving Konstantin Tarov. They stood on his left, each leaning to the right, as though if they leaned close enough to Daxton then some kind of protective force would reach out to cover and protect them.

Not likely. Not likely at all.

Paige Delroy had also somehow found and drawn close to Daxton – or he to her, or both to each other. Teacher guessed it was the last option: he had observed them a long time, and near as he could tell they were each other's heroin. Addicting, at times adored and at other times hated. But always the heroin was the source of perceived strength and of actual weakness.

This time, in this moment, Daxton and Paige had obviously managed to draw strength from one another. At the very least, they didn't look as frightened as the other kids in the line.

They also hadn't handed over their phones. Daxton's cronies, who stood on Daxton's other side, had handed theirs over. But not Daxton. Not Paige. The Lady spotted it, and it was now up to him to rectify it.

As he walked toward the kids, Orange, still painted from his elbows down with what had once been the unmourned and unmournable Mr. Slattery, moved to join him. Green moved forward as well.

Teacher looked at the Colors. He nodded at Daxton and Paige, and the Orange and Green yanked the kids roughly out of the line. Paige gave a short cry that sounded more like rage than fear. Daxton didn't make a sound.

"I know you have a Samsung," said Teacher to Paige.

Turning to Daxton: "And you bought a new iPhone a month ago. Where are they?"

Daxton's chin jutted out so far that it could have served as a perch for small birds. Teacher shook his head. "Don't make me ask again, Daxton."

For a moment, the teen's eyes widened in surprise. Then cold calculation took over. The eyes narrowed. The air grew heavy and the scent of grass that had hung around them all on the field seemed far too sweet in Teacher's nose.

"If you know who I am," said Daxton, "then you know why you aren't going to touch me."

Teacher smiled. He didn't even have to give the order: they'd more or less expected this outcome, so before Daxton had even finished speaking, Orange had drawn a handgun. An instant after the last word, at the same time Teacher felt the smile on his face, Orange pistol-whipped the eighteen-year-old.

Daxton fell, blood streaming from the gash Orange's strike had opened on his scalp. Orange kicked him then, and though Daxton's scream was loud, it wasn't quite loud enough to mask the sharp *crack!* as one of the teen's ribs broke.

***

Orange didn't kick Daxton again. Knock him down, kick him hard: those had been the orders. Those had been all Teacher wanted. For now.

Teacher leaned down. He finally saw what he wanted to see in Daxton's eyes: fear.

"I know who your daddy is," he said quietly but fervently. "But all *you* are is my new toy." He shrugged. "And sometimes I break my toys." He paused. Daxton gasped but didn't speak. Teacher's smile fell away. "Where. Are. The. *Phones?*"

Still no answer.

Teacher sighed again. He inhaled, calming himself,

preparing for what came next. The sweet smell of the grass had become even more cloying.

"I really wanted this to come later. It would have been better later. But you brought this on yourselves."

He nodded to Orange. Daxton flinched away from the Color who had just broken his rib, and Paige screamed. So did several of the other students.

Orange had no intention of touching either Paige or Daxton. He didn't touch anyone at all – not directly. He did, however, use the same pistol he had just used to crack Daxton's head open.

He pointed the gun.

"No, wai –"

Orange pulled the trigger. Yet one more thunder clap in the cloudless sky. The students screamed again, and it was almost amusing to hear that the highest-pitched shriek came not from any of the cheerleaders, not from the Computer Gurlz, but from Daxton's third-in-command, Konstantin Tarov.

The vocal tone was surprising, if not the fact that he was screaming. Teacher suspected that if all two-hundred-fifty pounds of Daxton's number two had fallen into him without warning, he might have screamed as well – particularly when the juggernaut of a teen had left behind five pounds of his head when Orange put the hollow point bullet through Zane Kennedy's left eye.

***

The Lady stepped forward.

It was gratifying in a way: the kids, all screaming as a man they either hated as a bully, loved as one of their Popular Kids group, or – surprisingly often – both at once, shut up instantly. The Lady didn't have to say anything, to threaten, to make a move toward a weapon. The kids just knew that if she was moving toward them, it was a bad sign.

She wondered, jokingly, if that was because they sensed she

was one of the people in charge, or just because she had spent the last few minutes overseeing the destruction of the electronic devices that for many of these kids represented their best or only confidants, confessionals, and companions.

The Lady had suffered losses herself. One of them in particular, the one that haunted her to this day, had been almost a dream at first. When she first heard the news, it didn't really sink in. But when she went to look for her car keys, to drive to her remaining family and share her grief, she couldn't find them. It was only then that the grief and pain and loss and agony all hit her. The actual news hadn't done it. The loss itself hadn't triggered her response to pain.

The keys, though. The little, mundane, everyday thing. That pushed her over the edge.

So maybe that was what was happening here. The kids had just seen several people killed, including one of their own classmates. They had been yanked violently out of their daydream lives, thrust into this nightmare scenario. But they hadn't started responding with the defeated panic The Lady wanted until she destroyed their phones.

The silence that had fallen was thick, desperate. The Lady knew that silence, too. She had lived with it for a long time. Years. Forever.

A voice broke the stillness: "I know where the phones are."

***

Teacher turned to face one of the people he had least hoped to see. He motioned, and Green moved toward the speaker. The kids nearest Jonas Chambers shrank back, but he patted the air as though to console them. His hands shook, but he didn't shrink as Green took his arm and pulled him – firmly but gently – to Teacher.

Teacher stared at the man who had spoken. Cocking his head, he said, "Neither you nor Mr. Wright were called in today, Mr. Chambers. Why come to school on a day off?"

Jonas Chambers looked uneasy. Teacher could see some of

what the man was concerned about: Jonas and Holden had been dating for several months. Teacher didn't think the teacher was worried about getting in trouble with the school at this point – though romantic relationships between staff members were against the rules, (which Teacher found ironic).

Rather, he thought Jonas was worried that telling too much might somehow put Holden Wright in danger.

"I know more about you than you could possibly dream, Mr. Chambers, so lying to me is unlikely to bear fruit. I'll ask you one more time: why are you here on a day off?"

Jonas gave a nervous laugh, then shrugged. "We both had work to finish, so we carpooled in, then stayed to help out when we saw that there were more students in detention than usual and the computer systems had all –"

He cut off. Again, Teacher saw the man calculating. Putting two and two together.

Teacher nodded. "Go on."

"We stayed to help out," said Jonas. "That's all."

Teacher smiled. The skin of his lips felt tight, the smile more a gash than a grin. "Kindness doesn't pay off, does it?" The smile, bereft of humor though it had been, now disappeared. "Where are our delinquents' phones?"

Jonas took a step, then stopped, then another awkward half-step. "They're, uh –" He had obviously started to go to the phones, then realized that could be misinterpreted as him stalling for time or trying something underhanded.

"Take a breath, Mr. Chambers," said Teacher. After a momentary pause, he said, "Where are they?"

Jonas pointed at Fertetti, who still lay unconscious on the ground where he had fallen after the door hit him.

Teacher nodded to Purple, who searched Fertetti quickly. He pulled out the kids' phones, then one more – Fertetti's own phone, a seven-year-old model on which Fertetti had saved images that turned Teacher's stomach to think about.

Purple tossed the phones to The Lady, who did with them as she had done with the others.

While they were still in the air, Purple started kicking Fertetti. The ribs. The groin. Fertetti moaned, then screamed as he woke to pain.

The scream cut off as Purple stomped down on the teacher's head with the thick sole of his combat boots. Again. Again. Each time he did, his boot got a bit closer to the ground as he pulped Fertetti's head underfoot.

Six stomps. Seven.

On the tenth, there was nothing underfoot but lumpy smears. Fertetti's neck ended at a ragged stump that looked like the mouth of a meat grinder in the process of making hamburger out of steak.

The kids had started screaming again.

Principal Gersham was crying, then turned his head and vomited.

Teacher allowed the screams to continue. They went in waves: louder, quieter, in, out. They would creep to the edge of silence, then one of the kids would take a shuddering breath and another would exhale a shocked moan and the whole thing would ramp up again.

He knew what people would think: that he did this because he loved the sounds of the shrieks and sobs, the terror and trauma he was visiting upon those present.

It wasn't true at all, of course. He hated the sounds. He hated the pain, hated the torment he now caused. But he wouldn't stop, because he couldn't stop. The world needed this. He would hurt some, yes – the ones who deserved it.

But he would save others.

He wasn't a coward, though. Wasn't one of those people who screamed about laws and order, but broke them at their convenience and then shrieked even louder about the unfairness of it all when they were caught. The world had become a place where responsibility was viewed ever more as a form of abuse; where accountability was something that served only to lower self esteem and therefore should be avoided at all costs in the continuing quest to "find your truth."

Teacher knew the foolishness of that. "Finding your truth" could be a worthy goal, he supposed, if everyone lived on their own private island and nothing they did could ever impact anyone else. But in a shared world, especially one growing ever more crowded and ever more cramped, "finding your truth" had to give way to "figuring out how to make it all work."

The world was one piece, the people in it inextricably linked. So when one person pushed away their responsibilities, it didn't mean they disappeared – they were just shouldered by someone else. When someone sloughed off a consequence, it didn't return to the *nihilo* before *creatio* – it fell on someone else's shoulders.

Teacher would not let that happen. He would shoulder the responsibility as much as he could. He would listen to the screams. He would pay the price.

I already did.

And so did she.

He did not want to think of that. So he turned and left at last, the labored weeping and breathy screams following him as he went to find the people scheduled next to die.

***

When Teacher arrived, everything was as it should be. Raymond "Ray" Gunne and Nicholas Vachnarian sat on two chairs in the IT room, both the school's computer gurus tied fast and their faces already showing livid bruises. Vachnarian's right eye was so swollen Teacher couldn't see so much as a sliver of white or color –

just a lump of purple and yellow tissue with a thin trickle of transparent fluid coming out of the thick masses that had once been eyelids.

All that was fine with Teacher. After all, *If thine eye offend thee, pluck it out.*

Teacher had never been religious. Less so in the last few years – God was a joke, and it was up to men and women to work any miracles the world needed – but the biblical saying carried weight here.

He would gladly have plucked out Vachnarian's eyes. But it wasn't time for such things. Not yet.

He looked from Nicholas Vachnarian to Ray Gunne. Like his coworker, Gunne had been lashed tightly to a sturdy office chair. Teacher appreciated the Colors' adherence to even the smallest aspects of the plan, though he doubted they really had to tie Gunne down: the man had two broken arms. No x-ray necessary to make the diagnosis, either: whichever of the Colors had broken Gunne's arms had done so with such brutality that raw bone, bloody and slick, jutted from ragged wounds on Gunne's right and left forearms.

Perhaps it had been Yellow, who stood guard over the men with his rifle, the muzzle wandering from one man to the next and then back again. Whoever had done it, though, Teacher wholeheartedly approved of the tactic.

Gunne seemed out of it, but Teacher's gaze brought him back to reality enough to focus his eyes on his captor, if only for a moment. Bright terror lit his gaze and he shrank away. The motion wrung a moan of agony from his blood-flecked lips.

Beside him, Nicholas Vachnarian whispered, "Please, what do you want?"

Teacher ignored the question. He went to the bank of computers that served as the nerve center to Reina High's internet and Ethernet connections and began typing on one of the keyboards.

"My friend," Nicholas tried again, motioning at Gunne,

"he's really hurt and –"

Teacher lifted one hand from the keyboard, held out his thumb and index finger in a "C," then slowly clamped them shut. Nicholas got the message and closed his mouth. Or perhaps he was just shocked to see Teacher continue typing with one hand, and to do so faster than most people could manage with two.

Teacher had seen that reaction before. He and The Lady were, modesty aside, extraordinary in more ways than anyone could prepare for or protect against.

***

Two monitors sat close to Teacher. One of them lit with a view of the IT room as he activated the webcam. The other showed IP addresses scrolling past.

Behind him, Ray groaned, then sagged forward. The motion ground his exposed bones together, and he screamed. Nicholas vomited.

Teacher waited until Nicholas was done heaving. He didn't want to start the video with something gross. He wanted to start it with a bang.

Once done, Nicholas sat up. His eyes were glassy with terror, as though his mind was already retreating from this moment, this place, this life.

Yellow stepped forward. He grabbed the back of Ray's chair and turned it slightly to the side. He repeated the motion with Nicholas, so both men were partially facing each other.

Ray groaned in pain when he was moved, but his glazed expression didn't falter. Nicholas whimpered, but mostly looked confused.

Yellow stepped back so that he was not in view of the camera.

At the computer, Teacher hammered a key. A bright red circle appeared on the screen showing the view of the IT room.

Recording.

Ray Gunne noticed the motion, and it triggered something in him. Despite the pain he must still be feeling, he scrabbled back with his feet as though he had seen the future, and did not like what was coming.

Teacher stood. Back to the camera, he drew a weapon from a holster at his side. He had not used it until now, because this was the only time he planned to need it. The rifle would be better for most purposes, but for this moment…

The Desert Eagle .50 AE Magnum Mark XIX. One of the biggest and most powerful handguns in the world, bigger even than the versions favored by TV badasses worried about their tiny penises. With its weakest loadout it was capable of punching a hole in brick,

And Teacher was using something far stronger than that.

"No," whimpered Ray. "P-p-please. P-p –"

Teacher pulled the trigger. Ray was silent. His broken bones no longer bothered him – his brain didn't care about such things anymore.

The bullets Teacher had chosen for this moment were 350 grain CCI jacketed hollow points. Already designed to mushroom upon impact, he had had the bullets specially altered, weakening the jackets to encourage both expansion and fragmentation.

Between the Desert Eagle and the huge bullets, Ray was not just dead. Most of the back left of his head had exploded, and Teacher knew that the angle of the man's placement would allow the webcam to view of the crater in the back of his head as well as the bone-and-blood-spattered wall behind him.

Nicholas started screaming. Teacher swiveled. Pulled the trigger. Nicholas stopped.

It had been vicious, violent, and visually arresting. Everything the viewing public was most interested in. Teacher knew that better than most, and he and The Lady had spent three weeks planning this moment alone.

Now, finished, he felt no elation. He didn't feel sorrow, either, or rage or fear or much of anything. It was just another step in the process.

***

Teacher brought up the snuff video he had just created. He clipped off a bit at the end, a bit at the beginning.

Then he typed.

Clicked.

Sent.

PART TWO:
WHEN I GATHERED

When I gathered flowers, I knew it was myself plucking my own flowering.

- D.H. Lawrence
  "New Heaven and Earth"

CHAPTER 7
Intended Response

Cops moved around the room. It was early in the day, but justice – and crime – never slept. Though, if he was being honest, Detective Rick Montano would admit that justice occasionally (often) looked the other way when given the right incentives.

He had joined the force to stop that kind of thing. He had come in to fight the good fight, and liberty and justice for all. And if the ladies liked a man in uniform, well… gravy.

It had been easy for him from the start. He didn't always like the *job* – the paperwork and politics that were mother's milk to any large bureaucracy – but he loved the work. The feel of getting some scumbag off the street. The knowledge that someone innocent made it through the night.

Becoming a detective, even at an earlier age than most, was almost a foregone conclusion, and it never occurred to him beforehand that he might not enjoy cleaning up messes as much as he did averting them. Especially when so many of them happened on holidays. Because not only did justice – and crime – never sleep, they never took state or federal holidays off.

"Why the hell are we even here, Eb?"

He didn't really want an answer. Eberhardt probably knew that, which was probably why he gave one.

***

Detective Rick Montano stands at five-eleven, with a well-muscled but slim frame that always makes this reporter think of a rapier: fast, dangerous, and always (if you'll forgive the pun) quick to the point.

In stark contrast, Montano's partner, Vincent Eberhardt, stands at six feet, two inches, and weighs in at over two hundred and fifty pounds. He is obviously well-muscled despite his age – pushing sixty, and recently retired as of this writing – but as imposing a specimen as he can be, the first time this reporter met him I was most intrigued by his ability to disappear.

Not in a literal sense, of course: Eberhardt can't put on a Cloak of Invisibility like that used in his favorite series (a surprise the first time I found out he was a Harry Potter fan). He can't melt into thin air like a ninja, either, hiding away in places impossible to ken.

But he stands in the background, and manages often to become indistinguishable from that background. A person who can melt into a scene and remain *un*seen. It's a great quality for an observer, and Eberhardt uses it to good effect. He stands quietly, and victims and criminals alike eventually start talking because they feel free to speak when no one is listening.

Of course, that kind of quality can also work against someone: they are less likely to earn the accolades and rewards that come to flashier types. It bothers some people like that. But not Eberhardt. When I asked him once, he shrugged and said simply, "I don't care who gets the credit for the job, just that the job gets done."

That was, in no small part, why he and Montano got along so well.

***

Montano and Eberhardt hassled each other, regularly and with a barbed wit that both enjoyed. That kind of relationship is about as good as you can get with a partner on the police force. Stilted politeness was terrible, with outright silence the absolute worse.

So when Montano asked, "Why the hell are we even here, Eb?" and Eberhardt opened his mouth to give him crap, Montano was already grinning before his partner said word one.

"Why are we here?" Eberhardt was almost twenty years older than Montano, and went into his "professor" mode: sitting back in his chair, steepling his fingers, looking over the tops of his imaginary reading glasses. "Because while innocent Americans prepare to get drunk and overcook their burgers on this beautiful Memorial Day, we, my partner, my friend, my young protégé and padawan, are the thin blue line between remembering our fallen on their day of recognition, and complete anarchy."

Montano waited.

Eberhardt grinned. "Also, God hates us and cops don't get Mondays off."

Montano laughed. "There it is."

Shaking his head, he turned back to his computer screen in time to see it flicker. The damn thing had been doing that a lot. One constant in life: if a government entity "improved" something – say, the computer network – it inevitably worked worse than before. "If it ain't broke, break it" should have been the Latin motto inscribed over the door, instead of the boring ol' "protect and serve."

The screen flashed again. Montano hit control-S, worried that he would lose the last hour's paperwork if he didn't save the report in time. "Again?" he mumbled. "If I gotta be here, I should at least get a decent computer."

"What's wrong?" said Eberhardt. He looked over from his own part of the report – updates on a robbery that had happened two days ago. "Boobs taking too long to load?"

"You wound me!"

Eberhardt's hand darted out and, before Montano could stop him, the older detective grabbed Montano's mouse, moved the cursor to the corner of the screen, and clicked. "Really?" he said, as the click revealed Montano's desktop background. "I think instead of 'wound' you should use the words 'accurately portray.'"

Montano shook his head, returning the image to the police report, covering up the brunette bikini girl, all sand-speckled skin and surf, who smiled out at him from the monitor. "That's not *boobs*, you dirty old man. That's *ambiance*. And I'll have you know she's an award winner."

"Of what?"

"Sports Illustrated's Swimsuit Model of the Year, 2019."

Eberhardt snorted. "I thought Mexicans only went for the girls in car magazines. And don't they have to have, like, *chola* eyebrows or something?"

Anyone else said something like that to Montano and they would have ended up eating their own teeth. But it didn't bug him when Eb said it, for two reasons:

The first was that Eberhardt was married to a Mexican woman, adored his wife like no one Montano had ever seen, and spoke near-flawless Spanish. So when he acted like a racist douche, Montano couldn't take it personally – it was an act, and part of the gallows humor most cops developed as a defense mechanism.

The second (and more important one) was that Montano ate at his partner's house every Sunday night, and gleefully repeated Eberhardt's jokes to Maricela, and then got to sit back and enjoy her tearing Eberhardt a new one.

She smiled when she did it, though. So in love, just like Eberhardt – and Montano in love with them both. They were a weird family, but family they were. And one of the most defining characteristics of any family was relentless badgering.

That was why, though Montano didn't adjust his partner's dental work, he couldn't just sit back and take the barb. Grimacing, he said, "*Chola* eyebrows? I don't even know what that means, you racist asshole."

Eberhardt blew him a kiss. "At least I'm not an all-around asshole like you."

"I don't know how Maricela puts up with you," said Montano.

Eberhardt nodded soberly, no longer joking. He never joked about Maricela. "She's an angel."

Montano smiled. He wouldn't joke about Maricela, either.

Some things are too precious to joke about.

**

Montano's screen flickered again, drawing his attention. "Come, *on*, you –" The report disappeared. Even though he'd saved it, Montano was suddenly terrified in a way he hadn't even felt when one of the 2nd Street Bloods pulled a gun on him three weeks ago. Guns weren't fun to stare at, sure, but Eb had had his back. Paperwork, on the other hand? If Montano's disappeared, Eb would let him twist in the wind. Eb hated paperwork almost as much as he loved Maricela.

Montano grabbed his mouse and moved it, intending to click the folder where he kept his draft reports. The cursor didn't move.

"*Dios y Maria*," he muttered. His mother's favorite words, though she got mad whenever he used them in anything but a prayerful tone. Certainly she would have given him a tongue-lashing for using them in a situation like this. So what if the mouse wasn't working? Especially since this was his last day at this desk before moving on to bigger and better things.

Still, stuff like this bothered him. It –

Montano froze. The cursor started moving across the screen. He might have thought it was a glitch – something wrong in the mouse, or some problem with the firewall. Only the cursor wasn't blinking in and out of existence like it tended to when that crap happened. It was moving purposefully. Down to the taskbar. A quick flash the way it did when Montano clicked the mouse.

Montano's email opened. The cursor moved to the top.

"What the…"

The cursor quick-flashed again, clicking an email. No subject line, nothing in the body. And, according to the header, no sender other than "@reinahighschool.com" with no username in front of it – not possible so far as he knew.

"Hey, Eb?"

"Yes, *Señor Chim-ee* –"

Eberhardt's sentence cut off unfinished. He must have seen something in Montano's face he didn't like, because he frowned and slid his chair over.

As he did, the cursor moved to the bottom of the email. Montano hadn't seen what was there at first, but now noticed the attachment: "**ReinaMemorial.mp4**."

Montano clicked the mouse. Moved it. Typed a few garbled letters and the tried-and-true control-alt-delete that should have let him force the email to close. Nothing happened. "Is this a joke?" he asked Eberhardt. "Is Dapper Dan doing this? You?"

Eberhardt shrugged as the cursor on Montano's computer screen flashed. The attachment opened.

Eberhardt shook his head. And, as the video played, as the two men saw what had been sent to them, as both grew uneasy and pale, Eberhardt added quietly, "This definitely ain't me."

***

Montano kept tapping keys with one hand, moving the mouse with the other, though the motions were absent, rote. Most of his attention centered on the video.

Two men sat in what looked like some kind of computer room. Several monitors and servers could be seen in the back. Both were tied to chairs, and both looked bruised and bloody. One was sobbing, crying out. The other moaned.

As Montano and Eberhardt watched, a man dressed all in black, face obscured by a ski mask, entered the shot, holding a huge gun at the ready.

The man who had not been moaning –

("*Damn, Montano,*" said Eb, "*What's wrong with his arms?*")

– whimpered, "No. P-p-please. P-p –"

The man dressed in black pulled the trigger, and even

through his computer's tinny speakers the sound seemed overly loud. Montano jumped as the sound erupted, as the gunman blew a man's head off.

The remaining man started to scream. The gunman turned toward the screams, toward the man.

Another shot. The screams ended.

All was silent. All was still.

***

The video ended, then began to replay.

Eberhardt pointed at the lower right corner of the screen, where a timestamp was displayed. Quietly, almost in a monotone, he said, "This just happened a few hours ago. Helluva way to start Memorial Day."

Montano, watching the images, found himself having trouble formulating words. Finally: "Was that real?"

Eberhardt cleared his throat. "It couldn't be. Just a YouTube hoax." He paused. Shook his head. "Nah. Couldn't be."

A door slammed open at the end of the bullpen, hard enough to turn the heads of the men and women in the room. The man who had done it didn't notice; he was rushing toward Montano's desk.

Seeing the man made Montano relax for a second, and he could feel tension ease off Eberhardt as well.

"One of Double-D's jokes," said Montano.

"I'm gonna ream him," whispered Eb.

"You'll have to get in li –"

Montano didn't finish. The man who had just entered the bullpen was at Montano's desk now, and the detective could see from the man's eyes that he wasn't playing any jokes.

Daniel "Dapper Dan" Hitomi is the department's head IT guy. He looks like a cover model, slim and well-muscled, always sporting a three-piece suit. The suits themselves are all expensive, some of them worth more than the entire wardrobes of some of his fellow officers. But whatever his appearance, Dapper Dan was and is a certified computer forensics genius.

"Did you get that email?" Dan asked, staring at the violence that played on Montano's desktop.

Montano nodded. "You got it, too?"

"Yeah. A couple minutes ago. The email domain belongs to a continuation school."

"We know anything about it?"

Dan shook his head. "I googled it, but all I got was that it's for kids with rich parents who care more about discretion than they do about their children."

Eberhardt shook his head. "Damn." Then he jerked his gaze to Montano. "You don't think there are kids there now, do you? On a day off?"

Montano was already looking up the school's phone number, dialing it as Dan said, "No way to tell from the vid. But if there are…"

Montano sighed, listening to the dial tone. A thundering headache had erupted behind his right eye. He rubbed it as the phone rang, rang, rang. "*This* is going to be my last day?" he murmured.

"I know," said Eberhardt. "This'd be the best job in the world if it weren't for all the work we have to do."

He was trying to joke, the way he always did. But the tones were uneven, jerky. He sounded like someone speaking a foreign language after a few months' study. An alien unsure what the words meant, let alone if they were true.

"Happy Memorial Day," said Montano.

"Mondays are a bitch," said Dapper Dan. Like Eb, he

sounded like he was attempting a joke. Like Eb, he failed.

The video clip ended. Started again.

The phone rang, rang, rang in Montano's ear. No one picked up.

***

Twenty minutes later, the day begun in earnest, Montano had almost reached Reina High School. No one had answered the phones, but given that it was Memorial Day, that wasn't necessarily cause for alarm.

"For now I'm unwilling to believe it's more than some rich kid trying to be famous without actually having to do all the work of leaking a sex tape. So Eb, you stay here and work with Dapper Dan to confirm or deny from this end."

"I'll keep phoning the school, too," said Eb.

"Copy that," Montano said. He swung on a jacket, patting his pants to make sure he had the car keys to the unmarked vehicle he and Eb had been assigned. The sound of metal on metal told him he did. It also sounded ominous in the moment – like brass casings falling around at his feet while men's heads were blown off on his monitor.

"Should we call the parents?" Eberhardt had asked.

Montano chewed his lip. He liked his work. Sometimes he hated his job. This was one of those times. Given the profile of Reina High School, did he really want to start alerting some of the wealthiest and most influential people in the world? What if it *was* a hoax? He didn't think they could do anything to stop his promotion from going through – the reason today was his last day in the 'pen with Eb – but what if they could?

"Not yet. Given what kind of people they are, I'd rather not open that can of worms just now. I'll drive out there and check things out. Anything weird and I'll call it in."

Eb nodded. Dapper Dan was already gone, buzzing back

into his computer/mad scientist lab, presumably to see what facts he could dredge up from the ones and zeros that ran his world.

Please let it be a hoax.

If it was a hoax, Dapper Dan would run down the "jokester," whoever he was, and Montano intended to dedicate his life to seeing the person tossed in a dark hole.

That was the outcome he hoped – prayed – for.

***

He arrived at the school. He'd never been here, but knew it in a general sense, the way all cops generally knew their areas. He wasn't surprised at the layout: sturdy wall, security shack where guards could keep the unwashed masses at bay.

The shack was empty. Dead-seeming.

Why would I think that? Dead-seeming?

Something tickled Montano's neck. The instincts he'd followed through promotion after promotion – including the one that started tomorrow – were warning him. Screaming at him.

Something's wrong.

But what is it?

It wasn't just the empty shack – it was Memorial Day, after all, so it wouldn't be a shock to see no one manning the booth today. There was something darker playing about the edges of his consciousness.

Montano pulled up to the lowered arm that marked the line between Reina and the rest of the world. Stopped the car and got out. He looked around at the wall, the gate, the forest behind him. The birds sang, the air was crisp with the last bits of morning fog that were melting away as the sun climbed higher in the sky.

Everything looked fine.

But the look of it was the lie of it. He didn't know how he

knew, but Montano was sure something terrible was happening, or had happened – or maybe was just about to.

He pulled out his phone and dialed.

"Whatcha got, *hermano*?" said Eberhardt. Another sign that his periodic jokes about "chola eyebrows" or the like was nothing but an act to get a rise out of the partner he loved: more often than not, Eb spoke Spanish automatically when he was at his most stressed or worried. "It's an emotive language. Beautiful," he'd told Montano over a beer after one particularly nice Sunday dinner. "I fall into it when I'm mad or scared." He'd squeezed Maricela's hand. "Or in love, *como contigo, querida.*"

Montano looked around again. Trees, wall, gate. Nothing. Everything. "I'm here. I don't see anything weird."

"Hoax?"

"Don't know yet. But my Spidey-Sense is definitely tingling."

"Dapper D wants to know if we should forward the video to a contact of his at the FBI. He says he hasn't found out anything determinat –"

"No!" Montano all but shouted. Then, calming himself, he added, "I don't want them butting in."

"Worried they won't get it done fast enough for –"

Eberhardt may have kept talking, but Montano didn't hear it over the sudden, sharp crack of automatic gunfire as bullets tore up the road nearby and began stitching their way toward him.

CHAPTER 8
Intended Response

If you had been there that Memorial Day, this is what you would have seen: a perimeter set up outside the gate, cops unrolling police tape. They also blocked the road with cars, wooden barricades. Everything about it screamed that classic, "Move along, nothing to see here." Which, as any reporter (or even any private citizen with a cell phone camera) can tell you is about as effective for keeping people away as a neon sign advertising free money, sex, or power.

That was outside.

If the police there had even suspected what was going on inside, they would have reacted differently. If any of my fellow reporters had moved faster?

We'll never know.

And that was part of what those inside intended. They were DJs, playing the songs as we danced to their beat. We never suspected that they were playing the songs we expected to hear… while they busily burned the nightclub down around us.

***

Montano moved fast, talking faster. The place had to be put under his control – not just because it would be good for his career, or even because it was the right thing to do. It was also to make sure that when-not-if the feds found out about this, he already had everything wired.

The best way to stay in the game, he knew, was to make himself the manager, head coach, and MVP all wrapped into one.

As he walked, uniformed cops came and went. Each one got a machine-gun burst of instructions:

"Make sure the back is covered."

"The trees make that harder to do and –"

"Do I look like I care?" Already dismissing the cop he'd been speaking to, Montano turned to the next. "The barricades up?"

"Yes, sir. Almost."

"Almost?" He rubbed his eyes. "Make it happen faster. Then make sure no one – and I mean *no one* – gets past them. And let everyone know that if the situation gets leaked I will hunt down and personally crucify whoever did it."

"Tough to keep something this size –"

"Put out word that it's a drill."

"No one's gonna believe –"

"No, but maybe they'll wonder for a minute or two. Any extra we can get."

The other cop hustled off as Montano arrived at Tac-Com.

***

The Department's Tac-Com is an armored motorhome with enough gear to overthrow a small country. Equipment hangs off every wall, save those covered in doors, behind which are shelves carrying still more equipment. Small cut-outs with smaller desks enable a dozen or more people to cram in and work any of the crisis scenes this place has been the center of.

When Montano walked in, he eyed the techs at their stations, making sure the lockdown was proceeding.

As he entered, Lieutenant Ilyssa Vickers rose from her station. In her late forties, attractive in a way that said she knew how to dance, but could also put a knee in your face faster than you could try any moves on her. She was the tactical commander, the person in charge of funneling all the information coming into Tac-Com, sorting out important from irrelevant, then making sure it got to the person in charge: Montano.

At least for now.

Montano grimaced at the thought, trying to banish it. Getting kicked off the command of a situation like this wasn't the way to move up in the department. It was also a pain in the ass because he was good at what he did, and hated turning over a project to anyone he thought might screw it up.

"What've we got?" Montano asked.

Vickers knew what he was asking about: she waved at a bank of monitors set in one of the walls. All showed nothing but blank, black screens. "We've tapped into the closed-circuit feeds."

"Hard to manage?"

She shook her head. "It's on a security system that the administrators very kindly gave us the passwords to a long time ago, in case anything horrible happened to their expensive students."

Montano made a face. He hated places like this, on the same gut level that many people have when faced with evidence of a life impossibly out of reach. The kids at RHS hadn't been born with silver spoons in their mouths – they held the rights to the silver mines.

"So if we have the feeds, what's this showing?" Montano pointed at the black screens.

"Our view inside the gym."

Montano frowned. "There's nothing there."

***

Vickers nodded. "Correct. And it's the only place in the school that we *can't* see."

Montano sighed. "Which tells us that these people are sophisticated, and that the gym is where they are."

"And we can't go anywhere near it."

Montano looked sharply at Vickers, the question plain on his face.

Vickers shrugged. "Because there are a dozen buildings

between the gym and us, and until we sweep them, whoever took a shot at you could hit any of us as well. Not to mention that they could have rigged explosives in the buildings, or any of a million other things I don't want to think about."

"Hell of a lot to do in a short time."

"Yeah, but some people move fast. Besides, even if the buildings are clean…"

Montano rubbed his forehead again. "It gets worse?"

Vickers sighed. "The gym itself is a nightmare scenario." She nodded at one of the techs. One of the dark screens flickered, and a set of blueprints appeared. Gesturing at each feature as she spoke, Vickers laid out the bad news. "The only windows are too small to get through, and too high up for us to do laser surveillance, so unless we can get the feeds online, we have no idea what's in there: how many bad guys, how many hostages, where both of the groups are in the gym, or what precautions have been taken against entry."

"Can't we –"

"I'm not done yet." Another deep breath, then Vickers continued: "The only doors in are heavy duty steel, and the walls are solid concrete and rebar."

"So we can still blast through it, can't we?"

"Sure. But any blast big enough to punch a hole in the concrete and rebar big enough to let us in would be likely to kill most of the people inside as well. And even if it didn't, that gym is a big empty room with no vertical support, which means –"

"Which means that knocking down a wall might cause the whole place to collapse and kill everyone inside," Montano finished for her. He chuckled humorlessly. He knew three things in that moment:

The press is going to have a field day.

The feds will *get wind of this, and take it over.*

And maybe I should be hoping for that, rather than dreading it.

***

"Fantastic," Montano said to himself, trying not to think of what would happen if some of the most powerful people in the nation saw their kids hurt on his watch.

Of course, there was also the other option, no matter how small: maybe he'd come out on top. Maybe he'd finish out his last day at his current assignment with a bang. Not the bad kind, but the rocket fuel that would propel him all the way to the top. Forget just being one of the youngest cops ever to land a position in the Special Operations Bureau, forget about moving beyond that – to the Crime Strategies Group or the Chief of Operations spot. This could be the thing that secured his long-term goal of becoming Chief of Police.

Sure. And maybe I'll go home to find someone has replaced every crappy piece of Wal-Mart furniture I have with bars of solid gold.

Nothing to do about it but win. Get ahead, and get these kids out and safe and take down whoever's doing this.

That was it. That was the right attitude: seek justice, preserve the peace.

Plus, someone had *shot* at him. He was pretty sure that the bullets had been intended to keep him away, rather than actually hurting him. But one way or another, he didn't like people who played with guns like that. Particularly when he was in range of the bullets.

He pulled out his phone and called Dapper Dan. The tech genius, even though not present at Tac-Com in the flesh, would be there in spirit – or in satellite connection, which was even better. Double-D was no doubt tapped into the tech-ops part of things here.

In fact, Montano suspected that Dan was probably the reason the people in Tac-Com had any view of the school at all, and he knew the white hat hacker would be pissed off at being locked out of the gym. "Big D, how far away are you from getting me eyes in that gymnasium?"

He heard Dapper Dan typing furiously in the background. Then he heard words he'd never heard or thought to hear come out of the man's mouth: "No idea."

***

Dapper Dan Hitomi is normally a happy guy. He dresses well, he gets laid regularly, and – most important of all – he is top of the world from a white hat's point of view. He's a self-proclaimed computer genius, which bothers some people until they get to know him, and realize he backs up the cocky attitude with actual ability.

So it bothered him, enraged him, actually, that he had been locked out of so many of Reina High School's computer systems.

The same email that played on Montano's computer had shown up at one of Dan's own stations. Dan's setup made Montano's crappy workstation look like an Etch A Sketch with a busted screen, so Dan anticipated being able to easily switch off the vile loop of the two men dying *ad infinitum*.

He anticipated incorrectly. The two IT guys at Reina, whom he'd ID'd as Raymond Gunne and Nicholas Vachnarian, died on his screen. Then the email started up again, and the whole thing replayed on an endless loop. Over and over, the two men got their heads blown off. He'd never seen something like that, so violent, and wondered if there was some sort of explosive in the terrorist's bullets.

Are *they terrorists?*

Dan's older half-brother had been a stockbroker at Morgan Stanley. And just as Dapper Dan had been born a tech genius, so Jason Hitomi had been born with an almost preternatural ability to divine the future of stocks and bonds, to invest in ways that made him rich beyond most people's dreams. He was going to retire, to live in comfort. To settle down and find love and all the things people dream about.

In fact, Jason had been in the process of briefing his replacements when some maniacs drove a plane into his nice office and killed him and, a short time later, three thousand more people.

Jason Hitomi died wealthy but childless. When his parents died a short time later – of broken hearts, Dan was sure – all his brother's money passed to Dapper Dan.

Dan was a wealthy man, and still is. But he never wavered from the decision he made that day, when the towers fell and he lost the big brother he'd worshiped: he became a cop, and determined to do what he could to keep innocents safe from the random acts of violence that have become such a mainstay of contemporary existence.

And he had a special place in his heart – a dark, dank, painful place – for terrorists. And he worried that whoever had tried to cap Montano belonged to that group, and was going to try and blow a smoking hole in the world where Reina High School now stands.

***

There was also the alternative, of course: that this was about nothing more exciting than money. That still presented its own dangers, he knew. But at least greed meant he wouldn't be dealing with fanatics, just people greedy for things they could never have. The avaricious could be reasoned with. They could be captured or even just convinced to give up.

Not so zealots. The True Believers would blow themselves to hell, take as many people with them as they could.

Terrorists? Dapper Dan didn't know. He didn't know a great many things, and that bothered him.

It scared him.

So did the other thing: that whoever was behind this, whoever had opened those damn emails and replayed them over and over, death in 4K, screams bright and sharp as blood spraying on walls, belonged to the tiny, extraordinary group of people who were simply better at computers than Dapper Dan was.

Was this about money? About ransom?

Maybe. But Dan didn't think so. Certainly the video being played on his computer over and over didn't feel like an opening gambit in a ransom negotiation.

It felt like someone wanted to send a message.

***

Dapper Dan Hitomi felt that from the beginning, and said so after – both at the trials and government hearings. He says them still: "I felt like they were trying to tell us something. We just had to figure out what." He always laughs wryly when he says this. "We didn't know then what we do now. But the worst part is this: now that people *do* know, most of them don't seem to care."

***

Now, on a Memorial Day he hadn't expected to cause him any real trouble, he had some shadow figure barring his way, and on top of it he had Montano barking orders at him. Most of the time, Dan was happy to listen and follow those orders. Now, though, he wanted nothing more than to start shrieking at the detective. He quashed the feeling, though: Montano was a rising star in the department, and you didn't get to play with the best toys by pissing off the other kings on their mountains.

"How can you have no idea? You're... you're Dapper-Damn-Dan."

"I know who I am," Dan responded, still working on carving his way through the walls that had been erected between him and the knowledge he needed. "And no matter who I am, I don't have eyes inside the gym and don't know when I will."

"Well, work fast."

Dan bit back the retort: he always worked fast. Even if he didn't normally, he'd be a moron not to do so now.

Continuing, Montano said, "And see if there's anything else you can find. Check the video for clues, and any web stuff you can think of."

That last was so wholly Luddite that it made Dan laugh. "What the hell does *web stuff* mean?"

Montano's tone tore the momentary mirth from Dan's voice. "No idea. But you do, so look for it. Anything out of the ordinary."

"Captain Vague strikes again."

"I don't know what else to tell you. But none of this smells right."

Dan shook his head. When he realized that Montano wouldn't be able to see that, he sighed dramatically. "Two people got blown away, Montano. It's not supposed to smell right."

***

Dapper Dan is not the only person who works tech at the police department. Reggie Meikle is his junior, which is too bad since anywhere else he'd likely hold the Biggest Computer Nerd prize. But Reggie doesn't seem to mind. He adores Dapper Dan, and even dresses like him.

Dan likes him, too. "He's not quite as stylish as me," he told this reporter once. "But he tries hard for a white guy."

This attempt at style is somewhat marred by the fact that Reggie Meikle's desk is covered by still life pictures he has taken, all of which feature exactly the same subjects: two apples and a banana in a bowl.

Freudian fixation aside, Meikle is quick to smile, quick to laugh. A good office companion, and as hard as he tries to dress well, he tries even harder to be, simply and completely, good at the job he loves, and which he thinks is a genuinely important one.

***

Now, Reggie was trying harder than he had in his life, and Dapper Dan looked over at him when he made a small grunt of frustration.

Still talking to Montano, Dapper Dan said, "Hold on," then

kicked his wheeled office chair in the direction of his friend and assistant. "What's that?" he said, pointing at a line of code.

Reggie responded in a loud voice that Dan knew was calculated to let Montano hear. Dan didn't mind that – credit where credit was due, and the move just saved him having to relay the information at the cost of time he sensed they didn't have. "They've got someone in there with a lot of computer savvy. When we couldn't get into the CCTV feeds directly, I thought about making an end run."

"What's that got to –" Montano began, cut off by Dan's terse, "Shut up."

Reggie nodded appreciatively, then continued. "Every RHS computer log I can access just... *ends*... a few days ago."

Dan thumbed the speaker on his phone, knowing Montano would have questions and, again, not wanting to waste time playing middleman. "– that mean?" Montano's voice said, tinny and ringing over the speakerphone.

"Meaning we're in their network," said Dan, "but it's like looking at a blank slate or a brand-new system. Nothing there."

"And meaning they're very good," Reggie added.

Dan put down the phone. He gestured, and Reggie slid out of the way, letting Dan move into his space and begin working his magic. "Whoever it is, they're not as good as I am."

"Which is why you're Dapper Dan," Montano said, sounding almost cheery: he had faith in Dan's and Reggie's abilities, and Dan knew the detective expected them to crack this problem. "Call me when you find anything."

"Will do," said Dan. Reggie ended the call, and moved away from the station Dan had just commandeered.

Dan worked, trying not to hear the last words. The ones he hadn't said, but which repeated in his mind in a loop just as endless as the one playing on the computer screen behind him.

Death, death, death on the screen.

And in his mind, over and over and over again:

I hope I do find something.

I hope I can crack this guy's walls.

I hope he's not better than me.

(But he might be. God help us all, he might be.)

***

In Tac-Com, Montano put his phone away as a man entered the room. "You the negotiator?"

The man nodded. He wore a perma-stressed expression on his face, which matched the wrinkles on his perma-rumpled suit. He stuck out his hand and said, "Noah Oberczofski."

The two men shook as Montano said, "The Carlston Bank guy? Glad to have you here."

***

The Carlston Bank situation was one this reporter covered. Six years ago, eight armed gunmen attempted to rob a bank, wounding six people in the attempt.

Noah Oberczofski was in his first month as a negotiator. There were three senior officers, all of whom should have taken over the situation. Two were out of town at, ironically, a conference for negotiators whose goal was "to enable all such professionals to deal with and overcome unusual situations they find themselves facing under any circumstance."

Nothing, predictably, in the conference description about how to negotiate long-distance during an out-of-state conference, or what to do if the third person in seniority is laid up with a burst appendix the night before.

Enter Noah Oberczofski, who not only managed to convince the bank robbers to let all the wounded go in order to "show good faith," but then followed it up by convincing the robbers to release half the hostages to "grease the wheels," ten more to "show the money guys that you're willing to deal fairly," and five more to "demonstrate that you understand the situation we're all facing over here."

It was a lot of negotiator jargon, but he wielded it effectively as any swordsman with a blade. The bank robbers eventually surrendered without bloodshed, and one of them even tidied up a mess in the bank's bathroom because he "felt bad after that cop talked to me about hurting people."

The would-be robbers were carted off to prison and quickly forgotten. But Noah Oberczofski wasn't forgotten: he became something of a legend through the course of that day, and deserved every bit of the credit he received.

He was good. Very good. Even excellent.

Which meant he wasn't anywhere good enough.

***

Montano felt a surge of relief when Oberczofski came in. Having a negotiator for stuff like this was protocol, but he had a low opinion of several of them. He was glad to have someone with a great record and a reputation of operating as support rather than trying to manhandle the situation on both sides of the barricade.

"Any contact yet?" Oberczofski asked.

Montano shook his head. "We've rung every phone in the school. No dice."

"How do you know they're in there?"

"Automatic weapons-fire tried to ventilate me when I got too close."

Oberczofski nodded without surprise showing on his face. Which Montano figured made sense: he'd no doubt been briefed at least that far as he drove to RHS. "We should set up a –"

The negotiator's voice was cut off by the shrill, piercing ring of a phone hanging on the wall. It was a phone dedicated to only one thing, and everyone in Tac-Com stiffened as it rang.

Oberczofski pointed at the phone, looking at Montano as he did. Montano nodded, and the negotiator picked up. "This is Noah Oberczofski. Can I ask who –"

A voice cut him off. The voice came from the speakers embedded in the wall above the phone, allowing everyone in the command center to hear it. "Put Montano on," said the voice. It was a relaxed, almost pleasant voice.

Everyone startled at that. Vickers and Oberczofski looked at Montano, who shrugged a "don't look at me, I just work here," then gestured for Oberczofski to continue.

"I assure you, I –"

Oberczofski's words died instantly as a sound cracked out over the speakers. It was one every cop knew instantly: the sound of a weapon being cocked. "I won't ask again," came the voice, never losing that pleasant *gee-golly-ain't-we-all-friends*? tone.

Oberczofski glanced at Montano, then held out the phone. Montano took it. It felt cold and somehow oily in his hand. "This is Detective Montano. To whom am I speaking?"

"I don't need a name. I just need to be heard." The voice paused. "But for clarity you can call me Teacher, and my associate is The Lady – though you'll only be talking to me, for the time being. And when you do speak to her, I doubt you'll know it's her until she wants you to."

Vickers mouthed, "Oh, shit."

Montano agreed. A simple demand for money would have been one thing. But this… it still wasn't clear what was happening, but the situation felt a bit worse with every passing moment.

"I'm listening, Teacher," he said. He ignored the comment about "The Lady," filing it away to follow up on later. But for now the focus was less on Terrorist Staffing than it was on getting the hostages out. "You want to tell me what you want? Other than to blow holes in my car?"

Teacher chuckled. "Right now, I want you to come closer to the gym."

Montano chuckled, too. Unlike Teacher's light, airy laugh, his was dark and angry. "Wait, I've heard this one. The punch line is: 'So I can shoot you that much easier,' right?"

"As long as you don't go past the Science Building, you'll be fine. You won't need to go much further than there to see what you need to."

Montano looked at Oberczofski. The other man gestured, waving his hands in a "keep going" motion. "Okay, we'll consider it."

"Don't consider it. Come now. I've got something you'll want to see."

"What?"

"Come see. Ten minutes."

"And if I don't?"

Teacher laughed again. Harder this time, and the cold handset Montano held somehow seemed to drop a few more degrees. "Not just *you*, Detective Montano. I want your whole group to come closer. So you can see."

"Fine. And if *we* don't?"

"Then I execute the first ten students, and one every minute after that. I bet you run out of resolve before I run out of hostages."

CHAPTER 9
The Plan

The late-and-unlamented Coach Fertetti's office is a windowless, tight space to one side of the RHS gym. This is where Teacher had called Tac-Com from, and when he finished he hung up the phone on Fertetti's desk and turned to look at the other two occupants of the office: Blue, and Principal Gersham.

Blue sat on the corner of Fertetti's desk, one hand on the trigger of his rifle, the muzzle of which rested easily against Principal Gersham's forehead.

As for Gersham himself, Blue had gestured for him to sit down on a wheeled chair some time ago. Gersham complied meekly, and neither moved nor spoke as Blue encircled his trunk, legs, and forelegs with duct tape, binding him tightly to the chair. His arms had been taped as well – bound together behind the chair back – and a final strip of the silver tape went over the principal's mouth.

Teacher took a moment to study the school's esteemed principal. Gersham seemed to be a different person than the one Teacher had snatched out of his cocoon.

Though Gersham is nothing so lovely or dainty as a butterfly. Neither was Fertetti.

A final strip of duct tape covered Gersham's mouth, then Teacher took his long knife from its sheath at his side. Like the huge gun and powerful bullets he had used to end the lives of the school's IT personnel, Raymond Gunne and Nicholas Vachnarian, this weapon had been chosen and prepared to make a specific statement.

Part of that statement would be a public one – meant for the police and, shortly, for the reporters who would come.

Part of it was a more private message. Much more intimate. Part of the statement was something that Teacher would say directly to the principal. He would not speak, but the message would be received, he had no doubt.

"Ready to be my attention-getter?" he asked the principal.

***

The man, who had been sitting absolutely motionless in the chair, smelled disgusting. He had voided his bladder and bowels. But it was nothing compared to the stink of unadulterated fear that now ran off him.

Teacher smiled. He held up the knife.

The blade glinted in the dim light of the windowless room. It looked sharp. But Teacher knew that appearances could be deceiving. The principal was not what he seemed, and neither was the knife.

The principal looked like the right and righteous administrator of an expensive and respected prep school. The knife looked sharp.

Both were lies.

Teacher put the point of his knife against Gersham's once-expensive, now ruined clothing. The man hadn't moved for what seemed an eternity, but upon feeling the knife he shook his head wildly and tried to stand.

Useless: all he managed to do was rock a bit from side to side.

It didn't stop Teacher. Didn't even inconvenience him. He just kept pressing down on the knife. Not stabbing the principal – that would be far too quick and far too kind – just... *pushing*... the dull piece of metal into him.

Slowly, slowly: he didn't want to kill the man.

Gersham began thrashing harder. Muffled sobs choked out around the tape on his mouth. Teacher reached up and yanked the silver strip. The tape had been on long enough that it had melded to Gersham's face, and it tore a wide strip of skin away from the man's mouth and cheeks.

Gersham gasped, but any screams were stolen from him as

Teacher pushed the knife in another inch.

A moment later, though, he did start screaming as Teacher stopped pushing the knife and instead began to *saw*. The knife was dull. The going was slow.

But that was just fine. After all, he had ten minutes to kill.

CHAPTER 10
Intended Response

Montano, Vickers, and Oberczofski all stared at the phone Montano still held in his hand. No one on the other end of the line, but he still heard the last words Teacher had spoken.

"I bet you run out of resolve before I run out of hostages."

Vickers broke the silence first. "There's no way we're moving in there. The whole place could be wired to blow, they could –"

"They could start blowing up kids, Vickers. *Kids*." Montano finally put the phone back on its hook on the wall. Without turning away from it, he said, "What do you think? Will he do it?"

Oberczofski said, "We have no information."

Montano turned to see the man holding his hands wide, shrugging. "What's your gut tell you?" he asked.

The negotiator chewed his lip before answering. "It tells me he'll kill them if we don't comply."

"What about you, Vickers?"

Vickers grimaced. Answer enough.

"Dammit."

Montano wasn't sure if he said it, or Vickers, or Oberczofski. And it really didn't matter.

***

In only a few minutes' time, Reina High School had become Montano's world. The gym was at the center of it, the beating heart of a body gone mad.

The things that had happened here had guaranteed a state of, at best, controlled chaos. Now, as Montano and Vickers coordinated the movement of their small encampment into the walls of the school, the controlled chaos became near-unbridled mayhem.

Officers moved forward, some on foot, others in cars. They were preceded by others in tactical gear, moving into the buildings, sweeping through them, trying desperately to clear rooms of any hazards while knowing they didn't have near the necessary time to do a good job of it.

Tac-Com moved in last.

The world had constricted.

The body had curled in on itself.

It is said that every human heart has a set number of beats that it can get through before it dies. This reporter does not know if that is true or not. Certainly, though, the camp drew closer, the beat grew faster... and death came all the more quickly for it.

Though more – many more – would follow, and though neither Montano nor any of the reporters already approaching the camp could know it, the first death they would witness and bear record of was only minutes away.

***

Tac-Com had barely stopped moving when the phone rang again. Oberczofski picked up. "This is –"

Again, Teacher's voice came from the speakers. "If I hear your voice on this phone again, ten hostages die."

Oberczofski handed the phone to Montano. Montano nodded at him: *Thanks. It was worth a try.*

To Teacher, he said, "Nine minutes even."

"Very punctual. Thank you."

"Thank you for not shooting us or blowing us up."

Again, Teacher chuckled. Montano considered commenting on it, but knew anything he said would come off as either sarcastic or angry – not a good way to help the students or staff of RHS.

"I wouldn't blow you up, Detective: that would be

counterproductive. That said, you can't really believe me at this point, and clearing the school buildings of explosives or possible booby traps will take some time, won't it?"

Montano thought about lying. Then he thought about the kids, decided there was nothing to gain from a falsehood. At least, not for now. "Yeah, it will. Anything could be in them."

"I'd keep that in mind."

"Or," Montano said through teeth he couldn't keep from gritting, "nothing could be in them at all."

"That's true," said Teacher somberly. "So how will you know to take me seriously? Should I kill one of the students?"

Negotiation 101: don't disagree with the hostage-taker. Try to build rapport, common ground. But Montano was having a hell of a time figuring out how to answer Teacher's question with anything other than a shrieked, "NO!"

"I'd... prefer it if you didn't. Maybe if you'd just tell me what you –"

"It's not time for that, Montano. But I won't kill students at this point. It would be premature." He paused, then said, "Watch the south side doors. You can send six people a bit closer to the gym when the time is right, but no closer than fifty feet under any circumstances. You try to move in closer than that, or send in more than six, and you'll find out just how big an explosion someone like me can rig in a few hours."

"When the time is right? What does that –"

Click.

***

Montano didn't think he'd ever run as fast as he did then, tearing out of Tac-Com, juking right like he was avoiding a tackle from a six-hundred-pound linebacker, then plowing up grass and sod as he tore between two of the buildings, running toward the cruiser that was closest to the south side of the gym. They'd drawn a hard line in the sand at the science building, just like Teacher had said to do, but there was still plenty of room between where they were and the far edge of the science building that jutted into the fields to one side.

He was aware of cursing, followed by a soft, oddly calming whisper: Vickers and Oberczofski. Both of them had barely hunkered down behind the cruiser with Montano when a group of men in full tactical armor appeared: C-Unit, Vickers' hand-picked group who always handled the most dangerous moments. Montano knew about C-Unit. Knew they were good.

And it occurred to him then, starkly and forcefully, that there were six of them. Exactly the number of people Teacher had said would be permitted to get close to the gym "when the time was right."

Was it a coincidence, that Teacher had provided a sort of hall pass for exactly the number of people Vickers would have sent given the chance?

Montano didn't know. But he doubted it.

That was his first inkling. The first moment where he suspected how far ahead of him Teacher might be.

***

One of the south-side gym doors slammed open. A flurry of movement in the darkness beyond, then a body was flung out.

Montano didn't have the information he needed. Not nearly enough. But he thought the guy looked familiar from the file. Principal? What was his name? Gershing? Gersh…

Gersham.

Gersham took a staggering step away from the building. Another. The door slammed shut behind him as he started running. Something about the way he lurched told Montano clearly: the guy was injured. Maybe badly. But he couldn't see anything of his body through the voluminous, light brown trench coat the principal was wearing. Nor was the principal going to tell him anything: even at this range, Montano could see that someone had tied the man's hands behind his back – probably the same someone who had also slapped a thick length of duct tape over Gersham's mouth.

Montano stood, every instinct he had as a cop and as a human screaming to him that he should run to the guy. But Oberczofski grabbed him, and at the same time Vickers shouted, "No! He could be wired!" To the men nearby she shouted, "C-unit, get out there and intercept him. Everyone else, stay down and move back if you can."

***

The C-Unit commander is a man named Robert Kale. The men in his unit call him Greenie for obvious reasons – and he permits it. Some men need to prove bravado by screaming and threatening. Greenie doesn't. During one of our interviews, he told me that he'd happily "permit" the men under his command to call him Greenie if that helped get the job done.

"And if it didn't?"

He smiled, and cracked his huge, scarred, calloused knuckles and said, "Then I'd stop permitting it," and I believed him without further question.

Greenie has a funny nickname, but there is nothing funny about him when he is on the job. And Greenie is *always* on the job.

***

Greenie led C-Unit as they sprinted out to meet the principal. Gersham's tottering run had turned into something like a ballet of tumbling almost-falls, the trips and flails growing more pronounced as he stumbled forward. The tan trench coat fluttered around him like a bird's broken wings.

The coat worried Greenie – terrified him, in fact. He couldn't see enough of the man wearing it to tell if he was really friend or foe, and if foe then that coat could be hiding anything. He wasn't on the bomb squad, but he'd done two tours in Afghanistan. He'd seen three of his friends turned to bloody chunks by a pair of IEDs, and he didn't like people wearing anything more voluminous than a g-string when explosives were a possibility, as they most definitely were at RHS.

When C-Unit was within twenty paces of the principal, Greenie started shouting, "Get down! Get down now, sir! *Now!*"

He was pretty sure at this point that the guy in the coat wasn't one of the bad guys – be that a terrorist; a kidnapper; or just a ten-year-old kid with ADHD, a gluten intolerance, a peanut allergy, and a need to be seen by his mommy and daddy. But terrorist or not, the guy in the coat was making strange, strangled, hacking noises behind his gag. They creeped Greenie out, and that wasn't a feeling he liked or was used to.

Greenie noted a spreading stain on the man's coat, around the crotch: looked like he'd pissed himself.

"Get down, sir. Get down or I will PUT you down!"

The man finally listened: he fell forward, flat on his stomach, his bound hands fluttering spastically behind his back.

Greenie and the rest of C-Unit closed on the man, half-encircling him, shouting commands and updates to one another: "Careful, careful!" "Not too fast!" "Watch the gym, watch the gym!" "Eyes on!"

The man in the tan trench coat had fallen facedown on the ground. He was still making those awful sounds, something that Greenie would continue hearing in his dreams until the present day. "Probably never forget them," he said when I last interviewed him.

But at the time, he just knew they sounded bad. Greenie had already doubted this guy was a terrorist. Now he was certain of it. "Turn him over," he said.

One of his guys rolled the man over, another reaching down to rip the tape off Gersham's mouth. The second the tape came off, the strangled, wheezing sound the principal had been making turned into a shriek of a sort Greenie had never heard before. It was agony on a scale he could not comprehend – either as to its intensity or its genesis.

Beside him, one of the men who had run onto the field was first to catch on. To *see*.

He turned and vomited.

All these men were tested, hardened. Greenie's first impulse was to reprimand the guy for puking. Then another man vomited. Both those men had seen it first, and when Greenie did as well, it was all he could do not to send the breakfast his wife had made spewing all over the grass.

***

Montano watched C-Unit race out. Saw them surround Principal Gersham's body. He felt like the universe – smaller and smaller with every passing moment – was now no larger than a man sprawled in the grass.

Beside him, Vickers shouted, "C-Unit! Get back here!"

Her voice was piercing, almost a shriek. Montano couldn't blame her: seriously weird shit was going down, and she was the one who bore primary responsibility for the safety of the men out there.

The biggest of the C-Unit members – obviously the leader of the group – didn't answer. Not until two of his men vomited all over grass.

"What the –"

The man straightened, and whatever Vickers had been about to say died on her lips. Montano felt the blood drain from his face. He couldn't tell what it was, but something had the guy out there spooked. His eyes looked flat, dead. "Like something had stripped away the best parts of his soul," was the way one of the police on-scene would later describe it in a deposition.

The leader of C-Unit spoke in an oddly quiet voice, as though to hold back the rising tide of madness Montano felt all around them.

The voice shouldn't have carried so far, but on a day about to tilt away from anything possible, it did carry, and Montano heard the guy say, "I don't know if we can move the –"

"Unless he's a threat I want him and you back here *now!*" Vickers shouted. Montano glanced at her. She was flicking her gaze back and forth: now looking at C-Unit, now at the Science Building. Montano was surprised to realize that in the past few moments he had totally forgotten Teacher's instruction not to cross that invisible boundary.

He tensed involuntarily, as though waiting for the explosion that would vaporize him and everyone else.

It didn't come.

Instead, C-Unit lifted Principal Gersham from the ground. It struck Montano forcibly how odd it was that they would carry him like that. He had been running a moment ago. Now, four of the men hoisted him – one on each arm, one on each leg – while the other two men in C-Unit walked behind them, aiming their guns, acting as both sword and shield in case of an attack from the rear.

They were carrying the man like a dead soldier being dragged from the battlefield.

***

As they came closer, Montano heard a strange noise. Gasping, bubbling. Like someone drowning – but not in water. This was the noise of sinking into pure agony.

As C-Unit reached the perimeter, one of them shouted, "Get EMS up here!"

There was a flurry of movement behind Montano, and a pair of emergency responders, onsite for just such a situation, rushed forward with a field gurney. Montano lurched out of cover, following without thought. Vickers and Oberczofski fell into step beside him.

C-Unit was sliding the principal onto the gurney as Montano

reached them. As they did, Gersham stopped making that strange noise. It was a relief, until he opened his mouth and… *howled* was the only word that Montano could think of.

"What's wrong with him?" Montano shouted.

As they slid him over, one of the EMTs leaned over and, just as the two men of C-Unit had done, vomited onto the grass. As he did, Montano saw clearly what had happened.

Gorge rose in his own throat. Vickers gagged behind him, and to his right Oberczofski whispered, "Dear God in Heaven," and crossed himself.

Gersham was still screaming, screaming, *screaming*.

The EMT who had vomited stood. Bile ran down his chin, spattered his otherwise white shirt with yellow, but he visibly pulled himself together. He grabbed the side of the stretcher with his fellow and ran off.

Montano didn't follow. Neither did anyone in C-Unit. They all just stood there in shock, transfixed by the sight of Gersham.

***

Greenie had thought the stain on his coat was urine; that the man had lost control of his bodily fluids as terror wracked him. Greenie had seen that before, and would see it again.

But he had never seen anything like *this*. Neither had Montano or Vickers or Oberczofski or anyone in the department.

Gersham's crotch had been hacked to pieces.

Not just cut, not even bludgeoned with a hammer or some other heavy instrument. Hacked. To. *Pieces*. Someone had gone at him with something dull, slashing and tearing at his groin until nothing was left but blood and loose shreds of flesh hanging off bone.

CHAPTER 11
The Plan

Teacher stood in front of the closed door that led outside. He listened to Gersham's screams as they rose, fell. As they drifted away to silence. He heard a siren – the sound of pain being ushered to aid.

He doubted anyone could help Gersham. And was glad. It would save him trying to figure out how to kill him later.

He looked at the knife – bloody, dripping. Gobbets of meat hung from parts of it, and a thin strip of skin draped off the point: what remained of Gersham's scrotum.

"Do I have your attention?" Teacher said. He was speaking to himself, but also willing the words across the empty expanse of field. Sending them to Montano in his mind.

He knew he did have that attention.

But would it be enough? He wanted attention, but only as a means to an end. After all, attention was different than listening, and listening a separate thing from understanding.

Teacher wanted that last; wanted *understanding*. Indeed, he would settle for nothing less.

***

He looked around the gym. To one side, the bleachers had been disassembled, then put back together in a different configuration. Where possible, he had used the nuts and bolts and joints already present to put them back in the shape he wanted, and needed for the plan. Occasionally they had to be simply welded into the shape he desired. That was fine: The Lady had her stick welder for that purpose – and for a few other purposes as well, though they were darker and more satisfying than simply turning bleachers into a new shape with a new function.

He turned to look into the cavernous center of the gym.

The teachers and students who still remained had been

spread out on the floor. Black hoods covered their heads, but he knew that anyone looking into the gym would be able to place them:

The Misfits, with their clothing that so loudly pretended to stand out, while only emphasizing how much the owners wanted to fit in.

The cheerleaders – especially Paige, with her outfit that verged on the microscopic.

Daxton Leigh, he of the dick pix, along with his remaining flunky, Konstantin Tarov – the boy with the hair so bright it hurt to look at, shared by nearly everyone in his family.

Isaiah Mulcahey and Jonas Chambers: the two surviving teachers; the former a piece of living scum, the latter a teacher who was a genuinely good person, so far as Teacher could tell. He was lucky, in a way, that Teacher had come along before the younger man could be corrupted in this cesspool.

Holden Wright, the office secretary. Like everyone on the floor, he had been hooded and forbidden to speak, though The Lady had ordered that he be laid out next to Jonas – she was kind in that way. She cared about how people felt. Of course, that also made her more cruel when the time came: she was empathetic. She understood pain. And, having traveled the byways of agony, she knew the map well enough to lead others in that same direction.

Teacher had killed some people today. He had maimed Principal Gersham. And it was nothing compared to what The Lady had insisted must happen, from the very beginning.

The Colors walked up and down between the hostages, their guns drawn, ready to use them. They understood who had to die, and who must not. They understood the order of things, and the way they had to happen. They would follow orders, of that Teacher had no doubt.

It was time to move ahead with the plan.

CHAPTER 12
Intended Response

Like just about everyone in the world, Montano would come to understand that plan. Like just about everyone in the world, Montano would reel, dumbfounded, at how Teacher and The Lady had played him.

But for now, he was reeling in a different way.

Gersham had been taken away. But the sight of him still hung there, front and center before his vision. He was imagining it, and part of him wondered if his imagination was making it worse than it had been. Surely no one could do such a thing. Surely no one could take a principal – someone who watched over *children* – and so thoroughly emasculate him that he ceased not only to be a man, but to be anything resembling a human.

But the rest of Montano knew the truth: that was exactly what had happened. What had been done to a man who, so far as he knew, didn't deserve any of it.

Whatever they want, whatever they're trying to do, I'm going to stop them. I'm going to stop that bastard, Teacher, and feed him his own genitals. See how he *likes it.*

Even as he thought it, Montano was already moving back to Tac-Com. He was a good cop, with good instincts. He knew intuitively what was going to happen next. He didn't know what would happen after "next" was done, but the first step was a foregone conclusion.

Even as he stepped into the mobile command center, Vickers and Oberczofski shadowing him with grim expressions and pale faces, "next" happened:

The wall phone rang.

Montano snatched the phone off the cradle, almost shouting, cursing the monster on the other end of the line. He felt a hand on his shoulder. A squeeze. Oberczofski, warning him to keep it together.

"You're all they've got, so don't screw this up. It isn't about what happened, it's about what you can stop from happening," said that squeeze.

Montano managed to get himself under control, mostly. "What. Do. You. Want?" he managed. His teeth ground together so hard that he felt something crack and would in fact later discover that he had split a molar.

Teacher was quiet for a moment. Montano heard breathing, but nothing else. He recognized the old negotiating tactic: force the other person to talk first. Keep *them* asking, keep *them* as the supplicant.

Montano could play that game. Heated wrath had nearly made him lose it a moment ago. Now, cold rage took over. He held the phone in his hand and waited.

Finally, Teacher said, "What I really want is something you can never give me, Detective."

"Try me."

Sounding like he hadn't even heard (and Montano was thinking more and more that Teacher was not just evil, but likely also insane), Teacher continued, "How about I give *you* something instead?"

***

Montano felt hope. Maybe this guy would let out a hostage. But the hope fizzled and died almost immediately: people who were going to let someone go right away did that *before* hacking a guy's privates to hamburger.

"What exactly are you going to give me?" he asked.

"Information," said Teacher.

"How can I believe anything you'd say?" said Montano.

Again, Teacher ignored him. Sounds of a struggle could be

heard. "Teacher? Teacher, answer me."

"Sorry to leave you hanging there, Detective Montano," said Teacher. "I'm just sitting here on the school bleachers, looking out at my little kingdom. I thought about giving you details, but realized you probably wouldn't believe me, so…" His voice shifted slightly. "A police officer is on the phone, Konstantin. Why don't you give him a progress report? Fill him in on all the fun we've had?"

Montano gestured at Vickers, but she was already moving, whispering "Find out who Konstantin is" into the ear of a tech, who started typing furiously.

On the line, a new voice spoke. The voice cracked, in part because of panic, sure, but also because the speaker was obviously in the throes of ongoing adolescence. "Oh, God, mister, please –"

"Talk to the detective, Konstantin," said Teacher, his calm tones sharpening to a dangerous edge.

Trying to head off any more death or torture, Montano said, "Hi, Konstantin. Can you tell me your last name?"

"Tarov."

Vickers gestured again, and the tech started calling up school and civic records, faces flashing across the screen before settling on what looked like a school picture of a kid who looked unfortunately like a weasel's untrustworthy, red-headed cousin.

Damn, even rich kids have shitty school pictures.

"Good to meet you, Konstantin," said Montano. "We're going to get you out of there. But can you help us out? Tell us what's happening around you?"

Konstantin began sobbing. "Th-th-they killed them."

Montano, already on high alert, now tensed so hard his entire body ached. "What do you mean? Who got killed?"

Silence. Teacher whispered, "Go ahead, Konstantin. Tell the nice man."

"The… the Vice-Principal, Mr. Ulric. Mrs. Welner in the front office. Mr. Gunne and Mr. Vachnarian and Coach Fertetti. They took off our hoods, then dragged them right through here so we could see. Right through. They beat up Daxton. Killed Zane. And the screams…" Konstantin coughed, and Montano suddenly remembered an image: the Three Stooges, all of them trying to shove through the same doorway at the same time, to no effect. The cough sounded like that – like every terrible emotion was struggling to come out of Konstantin at once, and none of them could quite get through.

"We can't hold out much longer," Konstantin whispered. "They're going to kill us."

The worst part wasn't that the kid obviously believed that last. It was that, more and more, Montano was realizing that Teacher was well prepared, and that everything to this point was going to his plan. More and more, Montano was wondering if the kid, Konstantin, was right.

"They're going to kill us," Konstantin whispered again.

***

Montano tried to stop from screaming, and only half succeeded. "I'll get you out, Konstantin. Promise. Is Zane another student?"

But he could tell he wasn't going to get any answers. Konstantin cried out and the shift-shuffling sounds of a phone changing hands emerged from Tac-Com's speakers. "I think that will do for now," said Teacher. To someone else, undoubtedly one of the "they" that Konstantin had spoken of, he said, "Put the hood and the tape back on him."

Konstantin screamed, the sound quickly muffled. Behind him, Montano could also hear other screams, just as muffled. Kids, teachers. All of them no doubt gagged just as Konstantin was now being gagged, all of them no doubt blinded behind dark hoods just as Konstantin was now being blinded.

Part of being a good cop was the ability to put yourself in the mind of the bad guys. But part of being a *great* cop was the ability to put yourself in the mind of the victims. Montano believed that was why there were so few great cops: the pain is just too immense. To feel the terror and agony of the victims is a weight few people can shoulder.

Montano had always felt he was one of those greats. Now, feeling that boy's terror, playing it over in his own mind as though he were in the gym himself, he wondered if the price of greatness just might be too high to pay.

***

"What just happened?" Montano found himself shouting. "What happened?"

Teacher's voice had returned to its laid-back, almost folksy tones. "Easy, Detective. The... *remaining*... kids are fine."

Montano rubbed his eye. A tension migraine was blinding him. "Just tell me what you want. You call yourself Teacher, so teach me."

Teacher chuckled. "Did you know there are over three thousand animal shelters in the United States? An astounding number. And don't just take my word for it. Google what I just said and you'll find out for yourself. The world is a funny place."

He hung up.

Montano slammed the phone onto the wall. "Shit."

He spun and all but shoved one of the techs out of her seat. He opened a web browser, brought up the search engine, and typed:

over 3,000 animal shelters in u.s.

Tac-Com had a good internet connection. The browser only took a fraction of a second to go blank, then return. It was covered with words and links, but Montano only saw the top few:

10,000,000 results.

"Shit," he said again.

"You thought it would be that easy?" said Vickers wryly.

"Hope springs eternal," said Montano.

No one spoke. There was only the tapping of keys as the techs continued working. The breathing of the living close by. The heavy sound of Gersham, still screaming in Montano's mind.

"Is the irony of that sentence lost on anyone?" Oberczofski finally asked, his tone sepulchral.

***

At the station, Dapper Dan Hitomi was pummeling his keyboard like it had insulted him. Reggie Meikle sat nearby, typing as well (though less viciously). They both stared at computer screens filled with something that most laymen would find as accessible and understandable as Greek by way of the Enigma cipher.

But whether onlookers could understand or not, Dapper Dan and, to a lesser extent, Reggie Meikle both did. A new item appeared on Dapper Dan's screen, and he shouted in triumph. "Got it, you bastards!"

Eberhardt had been standing nearby, going through what meager school records they could access outside of the school's own systems. When Dan screamed, he startled and dropped half of the pages he'd been holding.

"Damn, Dan. What the –"

"I've gotten into the school's network logs. Some of them, anyway," Dan said. He didn't look at Eberhardt, just kept his fingers flying on the keyboard.

Eberhardt walked over to peer at Dan's screen, which almost made Dan laugh given that no one this side of MIT (or Reggie) could have understood what he was doing. "Didn't you say there was nothing there? That it was blank?" asked Eberhardt.

Dan permitted a smug grin. "It looked like it, but it's active and connected."

Eberhardt frowned. "Why make it look like they erased everything, or hide their connection?"

"So they could keep their network up for communications, is my guess," Reggie answered.

Eberhardt frowned. "I don't know much about computers or nothing –"

"Very true," said Dapper Dan, as Reggie said, "Understatement."

"– but I do know you guys. How could they have done that?"

Dapper Dan's smug look dropped off his face. "No idea."

"Then what about this: why bother keeping it on? Why not actually turn everything off, rather than leave something on for you guys to backdoor your way into? It's not like they're going to send interoffice emails about the big ISIS vs. KKK Terrorist Softball game this Friday. They'd be better off actually cutting it, keeping it cut, and just communicating with walkie-talkies or burner phones." Frowning, he added, "And why bother with that? Far as we know they're all holed up in the gym. Just talking face-to-face would do it."

"They want to communicate with someone on the outside, obviously," said Reggie.

"Okay, but who? They coordinating this? Is this part of something bigger? Is there more on the way? Worse?"

***

Dapper Dan didn't have an answer to Eberhardt's question

– but then, he'd almost stopped listening at that point. Something had caught his eye. The execution video was playing out on his screen, over and over again. Gory, bloody. Boom, and one head gone. Boom, and another was pink mist and gray matter.

Boom, gone.

"Any words of wisdom, Danny Boy?" said Eberhardt.

Boom, dead.

"You listening?"

Boom, gone.

"Reggie, is he doing his silent monk thing?"

Boom, dea -

"Eb," Dan said, "look at this."

Eberhardt looked like he was on the verge of a quip, but something about Dan's tone stopped him. He looked at the screen. The execution played out again.

Boom, gone.

Boom, dead.

"I'm not seeing anything," said Eberhardt.

"That's obvious from your wardrobe," said Reggie with a smirk.

"Can it, Banana Boy," Eberhardt growled.

Boom, dead.

"There!" Dan shouted. He jabbed his finger at the screen. He tried to pause the video, then remembered he couldn't: it was still acting autonomously, unable to be stopped or closed down.

And how are they doing that? Who's good enough to do that to me?

Dapper Dan tapped a few keys. A red dot appeared on his screen. He waited until the video had played through several times, then clicked the dot and navigated to the file he'd just created and emailed it to himself.

He spun back to his other computer – the one that was still under his control – and opened the file

Dan smiled. He wasn't happy about this – who would be? – but he thought he'd seen something. Maybe a break.

They needed one.

***

Eberhardt watched Dan work. Everything the guy did seemed a bit like magic to the older man, but so long as it was useful magic, and helped him catch the bad guys, he was fine with that.

Dapper Dan opened an email file, and the video – a screen recording – opened on Dan's screen. The same video that was playing over and over on Dan's other computer. The other one, Dan had said, was doing it without his input, and resisted every effort to stop it.

But here, on this computer… Dan let the video play for a second, then tapped some keys. The video slowed down.

Something flickered on the screen. Eberhardt mirrored what Dan had done a moment ago and jabbed one of his big fingers at the screen. "What was that? A glitch?"

"Dunno." Dan slowed down the video even more. He clicked forward a single frame at a time. Stopped.

Eberhardt stared at the frozen image. So did Dan and Reggie. After a few moments, Reggie broke the silence:

"What the hell is *that*?"

***

The single frame of video didn't show much: just a dim shot of a wall covered by peeling green paint, with a bare dirt floor below it. And on that floor…

... an arm.

The arm obviously belonged to someone laying face-up on the ground outside of the camera shot. Visible from what Eberhardt guessed was four or five inches below the shoulder down to the hand, which was slender, feminine. Blood spattered it, and the fingers were curled into the particular, claw-like rigidity that marks a painful death.

On the upper arm, a small, raised circle could be seen. It drew the attention with a strange power. Even the blood was, for some reason, less jarring to those who saw it at that moment. The blood was horrible, and indicative of terrible events, but everyone in the room had seen blood on victims before.

Something about the circle seemed alien to the arm. Foreign.

"Is that a burn?" Eberhardt asked. Neither Dapper Dan nor Reggie could answer.

One other feature: a small, braided bracelet encircled the thin wrist. It looked to be made of dark leather – or perhaps had started out lighter and been stained to the richer tone by sweat or the passage of years or simply dyed by the blood that had painted the unknown girl's skin. Woven into the center of the bracelet was a glass bauble. Nothing fancy, just a bead that had been fashioned into a translucent heart.

***

Ten percent of all line-of-duty police fatalities aren't because a cop got shot or stabbed or bludgeoned: they are the simple result of heart attacks. The stress of the job in general, and of each situation in particular, is not something the human heart is equipped to deal with on such a regular, insistent basis.

Eberhardt knew this. And as he stared at the arm and hand, the bright blood and the stained bracelet with its glass heart, he felt his own heart tighten. He was old enough that it was a concern for him, and one of the reasons his wife had started pressing him to consider retirement.

Don't you dare kill me, you bastard of a ticker.

Eberhardt suspected that if Montano had thought that, it would have been followed up with: *I'm too pretty to die.*

For Eb, it was more straightforward: he wasn't going to die until he stopped whoever was doing this. Whoever had taken over a high school and in so doing committed what, for him, was a cardinal sin: endangering kids.

And now this. This unknown girl who looks like she died on a dirt floor, in pain and alone.

Eberhardt didn't question for a moment that the two things were related. How, he didn't know yet. But he decided that he would do whatever it took to take these people down. For the staff of Reina High School that he hoped were keeping their shit together. For the kids who'd been confronted with difficulties no *adult* should have to face.

And, now, for the girl in the video.

Whatever it took, in this case, meant doing something cops as a rule hate to do: call for back-up from another agency.

"You have someone at the Bureau who can work this video?" asked Eberhardt.

Dapper Dan nodded. "He's not better than me –"

"Of course not."

"– but federal dollars do buy a much nicer computer than this one, and the FBI files will make extrapolating information from the paint and the dirt and anything else a helluva lot easier for them than it would be for us." He hitched in a half breath, looking like he wanted to say something else.

"Spit it out, Double-D," said Eberhardt.

"I'll call them. It's the right call," said Dan. "But, for the record, Montano isn't going to like it."

Eberhardt returned his attention to the girl's arm, jutting into view. The claw-hand, the red-spattered skin, the blown glass heart.

"No one gets everything they want," he said. "Not even Montano."

Certainly not the poor girl who died in the dirt.

CHAPTER 13
Intended Response

Montano alternated between watching the phone and watching the monitors that were supposed to register the gym feeds. Both gave him the same amount of information, which was none at all.

Vickers hung up one of the many other phones in the mobile command center and approached Montano. Her expression was sour enough that he knew what she was going to say before she said it.

"The mayor is starting to get calls from some of the parents."

"Just some of them?"

Vickers shrugged. "From what I'm starting to gather, the kids at Reina are mostly borderline delinquents – and some of them not so borderline – and the parents are mostly rich assholes whose primary concern is keeping their names out of the papers. Most of them we haven't even managed to find – they're either on vacation or 'incommunicado for business purposes.'" She shook her head, a rueful expression on her face. "The ones we *have* found weren't even aware their kids were MIA – and I got the impression that's typical, and most of them don't know or care what their kids are doing for days or even weeks at a time."

Montano's mouth dropped open. "How is that even possible?"

His own parents weren't shining examples of perfection: divorced, a father who had the morals of an exceptionally promiscuous housefly, a mother who drank too much because of it and often forgot to do things like cook dinner or pick up her kids from school. But hell, at least if he was missing they'd have known about it.

By way of answer, Vickers rubbed her thumb and fingers together. "Money," she said.

Montano snorted. "Wow."

It flitted through his mind that he himself had more than a little affection for money – who didn't – but holy hell in a hamster wheel, parents like Vickers was describing were a whole other level.

Aren't they?

Turning away from Vickers – and by extension his own suddenly guilty conscience, Montano looked once more at the darkened gym feeds. He pursed his lips, then, in a sudden movement, snatched the dedicated phone off its cradle.

"There's a coach's office in there, right?" Montano said. Vickers nodded. "Ring it."

Vickers gestured to a tech. "On it."

Nearby, Oberczofski had been sitting on one of the small desks, his entire body jammed into the cubby between wall cabinets, obviously deep in thought. Now, though, he hopped up and said, "I don't know if that's a good –"

"We can't just sit here with our thumbs up our asses," said Montano. Eyeing Vickers, he said, "Unless you think maybe we can go in there after –"

Vickers jerked her head side to side so hard Montano thought she'd give herself whiplash. "We know they've killed people, but I also know that if we go in more than likely *everyone* in that building dies."

Montano looked at Oberczofski, eyebrows raised, silently asking if the negotiator had any better ideas.

"Ahhhh... dammit, go ahead." Oberczofski waved in apparent irritation, but Montano could tell the annoyance wasn't directed at him. The other man obviously felt every bit as worried and powerless as Montano. Maybe more so. At least Montano got to talk to Teacher, while the hostage negotiator had been sidelined, confined to shouting advice from the bench during a playoff game.

Montano listened as the phone in his hand went from dead

Malignant

to the evenly-spaced sounds of the line ringing.

The phone rang and rang.

No one picked up.

***

Montano slammed the phone against the wall. At the same time, he felt a buzz in his jacket, reached in, and pulled his cell. The caller ID read simply: *Eb.*

"Tell me something good, partner."

"I'm sending a screen capture to Tac-Com. Take a look at it."

Without hanging up, Montano relayed the information to Vickers, who had the image pulled up on one of the Tac-Com screens in seconds.

Montano put his phone on speaker. "What am I looking at?" he asked, trying to ignore the crawling sensation that moved from his toes to his testicles.

"It was buried in the video we got. The one with the two guys getting capped. We sent it to a friend of Dapper Dan's at the Bureau –" He cut off when Montano groaned, then growled, "Can it, kid. He agreed to look at the picture and do a preliminary analysis, but to stay out of it other than that. For now."

"Okay, and…"

"And Dan's guy already struck paydirt. He's going to do some deeper dives, but within a couple minutes he got back to me and said he cross-referenced the room's architectural features, the paint, and –"

"Cut to the punchline, Eb."

"He said the photo was probably taken somewhere in Eastern Europe. Maybe Belarus, but he's not one hundred percent."

"That doesn't sound like hitting paydirt to me," said Vickers.

"That Vickers I hear?" asked Eb on the line.

"Yeah."

"Tell her she still owes my wife ten bucks – and tell her I'm not done yet."

"Okay," said Vickers. "Impress me."

"I started some people looking into the faculty and employees at Reina."

"Checking for an inside job?" asked Oberczofski.

"You're there, too, Obe?"

"I drew the short straw."

Montano was a bit surprised. He had thought he knew Eberhardt well, but had had no idea the older man was so connected to so many people.

And that's not important right now, hotshot. Focus.

"Eb," Montano began, "can we –"

"Sorry." Eberhardt cleared his throat. "Yeah, Obe, I was looking for an inside job. We're still digging, but get this: at least four of the staff look like they have offshore accounts."

Montano cocked his head. "That *is* interesting. You find anything out about them?"

"Not yet. We're still digging. But it looks fishy."

"As a shark humping a sea bass," Montano agreed. "Which employees?"

"Janine Welner, Thaddeus Ulric, John Fertetti, and Ken Slattery."

With each of the names, Montano's gut twisted a bit tighter. "Dammit. Dammit, dammit."

"What is it?" asked Eberhardt.

"We just got word from inside, Eb. All the people you just named are dead."

***

A pregnant pause issued from the phone. "You gotta tell me stuff like that, partner," Eberhardt said quietly.

In an even lower tone, Montano said, "I just did." He closed his eyes. "And it wasn't just them, either."

"God," said Eberhardt.

Unlike Montano, Eberhardt was a religious guy. He and his wife went to church on Sundays when Eb's schedule allowed, and two of his kids had even been missionaries. So when Montano heard him say that, he heard not the empty wording of most cops: Eb was praying. Because if it wasn't just staff who died, that left the one thing no cop wanted to face: a crime with a dead kid at the bottom of it.

"Who was it?" Eberhardt said a moment later.

"A kid named Zane's been killed. Another kid named Daxton was beaten, probably badly."

The line went quiet. Somehow, Montano could tell his friend and partner was scared.

"Take me off speaker, Montano," said Eberhardt. Vickers and Oberczofski started to protest. He cut them both off with, "Guys, I love you both, but for right now shut the hell up and let me talk to my partner. *Alone.*"

***

In Dapper Dan's office, Eberhardt shivered as he waited the fraction of a second for Montano to take him off speaker.

"You're off speaker."

"You said *Daxton*, right?"

"Yeah."

"Uhhh... Daxton *Leigh*?"

"How should I know?" Montano asked, sounding pissed.

"We've been able to grab next to nothing from the school's files. They're not part of the district here – private institution, different charter – and the district they *are* in has been telling us they've got computer problems."

"Computer problems," said Eberhardt dully.

"Copy."

"Like we've been having."

"Copy."

***

Eberhardt felt a tug at his sleeve and looked down to see Dapper Dan pointing at one of his computer monitors. "Small bit of good news," Dan said. "Looks like we finally grabbed the files." He clicked an attachment, and a list started scrolling past: all the registration records for Reina High School.

"Check if –"

"Already on it," said Dan.

"What are we checking for?" asked Reggie, leaning over from his own desk nearby to peer over his mentor's shoulder. "Who's –"

Dapper Dan cut off Reggie with a curse. Looking at Eberhardt, he said what the cop had already figured out: "One Daxton at Reina, and it's Daxton Leigh. *The* Daxton Leigh."

Montano, obviously listening to the exchange on his end of the call, said, "Who are you talking about?"

"Kid's been in the news a bunch, Montano. Don't you check your Tweet Feeder for news?"

"It's Twitter feed, Eb. Stop beating around the bush and tell me what's going on."

Eberhardt sighed. "Montano, Daxton Leigh's father is Joel William Leigh."

Now it was Montano's turn to fall silent. Then: "As in…"

"Yeah. Daxton Leigh's dad is the majority leader of the United States Senate."

CHAPTER 14
Intended Response

Montano closed his eyes. He barely heard Eberhardt's next words: "Want I should call him?"

Montano knew what he was supposed to do: call the guy's office, call the FBI – pretty much call everyone.

He was the department Golden Boy. He was going places.

The smart thing for him to do would be to follow procedure, pass the buck, and make sure this didn't blow up in his face. And with any other case, that's what he'd do if necessary – or if it looked unsolvable.

But for some reason, a switch flipped in his head. Passing the buck would be the politically astute move in this situation. But he knew that would just cause the chaos to surge, and likely cause the kind of confusion and turf battling that *they* couldn't afford.

Who's 'they'?

The kids.

The staff.

Dammit.

So instead of saying, "Call him – hell yes, call him. And anyone else you can think of who can take over," Montano heard the words, "Not yet. Soon," come out of his mouth.

He dropped the phone from his ear. Before he could disconnect, he heard Eberhardt say, "Don't hang up just yet. Dapper Dan just showed me more."

Montano lifted the phone, even as he said. "No more. Not acceptable."

The universe didn't listen to him.

He finished the call with Eberhardt. He didn't say a word. Just took in what his partner told him, then ended the call.

It's not too late to dump this.

But he knew he wouldn't. Just like he knew that it was a choice that was more likely than not going to cost him everything.

***

Montano turned to find Vickers and Oberczofski standing close enough to him that he could tell what they'd each had to eat recently: nothing. The smell of sweat and sour, empty stomachs greeted him.

Without waiting for the obvious question to be asked, Montano said, "Most of the kids have billionaire parents. Entertainment moguls, real estate magnates." He hesitated, as though not saying the next thing would make it not true. "And the kid who got beaten up is Senator Leigh's son."

No one had to ask *which* Senator Leigh.

"Shit on toast," said Vickers. Her already-pinched face drew a bit tighter. "They are terrorists."

Montano shook his head. "We're still not sure about that."

Vickers' expression took on an angry cast. "Stop polishing your pedestal and face facts, Montano. Leigh serves on the Appropriation Committee, the Judiciary Committee, and he chairs the damn Foreign Relations Committee. Oh, and he's also the majority leader. He's one of the most influential people alive, and his only child is now under the control of – and apparently a direct target of – persons unknown. What else could this be?"

"I don't know," Montano admitted.

"And that's the point." Oberczofski's statement was quieter than Vickers' tirade, but had just as much force behind it. Montano understood: they *didn't* know. So they had to assume the worst.

Then, in the next instant, Oberczofski surprised him by *not* being on Vickers' side. Turning to the tactical commander, he said, "Whoever this person is, this Teacher, he's got us off-balance, guessing his motives. That's not typical of terrorists. They usually want something, they want it now, and they want the world to know it. The man we're dealing with is more... elegant."

Vickers snorted. "Well I'll put out the finger bowls. But that doesn't change the fact that I've gotta call Homeland."

"Yes," Oberczofski said with a nod, "but you can call them and sound terrified, or call to alert them of a possible problem that *might* implicate national security. I recommend the latter. The last thing we need now is panic – especially from this side of the line."

***

The Tac-Com door opened and the officer whom Montano had earlier ordered to put up barricades and keep the press in the dark stuck his head in. "The press is here," he said in the dead voice of someone worried about his professional future.

"How'd they find out?" Montano asked.

"I told you it'd be hard to keep this under wraps."

"Don't give me the cover-your-ass speech. Just answer the question."

"I did everything I could think of, but –"

Montano could tell the officer was sincere, and he wasn't in the habit of punishing people who weren't at fault. But he also wasn't in the habit of listening to excuses. "You find out who's responsible for informing the press, and do it now!" he roared.

The cop almost let out a yelp of terror as he left.

***

Montano counted to ten, calming himself as much as possible given the circus that was about to set up camp around him He left Tac-Com, straightening his hair and tie as much as possible as he walked.

Oberczofski trailed him out. "Thanks for standing up for me in there," said Montano. "Vickers can be a bi –"

"Vickers is an excellent cop," said Oberczofski. The man

spoke quietly – he always did, Montano noted, which gave him a surprising power in any conversation. And with the same quiet force, he reached out and gripped Montano's arm, stopping him in his tracks. "Montano, I know you're skilled. You're making good moves and I'll support those moves as long as they last. But don't go thinking I like you. You're far too in love with yourself for my taste, and the second you make a bad call, I'll say so. My only concern is getting the staff and especially the kids out of danger, whatever it takes. If that means taking a bullet myself or throwing your precious career under the bus, so be it."

Again, Montano surprised himself. He didn't usually react well to this kind of speech, but he just nodded, impressed. "You remind me of my partner," he said.

Oberczofski cracked a half-smile. "Like me, Eb is a good guy, and supremely intelligent."

"He has his moments. Ugly, though."

The negotiator shrugged. "I'll take it."

***

It was worse than a circus. A circus at least had a ringleader, a master of ceremonies. What Montano saw outside the barricades was more of a feeding frenzy.

Reporters clustered, pushing and shoving in a way that reminded him of one of those zombie films: tons of moving meat pressing at windows and walls until the pitiful boundaries between order and chaos fell to pieces.

Network news vans pulled up every few seconds, dumping out payloads of reporters, camera people, producers. More and more media representatives thronged outside the barricade.

But what bothered Montano the most was the single reporter he saw first: one named Connie Kendall.

Shit.

Montano thought Connie Kendall was beautiful (subjective),

fierce (another subjective judgment, though one most people agree with), and a complicating factor he did not want or need (objectively true). To Montano in that moment, I was just someone who knew where the bodies were buried, and had a detailed map of where to find any closet with a skeleton.

Not to mention his own personal history with me.

I waved at him, obviously wanting attention and answers. He turned away, pretending he hadn't seen me in the first place. Instead, he walked to the center of the line of barricades, which was also where the most reporters had clustered.

He raised his hands, patting the air. The reporters hushed. They could be loud, frenzied, terrifying in their enthusiastic quests for The Big Story. But they also knew when to shut up – like now.

***

"My name is Detective Montano, and I'm in charge of this situation. I'm prepared to issue a short statement, and I will answer no questions at this time."

Montano paused, waiting. Sometimes the "no questions" bit resulted in a *roar* of inquiries, and if that happened he intended to turn around and walk away. He wasn't, as he had claimed, anything remotely like "in charge of this situation." But he'd be damned if he lost control of the sharks circling just outside the school.

The sharks circled still – but continued in silence.

Montano nodded approvingly, then raised a hand. He held up one finger. "First: this police line is for your safety and for ours." Before the questions he heard beginning to bubble up could fully surface, he turned the single finger into a flat, warding palm. "You want a statement, or you want me to walk away?" he said. "Because those are your *only* two options right now."

The silence that fell was absolute.

"Good. As I was saying: the barricades are here to protect everyone. They are also not a suggestion: any unauthorized person inside this line will face immediate and very strident prosecution for interfering with a police investigation." He paused. The silence continued. Another nod. "Now here's what we know: this morning, armed assailants took an unknown number of school faculty and students hostage. No demands have been made, but our hostage negotiator –" He gestured at Oberczofski, whose mouth opened in surprise, and who began straightening his own tie. "– has been in contact and is making progress. And now we both have to get back to our jobs. Thank you."

***

He turned away.

"Nicely done," Oberczofski murmured.

"Yeah, I worked on that speech all night," Montano said with a grimace.

"Oh, no, not the information – that was passable at best. But the way you set it up: you're in charge, so if everything goes right, you get the medals. But you made sure to mention me by name as the hostage negotiator so if it all goes ass over teakettle you've got someone else to point at."

"I don't know what you're talking about."

"No," said Oberczofski with a humorless wink. "I'm sure you don't."

***

Outside the police barricade, reporters were making calls, recording tape, doing all the things that reporters do in the absence of hard information. Back at the studios, producers were calling in "experts" – i.e., anyone who looked and sounded competent, and who could be counted on to bloviate and speculate until anything real happened. The twenty-four-hour news cycle at its finest.

One reporter did not do any of those things. Instead, I did the same thing I did with every story: I started looking for an angle – which in this case meant trying to find a way past the barricades and a bit closer to the action.

***

Montano walked about twenty steps past the gate into the school. He turned to the right. To the left. Trying to think like the enemy.

It was something he was good at.

That was why, when I turned the corner around a small building, he was waiting for me, leaning on the cruiser he had driven to this spot.

"What a surprise," he said. Oberczofski, who had come along for the ride after Montano filled him in on what he expected to find, waved from the front seat.

Sixty seconds later, I was seated in the back of the cruiser, looking at the very real possibility of jail time. Still, jail or no, I rubbernecked as much as possible, taking in as much detail as I could. I could see Tac-Com from where I sat, with several people going in and coming out in a fairly constant stream.

Other than that: not much. Mostly cops hunkered behind cars, a few moving back and forth as they relayed messages deemed too sensitive to give over the radio.

Montano, who had joined Oberczofski in the front seat after escorting me to the place of honor, turned around. He flipped open the small sliding window built into the plastic partition that separated cop from perp.

"Who leaked the story?"

"How about we trade?" I responded. "I'll tell you something, you tell me something."

"Fine. The leak. Now."

I laughed. "The newsrooms of almost every outlet got an email telling them to check out Reina High."

Montano looked unimpressed. "That's it?"

"That's it."

"And on the strength of some kook's –"

I cut him off: "No. On the strength of an email that went to every mailbox and then opened itself. We literally couldn't ignore it, and every news IT department in the city is going nuts right now, trying to figure out how some of the most secure servers in the U.S. got pulled apart like Play-Doh."

Montano put the car in drive, then pulled up to what I would later find out was a spot right behind the no-man's land between the line of cop cars and the gym. I didn't know then what I know now, but I'd been a reporter – a good one – long enough to intuit that he was giving me a gift, wrapped in silver paper and with a lovely bow to top it all off.

He turned back to look at me. "I need you quiet for now." Before I could object – he knew me well enough to know I didn't generally settle for the first thing offered without trying to bargain up – he said, "And I'll let you stay inside the line. Exclusive access."

Christmas had come early that year. That was what I thought. I was ashamed of that later: contrary to popular belief, reporters *do* have feelings, and I still wake up some nights, the first thought in my mind simply, *You are a piece of shit.*

***

Montano held out a hand. "Phone."

I pouted. I didn't expect it to work, but sometimes a dash of the Damsel In Distress thing makes people give in when they shouldn't. "You don't trust me?"

Montano just stared, and kept his hand poked through that little window between him and me.

I sighed and reached into my jacket pocket. I handed him a nice phone – two years old, sure, but decent enough that most people bought it.

Montano didn't. He kept his hand out. I sighed even louder,

then pulled out a second phone. That year's model. "There. Happy?"

"As a monkey with a Playboy," he said.

He closed the partition. Thumbed a control on the door handle. The back windows cracked an inch. Probably less than he'd crack them for a dog, and it took a moment for me to realize that his offer of "access" had meant "so long as you stay in the back of the car."

"You bastard!" I shouted.

Montano was already out of the cruiser. He poked his head in and said, "I promised you exclusive backstage access. I didn't specify where you'd be sitting in the wings, or say you wouldn't sit there alone."

I started shrieking. I don't remember what, but several police officers I later interviewed said they heard some very choice words at a hundred yards away.

Montano shook his head. "You want to observe from here, or do you want me to send you to a holding cell downtown where you can wait for me to get around to booking you?"

He smiled his toothiest smile. I shut up.

After a second, I tossed him an equally toothy grin. We were two sharks circling each other, and I wasn't really sure if it was a mating smile, or an "I'm going to kill you" smile.

A lot of days, I'm not even sure there's much of a difference.

**

When Montano and Oberczofski got back to Tac-Com, Oberczofski was still doing what he had been since the moment they got out of the car.

"That woman's a *parasite*, Montano. There's no upside to having her arou –"

Montano, walking in front of him, stopped so suddenly that Oberczofski ran full-bore into him. He almost cursed, but the word

– along with everything else in his mind – shut down and disappeared as Montano said, "Hello, Senator."

***

Senator Joel William Leigh was, so far as I knew at the time of the RHS disaster, one of the rarest of people: a politician who genuinely wants to help his constituents. Not a perfect man – no one who gets to the rarified heights of power to which he has risen can manage to do so without getting their hands dirty – but one of the good ones.

He also looks the part of a senator: silver hair, blue eyes that have faded little with age. On the day he arrived at the location of his son's kidnapping, he wore a gold power tie, a navy blue suit, and an air of self-satisfaction that, unlike the other two main items in his ensemble, he never removed, not even to shower or sleep.

When Montano and Oberczofski entered Tac-Com, he looked at them. Waited.

Montano looked away. It was hard not to when Senator Leigh stared at you, and harder still when you knew, as Montano did, that you hadn't told the man all the things he deserved to know.

Leigh was a man who could destroy *presidents*. Destroying a city cop? It wouldn't even be a speed bump if he decided to do it – just the casual swatting of a gnat.

"We... uh, we were going to call you as soon as we got final confirmation but –"

Leigh interrupted Montano with a wave. "No need to explain, Detective Montano. Discretion is often indispensable. Still, I hope you understand why I had to come and crash the party." Without waiting for Montano's (unnecessary and likely unwanted) response, Leigh continued, "Lieutenant Vickers has briefed me, but only to the extent of her ability. It seems there's a dearth of hard information."

Senator Leigh had spoken to Montano as a cop, and in so doing had put the detective back on footing he understood. Montano glanced at the still-dark CCTV feeds on the wall and said, "Is there anything you might be able to tell us?"

Senator Leigh smiled that famous smile: just a slight tilting on the left side of his mouth. "You mean, 'Do I as a mighty United States Senator have any inside information?'"

"More or less, sir."

"I'm afraid the only thing I can say with certainty is… I love my boy. Daxton's always been difficult, always resisted his mother and me. And God knows it's difficult having me as a father. But we've always tried. We sent him to Reina in the hopes that it would help him."

To Montano's utter surprise – and the surprise of everyone looking on – Senator Leigh's eyes actually started to moisten. To their even greater surprise, his fear and worry seemed genuine. "I'll never forgive myself if…"

He shook his head, bowing it slightly to knuckle away tears.

"I'll not stay here," he said. "I'd only be in the way. But if I could remain somewhere nearby…"

Montano gulped. He'd just been handed salvation in a pretty little box… and was about to spit on it. "Sir, I'm uncomfortable letting you stay so close. We haven't even fully cleared any of the buildings, so –"

"Detective, it's my son. My boy."

Montano nodded. A moment later, one of the techs was leading the senator out. "We'll set you up in a car nearby and get you a headset that's tied into our feeds so that…"

The rest of the conversation was lost to the people who remained behind in Tac-Com. Oberczofski broke the silence: "Is it just me, or did he actually seem like a human?"

"He did," said Montano. "But then, the humans are the ones you have to look out for."

"What do you want to do now?" asked Vickers.

Montano cocked an eyebrow in Oberczofski's direction: *What do you think?*

"We can either call again, try to make contact," said the negotiator, "or we can wait."

Montano looked at the clock that hung over the door to the mobile command: 10:27 am.

"Let's wait. It'll give us a chance to dig some more so that next time I talk to this guy I don't feel so much like I'm bent over in front of him with my pants down."

CHAPTER 15
Intended Response

By 1 pm, little had changed, either on the grounds of Reina or back at Police Technical Investigations. At PTI, Dapper Dan still looked immaculate, Reggie still looked like he was trying too hard, Eberhardt still looked confused. The only apparent concession to time's passage was piles of empty coffee cups that littered the area on and around Dan's desk.

Eberhardt glanced at the truly admirable number of coffee cups and grunted, "How do you not have to pee?"

Dan didn't look up from his computer. "Peeing might ruin the lines of my shirt. Now leave me alone."

He hit a key, and his screen – covered in code that would make most Silicon Valley professionals run screaming for the hills – went black.

"What's that? You get in the cameras?"

"Does it look like I got in?"

"Well are you *gonna* get in?"

The click-clack of keys sped up as the answer came: "I am Dapper Dan."

In those words, Eberhardt could hear every minute of Dan's studies, of his love of and obsession with computers. He could hear the confidence in the voice of a man who had yet to meet his match in that world.

So why didn't Eberhardt feel encouraged?

What if they had finally come up against someone as good as Dapper Dan? What if they had finally come up against someone even better?

***

When the phone rang, Montano snatched it up. It was a

hurry up and wait game, and he wasn't good at waiting. Never had been, never expected to be.

As always, Teacher sounded pleasant, nearly disconnected from the tense reality unfolding. "I've got some people who are getting extremely hungry," he said.

"How hospitable of you," said Montano. "I mean, you've only been holed up in there, what, five or six hours? Usually people in your position don't start worrying about the people they're holding for at least a day."

"Well, it's been a long day already, wouldn't you say," Teacher said, still pleasantly, refusing to rise to Montano's bait. "And technically, it's been a bit longer than five hours. I had to take the school, put together a home movie – a few other things."

"Thanks for that corrective note," said Montano wryly. "I'll make sure to point that out on my Zagat review. And since you mention it: who's the girl in the video?"

Montano half expected Teacher to say, "What girl?" and honestly didn't know how he'd react in that case. But Teacher just chuckled and said, "Just a nameless girl of no apparent consequence in the world."

"You're a sociopath," said Montano. "Or is this a 'my mommy doesn't love me' thing?"

Beside him, Oberczofski seemed to lurch in place. Montano didn't blame him: this was not the way to talk to someone who held innocents' lives in his hands. But his gut screamed otherwise; he was acting on instinct.

"Don't piss him off!" Oberczofski hissed.

For a moment, Montano was worried that was exactly what he'd just done. Then Teacher laughed. "Your friend whispers very loudly. But don't worry, I'm not in the least bit 'pissed off.' I just want to be a good host."

"Maybe let them go then. Nothing says good hosting like

releasing the hostages."

"It's not time."

Now Montano's gut whispered again: *Stop pushing.*

Out loud, he said, "Any preferences? Pizza, sandwiches, Chinese?"

"I leave it to your very discriminating tastes, Detective Montano."

That last sounded odd – Montano felt a bit more, every time he spoke to Teacher, like this was someone who knew him well. A friend? An enemy?

No. Not even the perps I've put away. None of them could manage this.

"How many mouths?" he said.

"You mean you don't already know? I'd have thought you would have at least compared school registration figures to kids who are MIA and figured out the number of hostages by now. Unless I've seriously overestimated your skills. Of course, you were actually trying to get me to tell you how many people I have – rather clumsily, I might add. Still, my confidence in you has dropped."

"Well, I –"

"Tell you what," said Teacher. "You guess how many hostages I have in here, and if you guess right you win a shiny nickel."

A knot of hot lead settled in Montano's stomach with the words. He didn't say anything, avoiding the question that was hanging in the air. Teacher didn't speak, either, forcing it: "And if I guess wrong?"

"No nickel. But you still win."

"How so?"

"I'll save you some money."

"How so?" Montano repeated, dreading the answer.

"On lunch. Because there will be one less mouth to feed."

"Look," he said, trying to keep desperation from seeping into his tone, "I'm happy to get you whatever you want, and I'm sure you're right: the kids are hungry and –"

"Tell me how many hostages I have, Montano. You have fifteen seconds."

***

Vickers held up a whiteboard, where she'd scrawled: "10 minus 7 STAFF, 24 minus 1 STUDENTS." Montano nodded. Mouthed a thank you.

"You want the total, or just the live ones?" he asked Teacher.

"Good question. Let's have both. 2 seconds."

"You started out with 10 faculty and staff and 24 students."

"And how many are left?"

"Three faculty, twenty-three students."

Another pause, and the lead in Montano's stomach cooled into an uncomfortable knot that reminded him he hadn't visited a bathroom – or eaten or had a drink of water – since he got there.

"Very good. And now I think about it, I have a hankering for Mexican. Put the food in uncovered aluminum steam tins, then wheel them to the door we sent Gersham out of." Teacher paused, then laughed again. "Think he'll be back as principal next year? I mean, he's literally dickless, which I have to think would mess with a man's ability to abuse his authority."

Montano gritted his teeth. "What's with all the jokes? You think you're just that funny?"

Teacher's voice was nearly a whisper. "No. I think I'm just that right." More upbeat, he said, "Forty-five minutes to get the food, Montano. And five dozen water bottles. Don't think about drugging the food or water: my people won't be eating or drinking it. We brought more than enough food and water of our own to last for days, so only my guests will partake. And if any of them fall asleep or get inexplicably sick, I'll just send them out the same way I sent Gersham. Understood?"

"Understood." Again, Montano's instincts made him speak without thinking: "And I hope *you* understand there's going to be a reckoning."

Another laugh from Teacher. "I'm counting on it, my friend. Oh, and one more thing: *you* bring the food. I see anyone else move past your barricade, and you'll quickly find out that what you've seen so far has been me playing nice."

The line went dead.

Montano hung up the phone, his mind racing.

Vickers said, "This can work for us."

Montano shook his head. "You gonna bug the food? He thought of the possibility of us drugging him, so he'll have thought of that."

"Maybe. But I have an idea," said Vickers.

She told him and Oberczofski. Neither of them liked it. But neither of them had any better ideas, either, and everyone knew they'd been marching exclusively to the beat of Teacher's drum, and that if they kept doing that, only tragedy could ensue.

***

They were such fools then. We all were.

Because the tragedy was written out, planned, and all but executed. A good teacher knows the subject, the students, and the lesson plan. A good teacher knows the beginning from the end… and the end from the very beginning.

CHAPTER 16
Intended Response

Several dozen uniformed men and women sheltered behind cars, only heads and arms showing as they pointed every gun they had at the gym entrance. Snipers hid in the trees nearby, aiming as well.

None of which helped Montano feel any less exposed as he walked into no-man's land. He felt like vomiting, and the tins and boxes of food on the small metal dolly he was pushing exuded a thick smell that didn't help matters.

He wasn't afraid for himself. Not really. Just the kids. For what had already happened, what he would see if he got a look inside the gym. And for what might happen still, if Teacher got his way.

Whatever that is.

He was wearing a Kevlar vest, but knew how little that would matter: more and more of the bad guys' guns held cop-killers: bullets designed to penetrate most body armor. And even if they didn't, his vest wouldn't help him feel any better if he was shot in the face.

Or if they shoot my balls off.

The image of Principal Gersham settled in his mind. Only now he saw his own face, heard his own screams over the image of his body writhing, clutching at something that had been hacked to pieces.

Montano stopped ten feet away as the gym door cracked open far enough for a rifle to appear. It waved Montano closer. He moved in, trying to appear calm, to focus on pulling in whatever information he could.

A man waited in the doorway. Dressed completely in black, in some kind of combat fatigues with numerous bulging pockets. He also wore a ski-mask-style balaclava: nothing but eyes and a thin slit of a mouth visible.

In his hands, he held an AR-15. Even though Colt had stopped manufacturing the weapon for civilian use, the rifle was still made to sell for police and military units, which meant enterprising criminals could still get their hands on them. Plus, before they stopped being manufactured for non-military groups, the AR-15 was the most-used civilian rifle in the United States.

So Montano was facing someone with a popular, basically untraceable – at least from a simple viewing like Montano was getting – firearm.

But that wasn't the bad part.

***

The difference between a fully automatic and a semi-automatic weapon is simply this: if you want to fire a semi-automatic, you have to pull the trigger, one time for each bullet fired. A fully automatic weapon will fire, over and over, for as long as you hold down the trigger – whether it be for a short burst, or until the magazine is empty.

Contrary to popular belief, fully automatic weapons and AR-15s are *not* the same thing. AR-15s are semi-automatic. They can still fire quickly – an experienced shooter can pull the trigger repeatedly in the space of a few seconds – but the finger will get tired, and there is a cap on the speed.

In sum: an AR-15 is terrifying for a cop when she or he sees one in a perpetrator's hands. Any gun is, but rifles are more accurate, can shoot farther, and as a rule carry more of a punch than handguns. Still, an AR-15 isn't nearly as frightening as a fully automatic machine gun, which, again, most criminals can't get.

Which brings us to what Montano saw:

AR-15: check. Bummer, because he couldn't bring back anything really actionable based on that. But expected, since most people who owned a rifle would have something like it, and most criminals definitely would as well.

The bad part, though, was the modification: a Slide Fire stock. A Slide Fire stock, or "bump stock," replaces the AR-15 pistol grip with an interface that creates a bounce effect. Essentially, the shooter holds down his finger on a finger rest, and the Slide Fire's clever design uses the gun's own recoil to bounce the shooter's finger repeatedly against the trigger.

Is it technically an automatic? No – the gun is, technically, being fired only once for every "pull."

So is it legal? Yes.

As a reporter, I'm not going to get into the wisdom (questionable, in the opinion of many, perfectly fine in the opinion of others) of the Slide Fire or similar products – at least not here. The thing that matters for purposes of this recounting is that a Slide Fire, as Montano knew, would turn the AR-15 from a gun with a top firing speed of a few a second, into one that could empty a 30-round mag at almost the same speeds as a fully-automatic rifle.

Most people, shooting that fast, wouldn't be able to maintain any kind of accuracy – the first bullet might go where they wanted, but the rest would probably pull up and miss.

Montano also knew, however, that the people who had taken the school were not "most people."

The people who had taken over the school were anonymous and – so far, at least – unnamed. They were prepared. And now he knew that they were armed at a level that outstripped most of his officers.

***

The man Montano saw at the gym was partially shielded behind the metal door – enough that any shot would be difficult. Not that he really had to worry. The snipers wouldn't shoot unless the guy tried to hurt Montano. And even then, Montano thought it might be better if the snipers held their fire. Killing the head might kill the rest of the snake, but if this was a hydra, they'd just end up with *numerous* venomous reptiles inside. Who knew what would happen to the teachers and the kids then?

The man at the door waited until he was a few feet away. Just out of reach.

"Far enough," said a familiar voice.

"You're the host, huh?" said Montano. "Teacher."

Neither was really a question, but Teacher answered, "Yes. To both."

"Want me to set the table for you?" Montano offered. He took a step. He didn't want to enter the lion's den, but he would. If he got out, he'd be a wealth of information.

Teacher shook his head. He shuffled to the side, and two more dark-garbed figures slipped past him. They moved so quickly that Montano was taken by surprise, and even if he'd wanted to fight back or try some fancy footwork, he wouldn't have been able to. They just darted out, grabbed the dolly from his hands, and pushed it and the food back inside before he could take a breath.

He took in this much: they were men. Again, expected, since violent crime is largely confined to those who boast a Y chromosome. They were dressed like Teacher: unsurprising. They each had a sidearm, holstered, so he couldn't make out what kind, though his mind replayed the vivid colors of the video where two men had their heads turned into cratered half-moons.

One held an AR-15. The other held an AK-47: the most popular rifle in the world. Both modified with bump stocks like Teacher's.

The one difference between them and the man who was calling the shots was that the two others had armbands. One wore a red armband, one a blue. Interesting. Important, probably.

But Montano didn't know what they meant. Were they designations? Code? Did they mean that these people had certain jobs – like demolitions, or engineering, or hacking computers?

He didn't know.

He didn't know far too much.

***

Behind the line of cars, Vickers and Oberczofski watched. They also listened in: Montano had more bugs on him than a Roach Motel.

Beside Vickers, C-Unit waited. All of those men had been on standby, and the panic they felt when seeing the mutilated Principal Gersham had turned to quiet rage at the horror that had visited Reina High. When the gun appeared at the door, they tensed, but Vickers waved them to hold position, then repeated the gesture, larger and more obvious, so that no one pointing a gun got the idea that it would be a good idea to turn into a cowboy.

That, she knew, would spell disaster.

She didn't know the disasters that had already happened, or she might have charged in then. And maybe that would have changed things.

Probably not, though.

We were all still dancing to Teacher's tune.

Actually, on second thought, that's the wrong (and overused) comparison. We weren't dancing to a tune, because that would mean we heard the beat, and chose to participate. Teacher wasn't a DJ of some maleficent music, he was a snake charmer, weaving and bobbing and inevitably drawing first the attention and then the subservience of a snake that, though deaf, danced the way the master desired.

***

As soon as the men with colored armbands had grabbed the food, Teacher said, "You know, it's said that if you share your food with another person, your life expands. But if you cook and eat him yourself, so does your belly."

Montano did his best to ignore that. He scrutinized the men as they disappeared into the gym. Teacher noticed.

"Their clothes can be bought anywhere. Their guns are easily secured black market arms. You won't figure out who they are." He laughed. "Until I want you to, of course."

The men were already inside, but Montano moved as though to follow them. There was no way Teacher would allow it, he knew, but he had to try. Sure enough Teacher's gun came up, halting him.

"Let's lay our cards on the table," said Montano.

Teacher chuckled, sounding genuinely amused, and Montano was surprised to feel the conversation turn almost genuinely convivial. As though the man facing Montano genuinely respected him.

Montano hated Teacher, because he was a criminal, a killer, a torturer. But he had to respect him, too. Not in a kindly way, but the way a person had to respect fire or electricity. To fail to respect such a thing was to court disaster.

Further disaster.

"I agree. Let's finish this hand and, since you've showed me all your cards, I'll do the same."

Montano nodded. He tried to ignore Teacher's implication that everything Montano had done was utterly transparent to him, and tried even harder to ignore the feeling that Teacher was right.

"You undoubtedly know I can't see inside the gym," Montano said. "You know I don't know if you've killed anyone else. And you know I don't want anyone else killed. But how do I know you've even got anyone left in there? Why shouldn't I just send in the troops to blow you all to hell?"

Teacher nodded and pulled back a bit. He gestured for Montano to move slightly to the side, permitting him to see a slice of the gym.

***

Montano got a quick glimpse, nothing more.

He couldn't see the walls where he knew the bleachers would be.

And that meant he also couldn't see what Teacher had done with the bleachers; the contraption he had jury-rigged. That would come back to haunt him.

***

Here's what Montano did see: students and teachers on the floor, heads covered.

And an ignominious pile of bloodied, maimed bodies. A few staring eyes pointed his direction, glassy and empty in a way that told him instantly they were dead.

A few of the dead bodies didn't stare, because their heads had been pulped. No way to tell if they were students or teachers or unlucky visitors or anything else. They were barely even recognizable as human.

Montano managed to point at the hooded people lying still and silent on the floor. "They could all be dead," he said.

"True," said Teacher.

He turned and fired into the air. The people on the floor screamed. Some sounded like adults, but most were the cracking, adolescent sounds of teen voices in terror.

Montano was a good detective. He was good at noticing things, at making connections. But that wasn't all he was good at, so when Teacher fired into the air, Montano had drawn his own gun almost before the bullet finished punching a hole in the ceiling.

***

At the police line, Vickers screamed, "No one move, **NO ONE MOVE, DAMMIT!**"

***

Beyond the police line, outside the school, a few reporters looked confused at the sound. Others, mostly veterans, started blasting off emails or calling producers or recording tape: "Shots fired at Reina High School!"

***

Teacher just stared at Montano, the lack of worry clear in his eyes. "Not a smart move, Detective."

Montano grinned tightly. "Maybe I don't care about smart."

Teacher didn't smile back. But he didn't sound angry, either. Suddenly, Montano thought he just sounded tired. It wasn't a tired that Montano could take advantage of – one that he could use as a lever, playing the man's exhaustion against him, forcing him to make a bad decision that the detective could exploit. It was the kind of tired that scared him. It was the weariness of someone who's lost everything, and now exists only to arrange his own funeral before letting himself die.

"A man like you always cares about smart," Teacher said. "Maybe not always about *right*, but definitely about smart.

That stung Montano, not least because there was a shred of truth in it. The detective was good at his job, and he genuinely liked helping people. But he also had ambition vying for attention: the need to succeed, to climb the ladder.

Montano holstered his gun. "What exactly is it you want?"

"An end to villainy."

Montano, stunned, said, "Villainy? Like making a bunch of kids lay down in front of you with guns to their heads?"

When Teacher responded, that weariness Montano had noted disappeared, replaced by an intensity that chilled the detective. "Especially that." Teacher glanced over his shoulder. "I'll issue my demands after my new friends eat. But only if you play fair, and listen to my every word, and follow each to the letter." He looked past Montano then, looking around the high school, not seeming to notice the masses of police, all of whom aimed guns his direction.

Quietly, almost reverently, Teacher whispered, "This really is a lovely place, all things considered." Then he focused on Montano. "Now go."

Montano hesitated a fraction of a second, trying to think of something to do more than he already had, coming up blank. He turned away.

Teacher said, "Sorry, hold on."

Montano turned back to see something flying at him. He caught it reflexively as the gym door slammed shut and he heard the sound of locks engaging.

He opened his palm to see what he had caught.

It was a shiny nickel: the one Teacher had promised to give him if he guessed the number of hostages.

Teacher had done what he promised.

That was – and would be, and in many ways still is – Teacher's way.

***

Montano returned to the line of cops. He looked for Vickers and Oberczofski, didn't see them.

That was a good thing.

He ran to Tac-Com, where the two other cops were waiting.

"We get anything?" asked Montano as he entered, breathless from running to the mobile command.

Vickers waved for him to shut up as Teacher's voice came through the speakers. "We will pass out the food one person at a time. You may sit up when your hood is removed. Please note you will have at least one weapon aimed at you during the entire process, so –"

A clanking sound suddenly issued through the speakers, drowning out his voice. Then a high-pitched whine.

Montano felt sick to his stomach again. "Tell me that isn't what I think –"

Vickers looked at a tech officer, whose face went white. He was the one who had followed Vickers' instructions. The dolly had been the key, and though none of them knew if Teacher would take it along with the food, they had all banked on him having to act quickly with all the guns pointing in his direction.

They had also banked on the fact that he would check the food for drugs and bugs, but probably wouldn't be able to find the one they'd inserted in the hollow tubing of the dolly. They'd bored a tiny hole for the mic to listen through, then filled in the rest of the tubing with melted plastic. It looked like the plastic that might come in the tubing in the first place, to keep the housing from catching dirt or any other detritus.

The whining grew in volume. "It sounds like they're drilling or cutting metal," said the tech. No one had to ask about the implication: the bug had been found.

"They couldn't have," said the tech, sounding like he was partly in denial, partly just worried about his career prospects. "Not this fast. I buried it in the housing of the dolly. I –"

The metal sounds abruptly stopped, as did all sounds coming from the speakers.

"Did they destroy it?" said Oberczofski.

Vickers hollered, to no one and everyone, "What happened? Get it back. Get it –"

Montano's phone rang

***

Montano glanced at the phone. The caller ID read "EB" and he almost declined the call, but what if there had been a break? There was only dead air on the speakers, and a partner in the hand was worth three invisible terrorists – or more – on the line.

So he answered the call. "Not a good time, Eb. I have to –"

"Not even for little old me?"

Montano froze – if only for an instant – when he heard the voice. Not Eberhardt.

Teacher.

Montano waved for silence in the room. He put the phone on speaker, glancing at the caller ID again. It still said the same thing: "EB"

"Nice trick, Teacher."

"Have you played fair?" said Teacher. "Have you truly listened to every word I have said?"

No one said anything.

Until Teacher said, "I didn't think so."

CHAPTER 17
The Plan

Teacher nodded to Yellow. "It's time."

Yellow yanked Konstantin Tarov – Daxton Leigh's slimy little right-hand man – to his feet. Konstantin started screaming. Still hooded, he lunged to the side. His hands grasped, not consciously, but in the instinctive way an infant will clasp a parent's finger. He was trying to hold onto reality, onto life.

Konstantin stumbled and fell. But hands found something. Pulled.

Konstantin had jumped away from Yellow, which meant he jumped toward the closest thing on the other side: Daxton Leigh.

Teacher watched as the hood pulled away from Daxton's head. The once handsome face beneath was handsome no longer. It had been wrecked, beaten to the point where there was no pink flesh, just livid purples and blacks and yellows marking the bruises, just dark brown cracks where his blood had first flowed then coagulated as time went on and he remained filthy with his own fluids.

One of Daxton's eyes was so swollen that there was no possible way he could see anything. The flesh around it was lumpy and strange: a fractured orbital socket had collapsed into itself, pulping the eye beneath.

The other, eye, though, could see. Daxton blinked, then screamed as he saw his friend being pulled away by Yellow.

Daxton reached for Konstantin. Then he was shrieking himself as the butt of a gun slammed down on his spine. Red, who had acted so brutally – and, in Teacher's opinion, with perfect righteousness – put Daxton's hood back on.

Yellow dragged Konstantin to his feet again. More carefully this time, he brought the boy to Teacher. To the man who would serve him up a lesson he would never forget.

CHAPTER 18
Intended Response

Sounds came through the speakers in Tac-Com. First one boy's screams, then another. The screams rose in pitch, in panic-sounds, and Montano became dully aware that he was screaming, too: *"Don't, stop, please, we can work through this!"*

One of the cries ceased, silenced to a muffled whimpering. The other boy kept screaming for a moment. "Don't, please don't!" he shouted.

"Teacher," Montano hissed into the phone. "Think about this. Think –"

Teacher's voice cut him off. "Believe me, this is for the best."

The remaining screams changed, quickly and violently. And as bad as the terrified screams had been, the sound that replaced them was one no one in the mobile command would ever forget, and one that would haunt most of them in their nightmares and their waking hours alike.

The scream turned to a wet, strangled gagging. Then a strange, damp noise that continued for what seemed like forever, then turned into a hiccupping, slurping sound.

"What are you doing?" Montano asked, trying not to let the panic he felt show in his voice.

The terrible, wet sound continued as Teacher said, pleasantly, "Start to take me seriously, Montano. Listen. Follow my words."

As he spoke, the Tac-Com speakers came alive again. No voices, but a bizarre-yet-familiar *whssh… whssh… whsssh…*

***

If Montano had ever been a father, if he had ever gone with a wife or a girlfriend to have a sonogram, he might have recognized the sound. Or at least, recognized what it signified. But only one person in there knew immediately what he was hearing, and what it meant.

Whssh… whssh… whssh…

"No, God," said Oberczofski. It was the shortest and most heartfelt prayer of his life. He remembered –

(Whssh… whssh… whssh…)

– going to the doctor when his wife got pregnant with their first, and –

(Whssh… whssh… whssh…)

– the technician feeling around with a microphone on her belly, a father-to-be hearing for the first time in his life –

(Whssh… whssh… whssh…)

– the sound of a person's insides, with the comings and goings of fluid and air that were a metabolic constant and a metabolic necessity.

(Whssh… whssh… whssh…)

"I think he made someone swallow the bugs," said Oberczofski.

***

The monitors showing the gym feeds were still dark, inert. The one place they most needed to see was the place the police had the least sight. But they had set up other cameras, that fed into other monitors.

On one, they could see the outside of the gym.

They saw the door fly open.

They saw someone tripping out, much the same as Gersham had done.

Everyone in Tac-Com thought the same thing, or so close that the differences didn't matter: *No. Not again.*

***

C-Unit was, once more, the group that went into the danger zone. They grabbed the boy who had made it less than twenty feet before falling to the ground.

One of them, a ten-year veteran, glanced at the door. Greenie saw the look and said, "Don't even think about it."

"We gotta do something, Greenie."

"We are. We're taking this kid back."

None of them knew who it was. They just knew that this was a boy. He was already vomiting blood, and by the time they got him behind the line of cruisers, he was well into a seizure.

***

I didn't see the event with Gersham. I did see Konstantin Tarov, ejected from the gym. I saw the red-haired eighteen-year-old stumble a few feet, fall, and then be hauled by C-Unit to "safety."

I didn't see the details of what had happened – and none of us did, really, not even the EMTs as they took him to the hospital. But I saw the pain, and heard the terrible cries and then the even more terrible silence when Konstantin lost consciousness.

Like Gersham, the boy was whisked away.

Unlike Gersham, the boy did not even survive the trip. It turned out that he had indeed been fed the bug. That alone might not have killed him – the device was small, and could have been removed in a variety of ways.

But the person who did it had made sure Konstantin swallowed. At the autopsy, the medical examiner stated it looked like someone – most likely Teacher – had put the bug into the boy's mouth, then rammed it down using a hard rod. Splinters found in what was left of the boy's esophagus showed it was likely a piece of wood – a plunger or just a piece of the bleachers.

They also found that part of the bug was not in his stomach.

It was in his colon, and had been inserted there via his rectum in a similar fashion.

***

Montano held his phone so tightly he heard a crack as the housing started to split. He had to force himself to unclench – no sense making the whole thing worse by breaking his phone – but barely managed to say, "I am going to make you pay."

"Someone definitely should," said Teacher, and hung up.

***

While this conversation was happening, so was another one. Detective Montano was smart enough to know that I had given him a dummy phone. But he wasn't quite smart enough to think I'd sacrifice a brand new iPhone, and keep a much older, third phone on my person.

It chirped, and I answered the call. "Connie Kendall, Channel Nine News," I said. I expected it to be my producer.

It was not.

It was no one I knew, or expected to hear from. Certainly no one I was able to prepare for.

***

Everyone had returned to Tac-Com. It was the best they could do to maintain the illusion of control: they had a big RV full of cool electronic gizmos. That meant they were in charge. Didn't it?

Vickers, unsurprisingly, was the first to break the pall of silence: "How long before he kills the senator's son?"

"There are more kids in there than –" began Oberczofski.

"Yes, but this is about Daxton Leigh, which means it's about the senator."

Oberczofski said, "Even if that's true, we don't know Teacher's going to do anything to Dax –"

"Yes we do," insisted Vickers. "He's setting the stage."

"Then why isn't he out having a press conference? Why hasn't he demanded anything?"

Montano stared at the slim crack in the phone he still held. "This isn't a terrorist," he said quietly.

"Sorry, Montano," said Vickers, "but the 'gut instinct' of a hotshot doesn't hold any weight in my book. Not anymore. This is some shitwad terrorist –"

"You notice anything about the people we've seen?" asked Montano.

"The only thing we know is they have masks and guns that are a dime a dozen."

"And armbands," said Montano.

"Which helps us exactly hill dollars and bean cents," said Vickers.

Oberczofski was shaking his head. "No, Montano's right: that doesn't fit the terrorist profile. That's an identifier, like they need to know who the others are, but none of them knows the group well enough to be sure. Maybe they don't know faces, or names, or anything. The colors are just designations showing their place in Teacher's plan."

"Right," said Montano. "Terrorists either know each other intimately, so they don't need identifying marks, or their identities are immaterial beyond, 'You're the guy who blows up this stuff' and 'you're the guy who shoots those people.'"

"Think these are mercenaries then?" asked Vickers.

Oberczofski sighed. "That makes even less sense."

Vickers blew a raspberry. "Not sure that's possible."

Montano looked at his phone again. A pair of letters flashed through his mind: "*EB.*"

"This guy knows how to black out our cameras. He knows how to find a bug faster than we can put it in. He spoofed my partner's cell, and called me on my private number. He sent everyone a video file directly, and it opened on its own." Montano chewed his lip for a moment, then finished, "And I think he knows the school."

"That's obvious," Vickers said.

"No. I think he's been here, and not as a criminal. Not as someone preparing for this job."

Vickers started to protest, but Oberczofski asked, "Why do you think that?"

"Some of the things he said… I got the feeling he's been here before, maybe a lot, but never really looked around."

Vickers rolled her eyes. "Is this an 'I've just got a hunch' moment?"

Montano grimaced. "Yeah. It is." His expression firmed. "This isn't a terrorist. So the question is: who could do all this?"

Vickers laughed, her disbelief veering into derision. "I'll just ask at 'Killers R' Us' or maybe just check out anyone with a 'will take hostages for food' sign."

Montano knew that if he didn't make his next moves very carefully, Vickers would take control of things in Tac-Com, move Montano to the sidelines, and run the show in fact if not in name. The techs were already looking at her like she was the sane one in the room, the one that had all the answers.

The only problem with that was that Montano *knew* he was right, and knew that Vickers would get people killed by wasting time on the wrong assumptions.

He had to do something, so he picked up the phone on the wall. He turned to the tech who had planted the bug in the dolly, knowing he'd be the one most afraid of losing his job and hence the one most eager to please someone – *anyone* – in authority.

"Get me the coach's office," said Montano.

Oberczofski squinted. "What are you doing?"

"Teacher only moves when we do. He wants something, but it's like he wants us to figure out what it is."

"Maybe it's my ex," said Vickers. "He never told me what he wanted, either."

Maybe just someone who didn't give him crap as the default emotion.

Montano didn't say it. The phone rang once, and someone picked up. Teacher's voice came over Tac-Com's speakers.

"Took you long enough. I was getting lonely."

"You actually don't want anything," said Montano.

"Oh, I very definitely do."

Montano's stomach lurched. First wrong guess, and now more of the techs – even Oberczofski – were looking like Vickers was the front-runner in a race. For a moment, Montano felt like maybe they were right; maybe Vickers was the only one who could lead them through this.

No.

Grasping, his mouth operating on a direct line to his subconscious, Montano said, "But you don't want to tell me what. You want me to figure it out. That's why you picked me. And you *did* pick me, didn't you? Not just as the person in charge, but as a specific person you wanted to deal with." Pause, and then inspiration: "You sent the video to my computer first, when you knew I was there. You made sure I was the officer in charge, and if that hadn't worked out, you still would have demanded to speak to me."

"Perhaps. Maybe you've finally started to listen to my words. Perhaps even follow them." Then, sounding as though he were speaking more to himself than Montano, Teacher said, "But no, actually I don't think so. Appearances can be deceiving. Life seems to be coming up daisies, and then boom! Everything changes."

The call ended. It had barely clicked in his ear before Montano had his cell out and was dialing again. It passed through his mind that he might be dialing Teacher instead of Eberhardt, but apparently Teacher had only messed with the display, not the actual numbers, because Eb picked up.

"The kid didn't make it," Eberhardt said. "The Tarov kid."

Montano wasn't surprised that Eb knew what had gone down, or that he'd been the one to hear it first from the hospital. They'd call the station first, and Eb wasn't going to call his partner for an update that wouldn't help.

It still hit Montano like a punch. But he gulped and swallowed the dizzy pain that threatened to overwhelm him and started talking.

***

Eberhardt was still standing in Police Technical Investigations. Dapper Dan was still there, pounding on one computer, moving to another, working on it for a moment, then cruising to a third. The guy was as much a machine as any of his toys.

Reggie was mirroring his mentor, though not quite as quickly.

The rest of PTI had changed, though. A half-dozen other detectives and support staff were crammed into the room, following up on the threads Eberhardt had been pulling together on his end.

In his hands, he held a printout representing some of the biggest ones, the ones he hoped that, if he and Montano tugged them just right, would unravel Teacher's plan.

"New theory," said Montano. "This guy is someone local. Or at least someone who's been at the school. Can you check into problems relating to RHS?"

"Way ahead of you, partner. And that particular haystack is very, very big. We already knew the place was a sanctuary for future thieves, murderers, and congressmen. But the more I dig, the worse it gets."

"Anything stand out?"

"No." Eberhardt coughed, then delivered the second bad news of the call. "But heads up: the mayor's alerted to the situation, including what happened to the Tarov boy."

"How do you know that?" asked Montano.

The mayor had been elected by a plurality vote. He wasn't popular with most people in the city, and even less so with the police, most of whom thought he was a nosey, micro-managing prick who was more interested in shuffling projects to his political donors than he was in catching criminals or making the city a better place to live.

"I know that because the Mayor was the one who called to tell me so," said Eberhardt.

"Let me guess: he knows his donors' kids are in danger. He wants them saved so he can take credit and watch his campaign coffers explode. Failing that, he wants someone else's head in the noose and isn't particular about whose, so long as it isn't his neck stretching."

"He didn't say that in so many words. But yeah."

"And the hits keep on rolling."

Eberhardt was surprised at how down Montano sounded. They'd been together long enough that he thought he'd seen Montano's entire emotional range, but this was a new one.

Then a measure of strength returned to Montano's voice. Eberhardt didn't know if it was real or feigned, but sometimes one was just as good as another in a pinch. "If you had to pick one thing that sticks out from what you've found out, what would it be?"

In the background of the call, Eberhardt heard a phone ring.

Probably someone in Tac-Com getting more bad news, he figured, and started calculating what his pension would be if he retired today.

"What stands out?" he said, as much to quell that internal coward as anything. "Other than *all* of today?" He snorted, then glanced at the paper in his hand, suddenly remembering what he'd found, and his voice grew somber. "The rape: two kids were involved in a rape three years ago – allegedly.

In the background, a woman – probably Vickers, probably the one who'd answered the phone – started speaking in angry tones, though Eberhardt couldn't make them out.

Montano spoke again, catching the key word Eberhardt had tossed out. "Allegedly?"

"They weren't convicted."

"Who were they?"

"No idea. It was minors, so their identifying information was stricken from the record."

"Have someone dig into it."

***

Back in Tac-Com, Vickers was almost hollering. Montano was about to hang up, when it hit him:

"Wait, *two* kids?" he said.

"Yeah," Eberhardt answered. And Montano could tell his partner was thinking the same thing he was.

Montano said it anyway. Sometimes the words had to be said, even when he and his partner were reading from the exact same script.

Please God, let me take over the rewrite from this bastard Teacher.

"Have someone get into those court records. And I want you to go talk to the parents of Zane Kennedy and Konstantin Tarov."

"Think the kids who died are the rapists?"

"Not sure, but I don't think they were chosen accidentally."

"Why not?"

Again Montano spoke the words. Again, he knew they were the words Teacher wanted him to say. But just because they were in the play written by a madman didn't mean they were wrong. "Because our guy doesn't do anything accidentally."

Montano heard paper shuffling. "The rape was three years ago. The dead kids would have had to be freshmen when it happened."

"Unless they were held back between then and now. Either way, find out who the victim was, too, then send someone to her house." Thinking a moment, he added, "Or his house."

Montano heard his partner ask the question then. The Big One. "You think the victim's parents are involved? Maybe Teacher is an angry daddy?"

"I don't know, Eb. I know Teacher isn't a terrorist; I *know* it. But whatever he is, he's targeting specific people. I think the only way to find out who he is and stop him, is to find out about his victims."

"All right, I'm on it."

Montano pocketed his phone and turned to Vickers just as she slammed hers onto the cradle. "What's happened now?" he asked, knowing it wasn't going to be good news.

Nothing today was good news.

CHAPTER 19
Intended Response

Everyone has seen the news of that day – either as it was happening or in the infinite replays that populate most of the news when ratings decline. We watched OJ not do much of anything for hours. We watched as Clinton said the same thing over and over, and it was for some reason more exciting than the actual revelation at the end of it all. Nixon didn't admit wrongdoing until after he was out of office, and it didn't get the ratings of the allegations. Society seems excited by the anticipation of the event more than by the reality.

That's part of the problem.

But problem or not, by this point the throng of press outside Reina High School had become a mob. Blood was in the water, and the frenzy had begun in earnest.

Then something changed: information, real information, started coming in.

***

Channel Two News – *The Only News Team That's YOUR News Team*: "… reliable source on the inside…"

Channel Four News – *News You Can Trust*: "…reports have been coming in that multiple members of the staff of Reina High School, a private school for…"

Channel Seven Morning News – *The Only Morning News That Makes You Laugh as Much As It Makes You Cry* (no surprise, that one's ratings were the lowest): "… have apparently been killed, along with several others, including students…"

And where was Channel Nine – *News With Jim Murphy* (now *News With Connie Kendall*)?

We all know that, too.

***

Everyone in the city was glued to their TVs, or their phones, or their computers. They watched all of it unfold – the nothing of it all, until now.

The only one who watched with any understanding was a woman. Thirty-nine years old, attractive in a settled way. The kind of woman who handed out the best treats on Halloween – full candy bars, often king-size; none of those crappy Tootsie Roll lollipops or even crappier Dum-Dums (the Channel Seven of lollipops). The kind of woman of whom neighborhood parents told their kids: "Anything ever happens, you go to her house. It's safe."

Other than that, no one knew her. No one at all, really. But she knew everyone. She knew what was happening at the school right at that moment, and knew what it would mean.

She watched the TV, flipping from channel to channel, waiting for things to start happening, tears in her eyes, knowing that this would end the process of her death that had begun so long before.

***

And in news-speak, Back to Channel Nine News with Jim Murphy – let's go to our reporter-in-the-field, Connie Kendall.

I was on the phone when the door of the cruiser practically ripped off the hinges. Montano got in, wearing an expression I'd never seen on his face before – and I'd seen more expressions on his face than most, which was something Jim tried to hang me for when I was in the process of taking over his job, and which ended up sinking him since he looked like a bully and a misogynistic prick (all true adjectives).

So I'd seen Montano happy, sad, upset, ecstatic. I'd seen him in fits of pique, and in throes of ecstasy.

But I'd never seen him like this: *enraged*.

The second he was in the car, he barked, "Give me the phone."

I hesitated. Not for the reasons he thought. But that rage grew even stronger. "Connie, give it to me or I swear I will drag you out of here, strip search you for anything else you're hiding, then send you to jail and you can serve as first prison yard correspondent and resident expert on ass-beating."

I handed my phone forward, through the still-open window in the plastic wall behind which I'd been stewing.

Montano, still glaring as he took it, said, "I trusted you, Connie."

I admit here to making a very unprofessional noise when he said that. "A one-night stand doesn't equate to trust. Especially when one of us was cheating on his girlfriend."

"No. But the fact that you didn't rat me out and you've never used it as leverage does buy some trust. And out of gratitude I don't press charges when you sneak in, or even toss you out on your ass. I give you a front-row seat where you can –"

"You call this front-row?"

I had just gotten the most important call of my life, and I was bitching about a guy cheating on his on-again, off-again booty call. It wasn't important. But then, how often in life do we actually focus on what's important? Not often, and not nearly as much as we should.

"What did you want me to do?" Montano snarled. "Invite you into Tactical Command? This was the best I could offer, better than you deserve, and you know it. And then you do this."

I was a bit surprised, though I shouldn't have been. I still thought he had just caught me talking on the phone, which he couldn't blame me for, really, so I was surprised at the level of anger on his face. "Do what?" I said.

Again, Montano's rage kicked up a notch. Any more and I figured he'd either die of a heart attack, die of a stroke, or get sent to jail for murdering a reporter. "Don't. Just don't. You saw that boy die, then you called the bottom feeders at your network, and the word's out." He started to say something else, but changed his mind and started rubbing his eye like it hurt. "You know the only thing this achieves is putting people – *kids* – in even more danger?"

That was too much. I finally realized (though I should have realized it earlier) what he was mad about: he thought I'd leaked something that he didn't want leaked. I hadn't – Detective Montano was no Boy Scout, but when he promised me an exclusive, I believed it. I'd called my producer, sure, but we hadn't run with anything yet.

"I didn't tell anyone anything."

"Then how did all your friends out there get their information?"

"Probably the same way I did: I just got a call. A private number, someone who claimed to know what was happening inside."

"And you didn't call and tell me?" Montano yelled it so loud that it hurt my ears.

I'm not some wilting flower. My yell was even louder. "I've been *trying* to call you, Montano. I've been screaming for someone to come over so I can tell them about the phone call – funny that these front row seats don't have ushers – and when that didn't work I *still* didn't call my office. No, I tried to call you directly, but it went straight to voice mail and since then I've tried everything from your department number to the 911 'hotline.' I'll probably get fired because I tried to alert you first, so get the hell off my back."

"I didn't get any calls from you."

I pointed at my phone and said, "Check my call history."

I have to admit, the part of me that's managed to stay human in all these years observing inhumanity hoped he would refuse. That he would just believe me.

No dice. He scrolled through the call history before wincing. "Well I'll be damned," he said, then looked up and said, "Was it a man or a woman who called?"

"Man."

"Sounded hyper-confident?"

"Yeah." I couldn't resist the dig: "A lot like you."

Montano let that one roll right off his back. "What did he say?"

I pulled out the small notepad I always carried. "He gave me a breakdown of how many hostages he's got, and how many students and teachers are dead."

I'd heard the numbers, but repeating it aloud made it a lot more real. This was the worst thing I'd ever covered. It still is. Even knowing the details that came out, the hows and the whys. "It's bad," I said.

"Yeah. Did you say anything to him? Ask him any questions?"

I shook my head. "I tried, but he didn't answer. Didn't even seem to hear me."

Montano pursed his lips, and his eyes went far away, to whatever vista he viewed when deep in thought. "A recording. Or maybe he somehow mass-called everyone," he said, mostly to himself.

"Like the emails," I said.

He nodded, and looked at the car door. I knew he was calculating the best way to get out of the car without re-litigating the terms of our deal. But I wasn't in a mood to bargain. Like I said, reading aloud the information had stunned me. At this point, I forgot about reporting, if only for a moment. I just wanted this to end.

"Go," I said. "Just… can you send some water or food?"

"Sure," he said. "I hope you like cold Mexican."

"I love it."

I didn't know the role the food had played. I had seen the food carted in, and a kid coming out soon after, but I hadn't connected them, really. I just figured the cops ordered extra for themselves, and that he'd be sending me some.

That was all true enough, but when I found out exactly what the food had primarily been ordered for, I puked every bit of it up, and haven't been able to look at a burrito since.

***

The sun crawled across the sky.

The news frenzy continued.

Montano and the others looked at the gym. Waiting for the next thing to happen, trying to figure out some way to counter it or – better – to stop it from happening at all.

No one had any clue how to do either.

PART THREE:
MANIACAL HORROR

I SHALL never forget the maniacal horror of it all in the end
when everything was me, I knew it all already, I anticipated it
all in my soul
because I was the author and the result
I was the God and the creation at once;
creator, I looked at my creation;
created, I looked at myself, the creator:
it was a maniacal horror in the end.

- D.H. Lawrence
  "New Heaven and Earth"

CHAPTER 20
Intended Response

Though the sun crawled, Detective Eberhardt did not. He worked harder than he ever had before, trying to dig out the facts he and Montano would need. He called in every chit and favor he was owed, made any promises he suspected might help, and issued any threat he thought would work. It all led him to a cold, forbidding high-rise.

He entered, and after a brief conversation with the men stationed in front of the elevators – one which got heated, and ended with his observation that they would either let him in or spend the night in jail – he found himself pacing outside not just *a* corner office, but *the* corner office.

He'd been waiting for ten minutes, and that was nine minutes and fifty seconds too long. He marched over to the hatchet-faced receptionist, a woman named Lenore Peabody, who had been hired as much for her ability to intimidate as for her secretarial skills, and snarled, "Lady, if you don't let me through now, I guarantee that your boss is going to –"

"My 'boss' is concluding an extraordinarily sensitive business deal. And whatever you threaten, I promise, I won't let you in."

Lenore Peabody was used to dealing with intruders. But the thing they all had in common – even the cops – was they had more to lose than they did to gain by pushing the issue. Eberhardt, however, had not just been juggling leads all day. He'd also done an internal inventory, then called his wife to see if she agreed. Maricela did: they both thought he should stop the tragedy by any legal means, even if that meant taking steps that were unwise on a career level. Even if he ended up fired, they'd take the hit and make it work.

But Lenore didn't know that, so was completely unprepared at the police detective who, apparently not caring that he was barging in on a man who could end his career with a word, spun abruptly on his heel and marched past the receptionist.

"What are you doing, you can't –"

Eberhardt threw open the doors to the office of Xavier Delroy.

***

Largely (purposefully) unknown before the shakedowns that followed in the wake of the RHS disaster, Xavier Delroy is now known to most. In case you are blind, or have an aversion to watching television, here is a snapshot. Delroy is a short, oily man in his fifties. He typically wears a ten-thousand-dollar suit that molds itself to his frame, which is squat and froglike.

When Eberhardt marched into Delroy's office, the man was screaming at three other businessmen of similar cuts – though they wore suits of only five or six thousand dollars apiece.

"I don't care who he is, but I do care about interruptions to my –" Xavier Delroy cut off abruptly as Eberhardt barged in.

"Who the hell are you? Never mind, I don't care." Turning to Lenore, who had followed Eberhardt in, wringing her hands and looking like she was witnessing the end of days, Delroy said, "Call security. Or the police."

Eberhardt flashed his badge. "The police are already here. We've been trying to reach you for hours."

Delroy was silent for a moment. Every move he makes is the product of careful calculation, and he was calculating now. He nodded at the other men, and they filed out.

Turning back to Eberhardt, he said, "You have a warrant this time? Or should I call my lawyers again?"

"Sir, I don't know what you're talking about. I'm here to inform you about your daughter, and to ask about one of the men in your employ."

"What man?"

Eberhardt was so surprised at the question he momentarily forgot what he was doing there. What kind of man, he thought, would ask about a business associate when he'd just been informed – by the cops – that his daughter was involved in something?

Then he remembered. He remembered what he was doing here, what kind of a man he had already discovered Delroy to be, and what line of questioning he was here to pursue. "Aleksandar Tarov," he said.

Aleksandar Tarov was the father of Konstantin Tarov, the boy who had been force-fed and sodomized with a variety of devices. Eberhardt had not been able to track the guy down, but had managed to discover that he worked at Entercom, directly under Xavier Delroy – who also had a child at RHS.

Delroy, seeming supremely uninterested, waved a hand. "If you can find Konstantin, please let me know. He went AWOL on me."

Eberhardt refrained from laughing. "Assuming I believe you – which would be a huge assumption, I can assure you – when did you last see him?"

"Two, three days ago." Finally, Delroy asked about the person Eberhardt would have expected any normal human to focus on. "What about my daughter? What's Paige done this time?"

"So you do remember her. What a relief."

Delroy frowned. "Watch it, officer."

"Detective, actually."

Delroy cocked his head. "Do you know who I am, *detective*? Or how close you are to seeing your career go up in flames?"

Eberhardt ignored the threat, answering only the first question. "Actually, you're a tough guy to figure out. My people only managed to sort out three levels of shell holdings before they started pulling their hair out and downing Xanax like they were Tic Tacs. I'd appreciate some enlightenment. Or I can invite you down to the station to talk there."

Delroy turned his back on the detective, looking out over the city lights beginning to blink into being as the sun fell beyond the horizon. "I am a significant shareholder in seven different media conglomerates. I have pieces of various cosmetics companies in my portfolio, as well as a dozen different entertainment-related software companies."

"So, like video games?" said Eberhardt. In addition to being a good listener, he knew when to play dumb. People who thought themselves very smart – as he could already tell Delroy did – tended to speak far too much for their own good when they felt they were with an idiot. Their way of showing off to someone they knew in their heart would never understand enough to get them in trouble.

"Yes. Like video games. And I find it easiest to manage my affairs when I do so quietly. Under the radar. Where's my daughter?"

"You know what's happening at Reina?" said Eberhardt, surprised again at Delroy's sudden conversational shift.

"Her school? No. She doesn't share much with me."

"Whether you do or not, you would have found out looking at the news. I'm surprised someone as obviously *well informed* didn't know already."

Like Eberhardt, Delroy refused to rise to the proffered bait. He picked up a remote from his desk and pressed a button. A large flatscreen hanging on the wall blinked on. It was already set to a news channel, and though the sound was muted there was a picture of Reina High School on an insert beside the reporter with the title "Disaster at Elite Private High School" written across it in large stencil lettering.

"What's this about? What's she done?" Delroy demanded, turning to Eberhardt.

Damn, Eberhardt thought. What kind of girl is she that her dad would figure a national disaster at her school would be pegged to her?

"She's committed the high crime of being hostage to armed gunmen, *sir*."

Delroy eyed Eberhardt. More upset about the disrespect than his daughter. "I could ruin you, *officer*."

Eberhardt laughed. "Probably. But for now I think your time would be better spent telling me about the last time you saw your daughter, and answering my questions about her and about Mr. Aleksandar Tarov."

Delroy watched as a series of students' photos were shown. An image of Paige flashed across the screen – she was eighteen, so fair game for some of the less-ethical reporters – her leg held high as she performed a cheer routine at one of Reina High School's basketball games.

Delroy whispered his daughter's name, as though suddenly aware of the gravity of the situation. Eberhardt waited.

Delroy nodded. He finally seemed affected by what was going on. "I'll cooperate however I can."

"Then let's start with this: why would your daughter be taken hostage, Mr. Delroy?"

***

At Reina High School, Montano stared at the gym as though hoping the building itself would start speaking; start explaining what the hell was going on. Beside him, Vickers stared at the gym through binoculars. No word had come for hours, and Montano knew that Vickers was on the verge of pushing to enter. The only thing that had kept her from doing it were the arguments of Montano (of little value to her) and Oberczofski (whom she had a lot more respect for).

Oberczofski approached now, his face wan and pinched: more bad news.

"What is it?" asked Montano.

"Hospital just called. Gersham…" Oberczofski swallowed. "The principal just died."

***

Montano was drinking a coffee, warding off the night, the fear that everyone felt, the chill that had settled into his bones. For perhaps the first time, he knew that anyone looking would see the concern in his eyes. Not for himself, though he knew others might think so. He was just worried about the kids. Wracking his brain to come up with ways to help them. Coming up with nothing.

"How much longer do you want to wait?" Vickers asked with a sigh. She was drinking a coffee as well, though none of the warmth in her cup made it to her expression.

"Until we actually know something. We move without understanding this and all we'll end up doing is playing right into Teacher's hand."

Montano's cell rang. He pulled it out, glanced at it, then showed it to Vickers. The caller ID read "TEACHER."

Montano started running for Tac-Com, Vickers close behind.

"You program your phone to do that?" she hollered.

Montano yelled over his shoulder, "Nope."

***

They arrived at Tac-Com before the phone had rung three times. Montano answered and put it on speaker.

"I was worried you'd forgotten about me," said Teacher.

"It's been busy over here."

"No doubt. Discover anything interesting?"

"Plenty, but I'm still waiting for you to tell me how I can help you."

Oberczofski, who'd been in the mobile command center when Montano and Vickers arrived, gave him a thumbs-up, obviously pleased that Montano had – for once – responded the way a negotiator was supposed to.

Teacher wasn't so easily impressed. He gave a melodramatic moan. "So you haven't figured it out. That's disappointing."

Montano's cell beeped. Call waiting: "DAPPER D." He swiped to get rid of the call. Then he said, "Why not just tell me? You're talking to the press directly, why not me?"

"Because I want you to come to a conclusion, detective, rather than act like someone who takes what's given and then vomits it back for ratings. Besides, when was the last time you believed something a reporter told you?"

"Touché," Oberczofski whispered.

Teacher didn't hear it, and continued, "You have to discover the answers. And the fact that you haven't… I may have overestimated you."

"Maybe you have," agreed Montano.

Dapper Dan again tried to ring through on Montano's phone, who again swiped a finger across his screen to deny the incoming call.

"Doesn't that bother a man like you?" asked Teacher.

Montano paused. Then asked, "What do you mean, 'a man like me'?"

"It means that you still don't know how to listen. So… time to move on."

The phone on Teacher's side shifted, like he was moving. He whispered something. Montano felt like he was shifting, too – tilting to the side drunkenly, about to fall down. Teacher was disappointed, and about to "move on," and there was no good scenario there.

Montano couldn't think of anything to do; couldn't even think of anything to say, other than, "What are you doing? What –"

A sound cut him off. Tac-Com's low murmur of voices – the

techs, still trying to hack through into the CCTV system or Reina's computers – shut off as the sound of a single gunshot rang through the speakers. A moment later they heard it outside as well.

Students screamed – again audible both through Montano's phone and the walls of the gym. The sound of rustling cloth filled the line, and it was only too easy for Montano to imagine what he was hearing: a dark hood being ripped off someone's head.

"What's your name?" asked Teacher. The tone of his voice was tinny, far away; he was talking to someone on his end of the phone.

A weak, frightened voice answered. "Jonas, sir. Chambers, I mean. Jonas Chambers."

Vickers held up her whiteboard: "English teacher."

Still speaking to Jonas, Teacher asked, "What just happened?"

The quiver in Jonas' voice grew more pronounced. "Y-y-you just shot a student."

"That's correct, Jonas," Teacher said conversationally. "And which student did I shoot?"

***

It's the nature of reporting – and storytelling in general – to glance over the unimportant things.

People enter stage left, they exit stage right. While they're in the spotlight, delivering information that tells us about the plot, the setting, the characters, they matter. When they leave the scene, they disappear from reality. That may be why everyone is so desperate for their fifteen minutes of fame: proof that they not only existed, but once actually *lived*, in full color and brightly lit from above.

That's the reason I haven't spoken much about one of the key players. He mattered – not just to the situation, but to every single person reading this. But no matter how important a man he may be in our day-to-day lives, until now he hadn't been much more than a blip.

Now, however, Senator Joel William Leigh became more involved, more important, and more a factor in how things would work out. He sat forward in the police cruiser where he'd basically taken up residence since the morning. Heard the two words he most feared as Jonas Chambers answered Teacher's simple question: "Which student did I shoot?"

The pacemaker that had kept his heart beating steadily for the last six years stuttered a bit, his chest growing tight as Jonas answered, "Daxton Leigh."

Senator Leigh screamed in rage, pain, fear. Perhaps a little guilt.

Maybe even more than a little.

***

Inside Tac-Com, the reactions to this announcement met with less screaming, but no less turmoil.

Montano waved everyone to shut up as Teacher continued talking to Jonas Chambers in the gym. "Is Daxton dead?"

Everyone in Tac-Com held their breath. Then released it as Jonas said, "No."

Montano breathed, but didn't stop worrying. And those worries were validated when Jonas added, "You shot him in the stomach."

"Shit," said Vickers.

"God in Heaven," said Oberczofski.

On the speakers, Teacher said, "Thank you, Mr. Chambers. I'm truly sorry you were involved in this – neither you nor Mr. Wright were supposed to be here. You're two good men, and I'm sorry you got roped into this."

"Teacher?" Montano said into his phone. Then, when no answer came, he nearly shrieked it: "*TEACHER?*"

The phone shifted again. "What can I do for you, detective?"

Montano swallowed his first-through-tenth responses, all of which involved impossible sexual positions. Through a rain of terror and rage – one seeping into the other, both becoming a muddy, murky pool inside him – he managed, "Teacher, send Daxton out. Or let someone come in to help him." He added a word he hadn't said yet. He had screamed it, but never simply said the word, "Please."

"Ahh… humility. It suits you." Teacher's voice was unabashedly approving – everyone who heard it agreed on that afterward. Just as they also agreed that his voice grew hard and frosty as he said, "No one comes in. No one goes out.

"We just want –"

"This isn't all your fault, Montano," said Teacher. "Daxton Leigh was destined to suffer."

And he hung up.

***

Almost the instant Teacher was gone, Montano's phone rang again. He picked up. "Please give me good news."

Dapper Dan's voice answered. "I don't know about good, but I dug into the two kids who raped –"

"Allegedly," Montano said automatically.

Dan's voice sounded disgusted. "I'd bet my wardrobe they did it, Montano."

"Without a juvie record or jail?"

"That's where the third kid came in."

Montano blinked. "The third kid?"

"Yeah. There was another kid: someone with the leverage to make his friends' cases go sideways, to make his own charges disappear completely, and to get the whole thing buried."

Montano realized what Dapper Dan had just told him, and how to put it together with what Teacher had just done. "It was Daxton Leigh."

Dan chuffed. "You ruined the surprise! How'd you know?"

"I finally started listening. Who was the victim?"

"Haven't gotten that yet."

"Why the hell not?"

"You already know. Juvie rape victims' identities are sealed tighter than a convent on Mardi Gras."

"Okay, keep digging, Double-D. Good work."

"Of course it is. I..."

They both finished the sentence together: "... am Dapper Dan."

Dan hung up, leaving Montano laughing. It wasn't that funny of a moment, but sometimes "not that funny" is just enough to keep a grip on sanity, and this was one of those times.

***

Montano kept the phone to his ear after Dapper Dan hung up. His mind was spinning, twisting, trying to draw something up from his subconscious. Without thinking about it, he went to the closest cubby with a computer. A tech had been sitting there, but Montano shoved the man aside, murmuring, "What'd he say? What'd he say..."

Behind him, Vickers snarled. "We're done. *You're* done." Montano turned back to her, almost running into the finger she was jabbing at him. "You know the senator's around. And you know what he's going to want."

Oberczofski stepped forward, his normally easy-going expression replaced by a rock-hard determination. "We can't. We go in hard and everyone's likely to die. *Including* his son."

Vickers wheeled on him. "His son's dead no matter what unless we get in there."

As the two bickered, Montano turned back to the computer. His mind coughed up something Teacher had said:

"Did you know there are over 3,000 animal shelters in the United States? An astounding number. And don't just take my word for it. Google what I just said and you'll find out for yourself. The world is a funny place."

Montano opened Google and typed the words in quotes:

"Did you know there are over 3,000 animal shelters in the United States? An astounding number."

Before, with his more general search, he'd gotten millions of links. But he hadn't done what Teacher had told him to, had he? He had acted like a cop – grabbing the facts, then following them.

As a reporter, I understand that. It's what I do, too.

But sometimes maybe the facts aren't enough. Sometimes maybe we have to listen – to the pain, to the people, to the "more" that lies behind the facts.

In Tac-Com, Montano finished typing – not just the essentials, but the thing he'd been told to type from the very beginning. He clicked the search button.

One result popped up.

***

Usually, when an internet search returns a result, it returns a hyperlink formatted to make sense to readers – the name of the company, or "Get best mattresses here!" or whatever it may be. Below that, net surfers will find a description inputted by the owner of the website to help them find what they're looking for.

When Montano entered Teacher's words on Google, none of that came back. It was just a link composed of random-seeming numbers and letters that the detective knew would turn out to be some elegant, untraceable hack of the system. Just the kind of thing

Teacher went in for.

He clicked the link, and an article opened. Since then, it's become one of the most-read articles in the history of the internet, shared and re-shared across the world:

"The United States Sex Trade."

Montano began to read.

CHAPTER 21
The Plan

It didn't happen as Montano read it – even for Teacher and The Lady, with their careful planning and to-the-microsecond timing, such would have been impossible.

But there could also be no doubt that they intended Montano to read certain passages, and that they knew the detective (and later the press) would realize how they corresponded to what happened in the gym.

Or rather, in the late Coach Fertetti's office.

The door to the office was shut. Inside, it was dark, save a strange red gleam: the light of metal heated to glowing.

Nearby the gleam, girls wept. Some of the girls cried hysterically, some tried to hold it in but failed, their sobs escaping in painful-sounding gasps.

But all cried. And if they hadn't cried, I think The Lady would have waited. I think she would have waited until the girls wept, because she would have believed that this had to happen to the dreadful music of tears.

***

The article Teacher had intended Montano to read from the beginning described the people most victimized in "The United States Sex Trade:

"… *unknown numbers of faceless young women…*"

Each of the crying girls, standing so close to heat they could feel it, was faceless: each wore a hood. They were nothing but a means to a desired result.

Six girls were lined up in total. Two of them wore Computer GurlZ t-shirts that the entire world now knows once belonged to Winona "Win" Jackson and Beatriz Alcivar.

I say "once," because the shirts don't belong to them anymore.

They don't belong to anyone, really.

Other than the shirts, the six girls wore a mixture of clothing: some wore outfits that marked them as Misfits, some wore outfits you could find on any girl at any high school in the United States.

"… the silent sex trade around us all…"

"Shut up," said one of the Colors. None of the girls knew who said it. But they felt the hands of the Colors chosen for this moment – Green, Blue, and Purple – shove them against the wall.

The Colors lifted or cut away the girls' sleeves. Some of the teens resisted, and were slapped down for their efforts, then hauled back to their feet.

All of the girls had elastic bands tied around their upper arms, all felt the prick of a needle as they were injected with a dark substance later forensic examination of the discarded needles would confirm as heroin.

The girls still couldn't see the source of the heat, and in the state of euphoria that was dropping over them, they didn't much care.

They started to care, though, a second later.

The Lady had been absent for much of the plan, though she had helped prepare every aspect of it. There had been much discussion between her and Teacher about who would do what, and when, but on this point she was adamant: she would be the one to do this part.

"… girls branded like cattle…"

The Lady held a long metal rod in one hand. It looked a bit like a fireplace poker, only instead of a hook at the end, it had a simple shape. Using the stick welder the group had brought with them when they took over RHS, The Lady had heated the metal to a bright white glow, and now, one at a time, she pressed the end of it against the girls' arms.

Each girl screamed. A few fainted.

But they were all marked.

The brand was simple: a circle. The same as the one that Dapper Dan had found on a girl's arm in a picture buried in a video of death that played on a non-stop loop in his office.

CHAPTER 22
Intended Response

Eberhardt was driving through the city when he got Montano's call. Montano had just finished reading the article Teacher had pointed him to, and things were starting to fall into place. Not the who, necessarily, but the why.

Eberhardt glanced at his phone, even as he pushed his car to thirty miles past the speed limit. Picking up, he spoke first. "I just heard about the kid. How long's he got?"

"We don't know. But with a gutshot he'll wish he was dead a long time before he gets there. Where are you right now?"

Eberhardt knew Montano wasn't asking for his physical location, but for an update on his partner's findings in the case. "Still looking into the parents of the dead kids," Eberhardt said with a tired sigh.

"And?"

"Other than the senator's son, the parents all have ties to Entercom."

Montano didn't have to ask what that was. Most cops knew of it, if only peripherally. "You lean on them?"

Eberhardt shook his head. "I still haven't even *found* most of them. I tried to question Xavier Delroy – the head guy at Entercom – and he made it pretty clear he only answers to a signed warrant or a lawyer better than his."

Eberhardt could hear his partner's disbelief and disgust. "Even knowing his daughter's in danger?

"I get the feeling she's a distant second to his business interests."

"Keep at it. And stand by: I might have something else for you soon."

"Any hints there, partner?"

Montano hesitated. Then just said, "Not yet," and hung up.

Eberhardt drove into a night that, despite the lights of the city, seemed a bit darker with every passing moment.

***

At Tac-Com, Montano turned to the tech he'd shoved aside to do his Google search. "How do I hook into the department network?"

The tech reached around Montano, clicked two buttons, and the police logo appeared, with a login bar below it.

"What are you looking for?" asked Vickers, obviously curious in spite of herself.

"This guy knows the area, but I don't think he's from here, specifically. He's got serious tech skills. And he's got a grudge against these three kids who raped someone."

"The father?" asked Oberczofski. "A relative or a friend?"

Montano shook his head. "This seems a bit extreme for that. A baseball bat or a gun would be a lot easier if simple revenge was the goal." He logged into the system, then began running a search.

"Then what do you think this is?" Vickers said. "And what are you looking for?"

"I'm checking for disappearances. Girls, children of rich parents."

He scanned the results that came up. Even with the meager information he had entered, several names jumped out at him. He dialed his phone again.

"That was fast," Eberhardt said.

"I'm sending you some addresses to visit."

"Who are they?"

"Parents whose daughters went missing within the last few

years."

"Think it was Teacher?"

"Probably not. All of them were taken in different places, with different MOs. A very few eyewitnesses described different possible suspects each time."

"So a bunch of different creeps took a bunch of different girls. But you think it's related."

"Maybe. Keep your eyes open. And be careful."

Eberhardt put on a baby voice. "Aww, you do wuv me after all."

***

Next on the line was Dapper Dan, who had precisely one word to say when Montano called. "Busy."

Reggie's voice came on. "Sorry, Montano, the big guns are occupied."

"You'll do, Reggie. When you looked at the school's computer logs, did you find any evidence of porn?"

"It's a high school, Montano."

That was the answer that Montano expected. But he sensed more in Reggie's voice. "More than usual?"

"You bet your life."

"Can you pinpoint the biggest users?"

"Already on it," said Reggie. "The individual students' names are protected and encrypted, but based on terminal usage, huge amounts of porn were streamed in the Science Building –"

"As long as you don't go past the Science Building, you'll be fine. You won't need to go much further than that to see what you need to."

Montano heard Teacher's instruction as Reggie spoke, and another connection was made. "Gunne and Vachnarian."

"The RHS tech guys whose heads got 'sploded?" asked Reggie.

"Yeah. Get into their bank records."

"I'll have to wait on warrants."

"Drop everything and focus on that."

Montano hung up, then turned as he heard the sound of a door opening, and in came more bad news.

***

Montano's first impression was that Senator Leigh had aged twenty years in the past day. His second was that the man was ready to kill someone, and probably wasn't very particular about who it was.

"Sir, we're very sorry and –"

Gone was the man who had professed faith in Montano's abilities. "I intend to make sure your career is over by tomorrow morning." Turning to Vickers, steel in his voice, he said, "You're tactical?" She nodded. "How long to prepare an assault?"

Montano had been expecting this. Still, it hurt – not just because he saw his career turn to ash in that moment, but because he suspected it was the wrong thing for the kids.

He didn't expect, though, what happened next: Vickers crossed her arms, scowled her most impressive and impassable scowl, then said, "About ten minutes past impossible."

Leigh looked startled – no surprise there, given that this was a man accustomed to crooking a finger and changing the lives of millions. Then his expression firmed, the rage cooling to something icy and terrifying. "No, it's just difficult. Here's what you're going to –"

Vickers cut the senator off, going so far as to walk in close, crowding him in his personal space. "Sir, I respect your office, but it means dick right now. We go in and there's a good chance every single person in there – hostage and captor – dies. *Every. Single. One of them*, not to mention a significant number of my people. I won't take that kind of risk on such a small possibility of success."

Yet another surprise: instead of digging in, cajoling, or threatening, Senator Leigh's expression fell in on itself, leaving behind a well of grief, terror, and desperation. "He's my son…"

"And you forgot to mention that he was involved in a rape several years ago," said Montano, oddly satisfied to see the surprise that flashed across Leigh's face.

"How did you –" Senator Leigh began, then cut off his sentence and said, "Why would that be relevant?"

Montano wanted to start shrieking. Almost, he shouted, *Because it changes things from terrorism to revenge, you asshole!*

Then another thought intruded: *This is his father.*

The thought softened his answer. Quieted Montano's own rage. "Sir, we'll do everything we can to get him out."

Senator Leigh wasn't willing to take the olive branch Montano extended. "No. Not you."

Oberczofski, so quiet throughout the exchange, had also come to the conclusion that Montano was the only hope the kids had. So he spoke up now, reminding the senator what everyone else seemed to have forgotten: "They'll only talk to Detective Montano. He leaves, it's over."

Leigh's face grew a few shades grayer. He rubbed his hand over his eyes. "How long does my son have?"

"Impossible to say," said Oberczofski.

"But these kinds of wounds are often slow," Vickers said. Her voice was soothing now, softer than anyone in Tac-Com had ever heard from her. "There's a good chance that –"

"That he'll be in agony until he finally dies," finished Senator Leigh. He looked around pleadingly. "Please," he said to everyone and to no one. "Save him."

Montano nodded. "We will."

Leigh's shoulders sagged. He looked around, appearing lost, and then walked out of Tac-Com. Vickers, hushed, called a uniformed officer on her radio, ordering him to follow the senator – at a discreet distance – and "make sure he doesn't do anything stupid."

"He's a senator," said the cop. "Isn't that what they get paid for?"

No one laughed. Not tonight.

***

A few hours later, Montano's phone rang. Everyone grew hushed. The caller ID said, "EB," but he was tense as he put the phone on speaker and answered.

"Montano," said Eberhardt (and everyone heaved a sigh of relief, then another of worry because whatever Teacher was doing during his silence, it couldn't be good), "I'm conferencing Dan."

"What have we got?" asked Montano.

"I found the users who most frequented the porn sites," Dan said.

"I thought Reggie was doing that," said Montano.

"He was. But when I heard what he was doing, and realized where you were going with it, I took over. He's good, he tries for a white guy, but he's not me."

"Okay, so you worked your magic," said Montano. "And what did you get?"

"First, I got an interesting jump. Lots of porn – it *is* a high school. But there's the 'usual' amount, then there's a significant jump to a tier of people who have so much T&A going through their computers it's got to be some kind of record."

"Let me guess: there are thirty-two people in that top tier."

"How'd you know?" Dan asked.

"Thirty-four hostages. Take away the two who, according to Teacher, weren't supposed to be here today, and..." said Montano.

"Nice," said Dan.

"I don't think that's the right word for it."

"No, I guess not," said Dan, sounding chagrined. Then his voice changed. "But that's not all I found."

"Don't play coy, Double-D," Eberhardt interrupted.

"Not playing coy, just setting the stage," said Dan.

"For what?" asked Montano.

"For this: all the kids in that top-level of porn users have a connection to Entercom."

"We already knew that," said Eberhardt.

"No," said Dan. "Not just the dead ones, *all* of the porn addicts there. All their parents are either employed by or 'consult' for Entercom."

"So this is looking more and more like a vendetta against Entercom?" Montano frowned. "Why would a group of persons unknown go after an entertainment company."

Reggie's voice piped up in the background. "We don't know yet."

"Shut up, Reggie," said Dan pleasantly. Then, to Eberhardt and Montano (and everyone listening in Tac-Com), added, "We don't know yet. But guess what *part* of Entercom they're all connected to."

"This isn't the time for suspense, Dan," said Montano.

"Reggie, would you care to do the honors?" said Dan.

"Bright Dreams, Inc.," Reggie chimed.

Montano couldn't place the name for a moment. Then he did,

and one more piece clicked into place.

**

"Wait… the porn company?"

"Yup," said Dan. "Number three in America, with a yearly revenue of nearly one-hundred-forty million dollars."

"I've never heard of them," said Eberhardt.

Dan chuckled. "You're sweet, Eb. I question whether you're actually male, but you're very sweet."

Montano frowned, shaking his head. "That doesn't make sense, though: what are the chances of so many kids whose parents work at Entercom going to this specific school?"

"Eberhardt asked that question first," said Dan.

"Why I called you," added Eberhardt, obviously speaking to Montano.

"I was pleasantly surprised at his clarity of thought," added Dan. "He's usually sundowned by this time of night."

"I had the wife DVR *NCIS* so that my oldness would have some hope to find strength in," Eberhardt deadpanned.

"Now if we could only explain that a tie is meant to beautify, not make it look like your neck threw up," Reggie shouted.

"Agreed," said Dan, at the same time as Montano said, "Focus, people!"

"Sorry," said Dan. "I've had about six hundred coffees, and Reggie's consumption of Red Bull has probably skyrocketed their stock, so we're a little punchy." He cleared his throat. "At any rate, I looked into it, and it turns out having all those kids there isn't that shocking. Reina is a continuation school, so it's there for kids with severe emotional and behavioral problems. And while I haven't had a chance to delve into it completely, I'd be willing to bet that finding out your mom or dad work in the sex industry is probably going to have some psychological impact."

Montano, mind racing, said, "Eb, go back to Xavier Delroy. Lean on him. And Dan: have you found anything else in the teachers' financial data?"

"Just a coincidence with a high weird factor: we got the warrants in for the bank records, and for once we got the banks on board in record time."

"How'd you do that?" said Montano.

"I called the governor, the governor called the banks," Eberhardt said.

The night of surprises continued. "You called the governor? Directly? Shit, Eb, are you a superhero in your time off?"

"No. The wife is. But I do sidekick work," said Eb.

"You do look good in tights," said Dan.

"D," said Montano, a note of warning creeping into his voice. "What did you find?"

Sounding confused, Dan said, "The dead teachers all got some rather odd deposits."

"What kind of odd?" asked Montano.

"They seemed random at first, but Reggie thought to look at the school calendar, and it turns out the deposits happened like clockwork on the day before any of Reina's sports teams played an away game."

Vickers, who'd been glued to the conversation, whispered, "What the hell?"

Oberczofski nodded his agreement.

What the hell? indeed.

***

Montano was just as confused, but he followed the logical train of questions: "How big were the deposits?"

"Various amounts," Reggie piped up. "Slattery, the dead

gym teacher, got a few hundred each time. Same with the dead secretary and the vice principal. Fertetti, the head coach, got a thousand each time."

"And the principal?" asked Eberhardt.

"Between five and ten," said Reggie. "The biggest payout."

"And the most painful death," said Montano, mostly to himself.

Vickers held up two fingers. "What about the IT guys? Vachnarian and Gunne? And the two others – Jonas Chambers and Holden Wright."

"Nothing on Chambers or Wright," said Dan.

"Who weren't supposed to be here," whispered Oberczofski.

"– and I'm still trying to make sense of Vachnarian and Gunne," Dan finished.

"Whaddya mean?" asked Eb.

Montano heard the clicking of fingers on a keyboard. "Their accounts are weird and they obviously did some shuffling to mask what they were getting and from whom."

"What about the other gym teacher?" Oberczofski asked. "What was his name?"

"Isaiah Mulcahey," Montano said. Inwardly, he cursed: he had forgotten that the other gym teacher was also a hostage. Easy to forget things in a situation like this, with so many moving parts and so much at stake. But easy or not, he couldn't afford that kind of forgetfulness: it could cost people their lives.

He was tired, he was stressed. But he wasn't done, and sleep wouldn't come until this all ended, one way or another.

"Mulcahey also got paid the day before the away games. A few hundred each time," said Dan.

"So why's *he* still alive?" asked Vickers.

"Don't know," said Dan. "But based on the trends, I'd say his chances at continuing that way aren't great."

"Anything else?" asked Montano.

"Not at present."

"Okay, keep digging, D. Eb, you push Delroy about Entercom and Bright Dreams. Hard."

"Right off a cliff, if I can," said Eberhardt.

CHAPTER 23
Intended Response

Things hadn't been happening outside the "front-row seat" Montano left me sitting in. But being confined to the back seat of a police cruiser didn't stop me from writing. Somehow I knew that this night would not only be huge for me, but for the world. So I was filling up pages with notes of everything from the description of the gym to the layout of the cars and the mobile command to the number of cups of coffee I'd observed being consumed.

I was so deep in my observations, in fact, that I failed to notice the things closest to me. I'm sure there's a pertinent lesson to be learned there, but the upshot in this particular moment was that I just about jumped out of my skin when the cruiser door opened.

After I peeled myself off the roof and managed to get my heart beating again, I saw that a uniformed officer had stuck her head in. "Montano sent me to see if you need a bathroom break?"

I did. In fact, part of the reason my note-taking had grown so furious in the last few minutes was to take my mind off the fact that I was in serious danger of peeing in the back of the squad car.

I nodded. The officer shut the front door and opened mine. I slid out, my legs cramping a bit after all the time on the hard plastic seat in the back of the squad car.

The officer was already walking, clearly intending for me to follow. I thought about trying to ditch her, to see what information I could get before I was found and ejected. I rejected it, though: there was still that exclusive Montano had promised.

The train of thought kept me from noticing where we were going. It wasn't until the officer stepped up to the door to Tac-Com that I realized what was happening.

"In *there*?" I said.

The officer winked. "I think Detective Montano felt bad about leaving you in the car for so long."

The need to pee – so immediate and important only seconds before – disappeared completely. I felt like I was having an out-of-body experience as I walked into the mobile command, barely hearing myself as I whispered, "All is forgiven."

***

No one really noticed me as I entered. Vickers was hanging up a phone, then walked toward where Montano was staring at a bank of dark monitors.

"I just got off the horn with the FBI," Vickers said.

Montano groaned. "They're taking over," he said.

Vickers looked a bit confused. "I would have guessed that's what they called about, but honestly? I don't know. The liaison acted cagey, and I got the sense that something weird's going down."

Montano thought a moment, then said, "Must be Leigh. He's stirring up –"

I interrupted him. This was the first time I truly injected myself in the story. I didn't just observe, I didn't just ask questions. I was even past telling Montano about the information I and the other journalists had received from the man everyone still knew only as Teacher.

"The Senator is a nonentity," I said.

Vickers whirled and snarled, "What's *she* doing here?" in a tone you or I might use if we realized Hitler had just walked into a synagogue. She took a step toward me, obviously figuring on a very forceful ejection.

Montano grabbed her arm. "Let her talk," he said.

Vickers stopped moving, but I could tell from her expression I had about six seconds to prove my value before getting tossed out, maybe thrown in jail.

"I assume you're talking about Senator Leigh," I said.

"How do you –"

I put on a coy look as Montano gestured for Vickers to shut up. Then, talking fast, I said, "Most don't know this, but he's retiring in a week. He's not going to be on any of his committees, and his pull in Congress is already somewhere between zero and the gunk under your fridge."

That landed. Hard. Which wasn't surprising. I'd just found out myself that morning, and it would have made all the headlines if it weren't for the story I was sitting at the center of right now.

When he recovered from his momentary surprise, Montano said, "All right, he can't run Congress, and it certainly points toward this being something other than run-of-the-mill terrorism. He's gotta still have the pull to take over a crisis like this one if he wants, and besides, that doesn't tell us why the FBI isn't following their usual playbook of either ignoring us completely or taking over and sidelining everyone without the word 'federal' in their job title."

That I couldn't answer. But between the information I'd served and Montano's insistence, I got to stay at Tac-Com for a while. I resolved to stay quiet, because you couldn't beat courtside seats like this one.

That resolution lasted a very short time. Soon I'd be taken out of the stands and tossed onto the court myself, to play or die.

***

Beyond Reina's walls, nothing new was being said. Mostly just repetitions and speculations by the reporters who were being yelled at by producers through their earpieces, told that the ratings gold situation was in danger of dulling to silver, and from there to bronze and then to the dustbin of yesterday's news.

They tried to keep things interesting, and largely succeeded, though everything they said amounted to speculation, with these two facts at the center: it had been nearly eighteen hours since armed gunmen took over Reina High, and there had been nothing from inside the gym for hours.

***

The woman who had been watching the news earlier, that woman who looked so kind and loving, continued watching. She checked her watch regularly, surprised and relieved in equal parts that no one had come knocking on her door.

She cried off and on. Mostly, though, she was numb. For her, the important facts – the ones that everyone needed to know and understand – were over, though she still had a part to play in what was happening at RHS.

Occasionally, she cleaned. She had always kept a tidy house, even when passing through the dark times, the crazy times. The times when she didn't want to accept reality and, to a certain degree, managed to make her wish come true.

She cleaned, she watched. She vacuumed, then dusted, not noticing that she had done things backwards. Many things were backwards. The world itself was all wrong, at least as far as she was concerned, and had been for a long time.

CHAPTER 24
Intended Response

It was at this point that a man and woman entered Tac-Com. Perfectly pressed-but-cheap suits plus conservatively cut and immaculately styled hair screamed "I'm with the government!" far louder than their badges.

Vickers, already knowing the answer, said, "Who are you?"

The man showed his ID to Vickers. "Special Agent Ryker, FBI."

The woman mirrored her partner. "Special Agent Heigl."

Ryker looked around, his expression hard as he spotted his prey. "Detective Montano?"

"Guilty as charged," said Montano. "Though if you're here about the cocaine in my car, it's just recreational." He was joking, but it was more to control his burgeoning anger than to jolly the agents out of what he knew was coming.

Ryker's diamond-edged expression didn't soften. "We're here to inform you that the FBI is assuming control of this situation, effective immediately."

Montano grimaced at Oberczofski. "Guess Leigh still has some pull."

It wasn't lost on Montano – or Oberczofski, or Vickers, or me – that Ryker had said he was "assuming control" of the situation. And all of us had the same mental response: *Good luck with that.*

Ryker turned to Vickers. "Lieutenant Vickers?" Then, seeming to notice that Montano was still there, he turned back to him and said, "You can wait outside."

Montano was clearly boiling, but there wasn't much he could do. For now.

***

On Ryker's orders, Agent Heigl escorted Montano from the vehicle. Heigl was the junior of the two agents, and deferred to Ryker whenever possible. But she was also a good agent – good enough to recognize how extraordinary this situation was.

With that in mind, as soon as they were outside, she said to Montano, "Everyone knows you're doing okay. This is political."

Montano spat back, "I'll tell that to the parents of all the dead kids you'll be carting out in a few hours. I'm sure that will console them."

Agent Heigl nodded as though understanding Montano. "I understand you're changing teams," she said. Montano was surprised that Heigl would know about his job plans, but nodded. Heigl smiled. "Then I'd leave as soon as possible. Like, now.

"Why?" asked Montano.

Heigl shrugged. "Plausible deniability. When it all hits the fan, you've distanced yourself and hopefully none of the shit gets on your suit."

Montano thought about that. The agent was no doubt correct in her assessment, and before yesterday that probably would have been the biggest factor determining Montano's response.

Today, though, was different. Something had changed in him, fundamentally and completely. He didn't understand what that thing was – not yet – but he knew that leaving was the wrong thing to do. For better or for worse: "No. I'm staying on-scene."

Heigl heaved a sigh. "You can't. I was trying to be nice, but either way, you're leaving. You're going to be escorted off the site, and if you or your partner are seen within a mile of here you'll be arrested." The agent looked away then and, speaking in a low tone, she said, "But I can't stop you from following up on any leads you have, can I?"

Montano nodded and turned to leave.

"Remember," Heigl said, "plausible deniability. There's the

right way, and then there's the smart way."

***

Those words repeated in Montano's mind as he slipped past the mob of reporters. The fact that no one seemed to notice or care that he was leaving drove home the truth of what Agent Heigl had said: word had already spread that Montano was no longer a part of things. He had gone from being center of everything to not even worth a second glance. It hurt, and made him wonder how much worse it would be if he'd stuck around and watched the ship sink on his watch.

He headed to his car, which was still parked in the trees, past the reporters, where he had left it after being shot at what seemed like years ago.

That thought gave him pause, too: staying here *might* have shoved his career that much higher into the stratosphere – but only if he got everyone out. And what chance was there of that? None. Not just because several people, including *kids*, had already died, but because Teacher was so far ahead of the people trying to stop him that Montano honestly didn't know at this point if he or anyone else could stop the guy.

Agent Heigl was right – getting away was the smart thing to do. Go home, catch some much-overdue shuteye. Leave this place to sort itself out.

And the kids?

He was aware that only seconds ago he had been convinced that their only possible escape lay in him. But with every step away from Tac-Com, that conviction faded.

By the time he'd reached his car, his position had reversed. He should definitely go home. He should definitely get a few hours' sleep, then go to the station and start writing up the gazillion forms and statements that would be necessary for the record. Forget about this place, distance himself from it as well as he could. A blemish, certainly – giving up and leaving wasn't a good thing, let alone being tossed out by the FBI – but not an insurmountable one.

He'd decided. And he would have done it, too – gone home, tried to stay low-profile, if his phone hadn't rung then, with the call that would start the process of blowing the case wide open.

***

Montano's fingers had actually curled around the door handle of his car when his phone rang.

"Detective Montano speaking."

The voice that responded was wheezy, out of breath, like the speaker had an asthma attack just around every corner. "Detective, my name is Wayland Koch. I'm a private investigator."

Montano groaned inwardly. Like most cops, he had little love for PIs. They were the ambulance chasers of police work, and loved nothing more than to pretend to greatness when in reality most of them did nothing more glamorous than following cheating spouses for the purpose of taking pictures *in flagrante delicto*, then presenting the tawdry things to wrecked husbands or wives.

He assumed that Koch wanted to talk to him about something unrelated – just because terrible things were happening in one place didn't mean they stopped everywhere else. "I'm sorry but now's a bad –"

Koch talked right over him. "One of my clients has provided information to me, with instructions that I pass it on to you – and only you – at this time."

Montano, one hand still on the door, his mind already on the way home, said, "What do you mean, at this time?"

"I mean, I had instructions to call you at this number, at this exact time of night, so that I could give you some information."

Montano grew rigid. Who would have something for him, timed to the minute?

Teacher.

"Who's the client? And what's the info?"

"I've been instructed to speak to you only in person. There's a business called LightGo. I'll be waiting in the parking lot when you get here."

Koch hung up without waiting for a response. When Montano called the number back, no one picked up.

Montano got in his car. He started to drive.

He was not going home after all.

***

Montano found the location easily: like most places in the developed world, anything could be found if you had an internet connection and the right app. When he got to the destination, he found a modest building, though its placement among much larger buildings and the size of its parking lot in a real estate market that grew tighter every day spoke to the business' profitability.

In the parking lot, an old but well-maintained Buick sat beneath a dim halogen streetlight. Wayland Koch, a fat man with a suit that was always wrinkled and a chin permanently darkened by five o'clock shadow, leaned against the car.

As soon as Montano got out of the car, Koch pushed himself upright. "Detective Montano?"

"Yeah. What's this all about?" He noticed that Koch was holding a manila envelope. "And what's that?"

The private investigator ignored his latter question. "Two years ago I got a case. A family wanted me to find their daughter."

Montano flashed to the picture Eberhardt had sent him. The girl's arm on the dirt floor.

"What family?" he asked.

"Thomas and Elise Easterly," said Koch. He jerked a thumb over his shoulder, gesturing at the LightGo building. "This is their business. Was their business."

"Who was their daughter?"

"Her name was Bella. A senior at –"

"Reina High School?"

Montano smelled Teacher's scent, more and more. So it had to be Reina.

But, again, though he saw Teacher's hand, he couldn't figure out what trick he was playing. He guessed wrong again.

"No," said Koch. "She went to a place called Hathaway Prep."

"Never heard of it."

"It's about sixty miles west of here. Their daughter went missing, cops had nothing, so they hired me."

Montano gave Koch a more careful look. He came away with the same impression he'd had on first seeing him: the guy was a slob. Hardly someone the police would turn to when even they hadn't found anything.

Koch seemed to understand what Montano was thinking, and didn't appear shocked or upset. He just shrugged, chuckled, and said, "Hey, looks can be deceiving. I'm very good at what I do."

"Okay, taking that on faith, what did you find?"

***

Koch didn't give Montano the answer he was hoping for: a smoking gun that would make everything fall neatly into place. "I found a trail that led out of the country. Not sure where after that."

"You didn't keep looking?"

Koch shook his head. "I was willing – they'd paid me enough to be willing to do just about anything short of murder – but they said no. They just handed me a wad of cash, said thanks, and that was it."

Montano folded his arms across his chest. "All of which is

interesting, but why did they want me here? And what's that?" He pointed to the envelope again; again Koch didn't hand it over.

"A few days ago, Mr. Easterly gave me another wad of cash along with this envelope. Said the cash was a retainer, and he'd call with instructions about what to do with the envelope. He called me right before I called you. Gave me your number and told me to meet you here and give it to you."

Koch made as if to hold the envelope out to Montano, who snatched it out of his grip so fast the pudgy man jumped back. "Hey!"

Montano opened the envelope. Inside there was only a single sheet of paper, which he pulled out. The back was blank, and Koch wasn't at the right angle to see the front.

"I, uh, have to admit to being curious," Koch said.

Now it was Montano's turn to ignore a question. "What does Easterly do?" he asked quietly.

Koch looked like he was considering whether to ask again, decided against it, and said, "I'm really not sure; the specifics are a bit technical for me. But it's software stuff. Computers and telecom and like that for the military, some big companies."

"Either of them ever mention a company called Entercom?"

Koch thought a moment, then shook his head. "I don't think so."

Montano held out the paper, showing Koch. All it had was an address in the city, below it some words.

"You know that address?"

Koch nodded. "I think it's the Easterlys' house."

"What about this?" Montano asked, pointing at the words below the address.

"No idea."

Montano spun on his heel, heading quickly for his car. He

got in, thought of something, and rolled down the window. Koch was already getting into his car as well, but turned back as Montano said, "You said this *was* their business? Not *is*?"

"Yeah. Went under, about six months ago is what I heard. Their last job was almost a year ago, I think. Not surprising, considering how much time and money they sank into finding their girl."

Montano started his engine.

"Hey," shouted Koch. "You ever hear about what happened to them? Know if anyone else found their girl? I looked into it, but couldn't find a thing. It was like the Easterlys got wiped off the map."

Montano pulled away without answering. Thinking, Not wiped off the map. Just hidden. Hooded. Masked.

He drove as fast as he could, glancing occasionally at the paper beside him. The address, and the words below it:

"The lost can never truly be found."

CHAPTER 25
Intended Response

The address was nearby; so close, in fact, that by the time Montano finished talking to Eberhardt, he was already parking across the street from his destination.

"I don't like you doing this," Eberhardt was saying as Montano killed the engine. "You should wait for backup."

"And run the risk of getting arrested or having some moron take over? No thanks to both."

"Either one might be preferable to the alternative, partner. When this thing goes sideways, you can claim it wasn't your fault: no one listened to you, they tossed you in jail, and look how it all turned out? 'Oh, if they'd only listened to me' et cetera et cetera. Right?"

Eberhardt's question wasn't for himself, Montano knew. The older detective was in this to the end, come what may. But the inquiry *was* perfectly in line with Montano's reality as it had been the day before: watching out for his career, watching out for himself. But that was then, this was now. Things had changed, and Montano cared a little less with each passing moment about his future in the department.

He got out of the car. "Just remember: if I don't call in ten minutes, you come running in here with the cavalry."

"Will do. Stay safe, partner."

"Copy that."

Montano walked across the street, wondering if he had just made a promise he couldn't keep.

***

It was the middle of the night, creeping toward dawn. That was why the sound Montano heard as he walked toward the house was a surprise: it was a bit late (early?) for anyone to be vacuuming their home.

He knocked, keeping his jacket open, ready to pull his gun should he need to.

The vacuum stopped. The door opened. A pleasant, slightly plump woman with kind but tired eyes opened the door. "Elise Easterly?" he said.

"Yes?"

Behind her, now that the vacuum was turned off, he could hear news reports. People talking about "the crisis at Reina High."

He flipped open the wallet that carried his badge and i.d. "My name is Detective Montano. Sorry to bother you in the middle of the…" He made a show of looking at his watch. "Geez, four in the morning." He looked back at Elise Easterly and smiled his best and most winning smile. "You're an early riser, Elise."

She shrugged, the tired look in her eyes growing as she did so, like she had just shouldered a burden no one else could see. "I don't sleep well these days." She waited a moment. "How can I help you, detective?"

Montano, waiting for this, gestured. "Could I come in?"

Elise looked genuinely chagrined. "Oh, of course. So sorry."

Montano entered the house.

**

Outside, everything about the Easterlys' home was clean and neat: the grass trimmed, the garden weeded, the walls of the house bereft of spiderwebs or dust. Inside, Montano saw more of the same. The only evidence of any possible mess was the vacuum sitting in the center of the rug.

Montano noticed the lines the vacuum had pressed in the carpet. They weren't the steady back-and-forth lines of someone doing a careful job. They were jagged, stopping and starting in different places. The work of an insomniac, perhaps, but more likely this was a sign of someone with – to put it mildly – a lot on her mind.

He looked around, noting that the walls were adorned with family pictures: Elise, a man Montano presumed was her husband... and a pretty young girl he knew was the one Koch had been hired to find. The one he had failed to locate.

Montano pointed at one of the images. "Is your husband home? This concerns him as well."

"No. Tommy's been out working on a business project all night. I was actually just making an early breakfast for myself."

Montano turned back to face Elise as her vocal quality changed, realizing only then that she'd left the room.

He followed, going from a neat and tidy front hall/living room to an equally neat and tidy kitchen.

In the kitchen, another television – different than the one he'd been hearing – showed muted images from Reina High. Eggs, cheese, and some vegetables sat on a center island, obviously an omelet yet to be born.

That was all of passing interest.

What grabbed Montano's real attention was that Elise Easterly was holding a very large knife.

***

He almost grabbed his gun, but Elise turned and began slowly chopping vegetables. She glanced at the television. "Sad what's happening there."

Montano nodded, his eyes not straying from her hands on the knife. "Yes. Isn't it."

She started chopping vegetables. They sliced quickly, effortlessly: the knife was sharp.

***

Back at Tac-Com, Agents Ryker and Heigl looked over the scant information gleaned to this point. Vickers and Oberczofski watched on, both of them obviously angry at the way the FBI had come in and "taken control" of things.

One of the techs shouted nearby, so loudly that everyone in the mobile command center jumped. "Got it!"

As he hollered, the monitors that had stared with dark, sightless eyes finally flickered to life, showing the gym.

"Looks like we've got eyes," said Agent Ryker, in a tone that indicated it was solely thanks to his divine, federally-appointed presence that this had happened.

Vickers and Oberczofski both picked up on the tone. Neither said anything. What would be the point?

And there were bigger things to talk about, now that they could see what was happening in the place they most needed to see.

***

Agent Heigl at least had the good grace to try and sound a bit less self-assured than her partner. She partially succeeded, but only partially. "Now we're cooking. Okay, so we'll hit them with tear gas first –"

Vickers said, "No good. First of all, we haven't even cleared all the rest of the school's buildings, so if the perps have them wired they'll have plenty of time to detonate any explosives while we fumble our way in. And what if the targets are wearing gas masks? Plus, even without that, since hostages block the main entry points the first things we'd hit is the students and staff, which – again – would give the hostage-takers time to respond… and we know they don't have a problem killing kids."

Oberczofski had been staring, not at the monitors, but into an empty space beside them. Thinking hard as he said, "I'm not sure about that last."

Agent Ryker didn't even look at the negotiator who had been there since the beginning. "When I want an opinion from someone who's added absolutely no value during this situation, believe me:

you'll be the first person I call."

Oberczofski shrugged. "Okay. I'll just find someone else to share my information with."

He headed to the door. Everyone stared at Ryker (including his own partner, Agent Heigl). Agent Ryker twitched, obviously in the throes of an internal struggle between wisdom and ego.

He called to Oberczofski as the negotiator's hand hit the door. "Fine. Tell me what you have." The agent's thick brows drew together in quiet anger. "Then you're dismissed from the command center. Permanently."

Oberczofski waited, obviously uncowed and unimpressed. Vickers, unseen by Ryker, had a grin on her face larger than anyone under her command could ever remember seeing before.

Heigl put a calming hand on her partner's shoulder, then said, "What can you tell us?"

Oberczofski didn't say a word. Nor did his hand move from the door.

Agent Heigl heaved a sigh. "And of course after you've provided your, uh, valuable input, you're welcome to stay. Isn't that right, Agent Ryker?"

Again, Ryker paused. He gave a short nod, barely a twitch.

Oberczofski finally turned back and rejoined the group standing in front of the monitors. "Glad to see you remember we're on the same team," he murmured. Then, before Agent Ryker could either have an apoplectic fit or throw him out – either or both of which seemed likely – he said, "Montano told us that when the principle hostage-taker – Teacher – killed one of the kids, he told him it wasn't Montano's fault; said the kid 'was destined to suffer.'"

"Which we already knew," Agent Ryker said with a sniff. Looking at Vickers, he said, "'They have no problem killing kids.' Weren't those your words?"

"But that's wrong," said Oberczofski. "They don't want to

kill *all* the kids, or make them all suffer."

"Of course not. That leaves them with almost no leverage," said Agent Ryker.

He wasn't understanding Oberczofski's point, but Vickers did. Comprehension dawned in her eyes. "They're only targeting certain people. Their victims were predetermined."

"They planned to kill them no matter what we did," said Oberczofski. "I've been playing through it over and over. Each of the students were connected via their parents' interests – which we knew, but that might be a coincidence given how many of their parents are involved in those interests. But then there's also the speed of Teacher's response. He had the people ready and waiting at each point. Principal Gersham, the Tarov boy. But the others haven't been touched. I think they're safe, as far as Teacher and his crew are concerned."

"Nice theory," said Agent Ryker.

"Can you confirm it?" asked Agent Heigl.

"No, but Montano –" Vickers began.

Cutting her off, Agent Ryker said, "Next person says *Montano* in this room will be escorted offsite just like he was."

Heigl had been examining the CCTV feed of the gym. She leaned in close. Frowned. "I can't see the Senator's son." She turned to the group. "Anyone else spot him?"

The momentary spat forgotten, everyone looked on the monitors. No one could see anything that would really identify the students. There were cheerleaders, obvious from their uniforms, but beyond that they were all just a bunch of hooded forms on a grainy feed.

Even so, Daxton Leigh would have been easy to spot – he had been shot in the stomach, and wherever he was, he'd be writhing in agony or laying in a pool of blood or both.

Easy to see, but no one could spot him. Heigl was right:

Daxton Leigh was no longer in the gym.

***

"He might be in one of the rooms off to the side," said Vickers. "There's the coach's office with a small equipment room attached, and some bathrooms."

Agent Ryker nodded. "Probably. Regardless, we have to assume he's alive – the Senator made that clear – and that he doesn't have long to live… which means we can't wait any longer. We have to prep an entry plan."

"No! We don't have enough information. It would put every hostage and officer at risk and –"

Glaring at Vickers, Agent Ryker said, "Those are my orders, Lieutenant Vickers. You can either aid me in the process or be relieved."

***

Across town, Elise Easterly was still cutting food, Montano was still watching on high alert.

"I was wondering if you could talk to me about your daughter," he said. He felt odd, like he was reciting lines in a play. One that Teacher had written and was now directing.

Elise stopped moving, the tip of her knife touching the cutting board, the edge poised higher. Her knuckles were white around the handle. "Have you found something new?" she asked.

Even in the midst of his confusion about what was going on, and his concern for the large knife in Elise's hand, Montano could hear the pain in the woman's voice. It wasn't just palpable, it had *weight*. It made his shoulders stoop a bit, even as he said, "Do you have a picture of her?"

Laughing sadly, Elise gestured with the knife. Just as in the front room, the kitchen was adorned with family photos. "Lots of them."

"I mean a recent one. As recent as possible, if you can point me to it."

Elise nodded, and pointed with her knife to a space on the wall just behind Montano. Framed pictures hung there, too. Montano saw Elise, looking happier, younger. "What's your husband's name?" he asked. He knew it, but everything he said at this point was a test, a measure of how Elise Easterly responded.

Behind him, she began chopping once more. His shoulders twitched every time the knife fell. "Thomas," she said.

Montano looked at the man in the photo. Vibrant, tan. Smile lines around his eyes and at the corners of his lips. Montano tried to place those eyes and lips in the ski mask Teacher wore. The same? Maybe.

He shifted to look closer at the girl in the photos. Bella Easterly was brighter than the sun: a stunning blonde girl with the smile of someone both loved and loving. Beautiful in an evergreen, fresh way that looked like summers at the beach and winters cuddled up in front of warm, crackling fires.

Montano smiled at the image of her, even his fear and cynicism insufficient to blot out the happiness that a simple image of Bella Easterly could communicate.

The smile froze as he saw her hand, perched on her father's shoulder as they laughed on a carousel horse.

She was wearing a t-shirt with high shoulders. No brand on her arm like the one Montano had seen in Teacher's semi-hidden photo.

But the bracelet she wore was the same as that girl who lay in the dirt, half a world away.

***

Montano spun around, drawing his weapon.

Elise hadn't moved. She just stood there, smiling sadly, tears in her eyes. She still held the knife, though it was no longer cutting anything.

Yet.

Montano's throat and mouth felt like they'd been stuffed with cotton, the crevices packed with sand. "Elise, I want to help you. Just stay calm and –"

Elise laughed almost hysterically. "*Help* me? How can you do that if you don't even know who you're chasing?"

She took a small step toward him. Montano's pointer finger slipped from the side of the gun onto the trigger.

"Don't move, Elise. I want to help you, but don't take a step or –"

Elise whispered. "I won't go anywhere." She stared over Montano's shoulder. Again, his shoulders twitched, even though there was nothing there but a wall showing photos of happiness lost.

Elise refocused on him. "Today's her birthday, you know. We thought that was right, that it all be finished today."

"No!" Montano screamed.

It was too late. Elise had already opened a deep gash along her forearm. The kitchen, so neat and organized only a moment ago, was suddenly painted in abstract streaks of red as blood gushed from the wound. The gushing turned to a pulse, her heartbeat driving blood in long, thin arcs that further streaked the once-inviting space.

The knife fell.

Montano grabbed a towel off the counter. Leaped forward.

Elise was falling, falling, and he wouldn't be fast enough to catch her. She slipped through his outstretched arms, bounced off the center island, then slipped to the floor as Montano heard her final words in his mind.

"Today's her birthday, you know."

CHAPTER 26
Intended Response

Eberhardt had ignored Montano's instruction to call in the cavalry after ten minutes, heading to the Easterly home the second Montano gave him the address. He arrived only a few minutes after the ambulance carrying Elise had left the property, about the same time local police began descending on the house like a plague of locusts.

He ran into the house, looking for his partner, his nose twitching as he smelled the acrid scent of blood. He followed the odor to the kitchen. Montano was there, sitting at a table amid swarming cops.

Eberhardt's partner held a photo in his hand. A family – the Easterlys, including their daughter, Bella.

Montano didn't look up, not even when Eberhardt touched his shoulder.

"They think she's going to make it," Eberhardt said. "You saved her life."

Montano didn't answer. He touched the picture of the family. Beside him, on the table, Eberhardt saw that his partner had placed his cell phone. The screen was illuminated, showing the picture of the girl's – Bella's – arm.

"She was branded," Montano said. "Taken from her family, and branded."

Oberczofski had no words.

Montano pointed at something else: a folder beside his phone, blood staining its front.

"What is it?" Eb asked.

"I found it on the counter. They wanted me to."

Eberhardt opened it. It looked like a contract of some kind.

A moment later his mouth fell open.

"Is this what I think it is?"

Montano nodded. "LightGo's final job was installation and updates of all telecom and computer systems for Reina High School – including an auto-dial system that would make it easier to call in students and staff on days off."

Eberhardt passed a weary hand over his eyes. "Which was why it seemed like he'd been there, but never noticed it. He had been – but as a contractor, not a sightseer."

Nodding, Montano said, "And how he and his wife ensured that exactly the right people showed up on Memorial Day – save the few good Samaritans who just got caught up in the mess."

Montano's phone rang.

He and Eberhardt looked at it as the picture of Bella disappeared, replaced by a single word: TEACHER.

***

Montano accepted the call and put it on speaker. "You found my house," said Teacher. As he did, the phone flickered. The word *TEACHER* disappeared, replaced for an instant by the word "**THOMAS**" and then "**BELLA'S DADDY.**"

And then by a blank nothing that made Montano shiver.

"Is your wife a part of this?" asked Montano.

"Ask her."

"She's on her way to the hospital after trying to kill herself."

"You saved her?" Thomas Easterly said. He sounded surprised. That was the first time Montano had heard that sound in Thomas' voice. He resolved to make the man sound that way again. Soon.

Thomas was silent. Montano and Eberhardt didn't speak, either. The moment stretched out.

"I think it's time we meet," said Thomas. "Face to face, instead of face to mask."

"Sorry," said Montano. "I've been kicked off the case, so I can't get to you on the school grounds. How about we meet at Starbucks?"

Thomas chuckled, but the sound was empty. Hollow. "No thanks. You can come to me. You're a smart fellow. You'll figure out a way in."

"Then what?" asked Montano.

"We talk," Thomas answered. "You, me, and Xavier Delroy."

Montano and Eberhardt shared a look. It didn't surprise either that Paige Delroy's father, the head of Entercom, was a part of this. But why would Thomas Easterly ask for him to be brought to him – a request he had to know wasn't going to happen.

"What's his place in this?" Montano asked. "He kidnap your daughter?"

"You've been looking at the staff's financial information," Thomas said. "But you haven't found the right connections. Not yet."

"Okay, so tell me."

"Come see me," Thomas answered. "I'll explain it all to you and Xavier Delroy."

"You going call him and ask him to sneak in as well?"

"No, I figure you'll bring him."

Montano, suddenly tired of whatever dance they were doing, said, "I don't think so."

Another silence, before teacher whispered, "Fine. Then the entire school goes 'boom.'"

Eberhardt finally spoke up. "What do you –"

"I want you, Montano," said Thomas. "Just you and Delroy.

Just to talk. I promise."

"You *promise*? That's a laugh," said Montano, and then he *did* laugh.

Thomas Easterly did not. "Have I lied to you even once during all this? If I haven't told the truth, I've been silent. The only one who's tried anything devious has been you, like with your little bugging scheme."

"Which you planned on. You had to have. And you did that to a *kid*, goddam –"

"He deserved to know what it felt like," said Thomas. "You and Delroy. Two hours."

"He won't come."

"He will," Thomas insisted. "No matter how little he acts like he cares, he's been monitoring all this, very closely."

"Still won't come."

"He *will*!" Thomas screamed the last word, his voice rising to a fever pitch. Then, calming, he said, "Tell him I want to talk business. And tell him that if he doesn't come, then what happens in Novi definitely won't stay in Novi. I guarantee he'll beg to come. Time's ticking, Montano. I'll give you two hours. Then things are out of my hands."

***

The sun was coming up as Montano and Eberhardt hurtled down the street, headed back to RHS. Montano drove while Eberhardt white-knuckled his way through the drive.

"Something's been bothering me," Eberhardt said through gritted teeth.

"Just one thing?" Montano snorted.

"How'd he know you didn't make the right connections? How'd he know to call you, or to call the private dick and tell him to call you?"

Montano grimaced, not liking what he was about to say, but knowing it needed to be said: "He was assuming I'm an idiot."

Eberhardt shook his head, his brow furrowing in thought. For a moment he actually forgot he was moving about twenty miles an hour faster than department policy, and forty miles an hour faster than the car tires were rated for. "No. It's almost like he's been following us around. Like he…"

Both detectives realized it at the same moment. They looked at each other, and said the words together: "The phones."

Montano, digging at his pocket with one hand (which didn't help Eberhardt's peace of mind at all), said, "He hacked our phones and turned them into bugs."

"Then that means he knows everything we know –"

"– and everything we're planning to do," Montano finished.

Eberhardt and Montano got their phones out. They had a list of numbers they were going to call. Teacher would hear, but it was more important to let everyone know that all communications were compromised than it was to pretend Teacher still had the upper hand, or try to feed him false information in an attempt to trap him with it.

Both men looked at their phones at the same time. Both frowned. Both tried to call.

Montano screamed, "Dammit!" as Eberhardt growled, "I got nothing. How the hell is he blocking us from Tac-Com?"

"From everything," Montano corrected. He was on the verge of pitching the phone out the window… when it rang.

***

"So we get incoming calls?" said Eberhardt.

"Of course. Otherwise how could this psycho call and gloat?" Montano checked the display on his phone. "It's Connie."

"Or it's Teacher screwing with us," Eberhardt said. In a

lower voice, he said, "If it *is* her, tell her to talk to Vickers."

"Connie?" said Montano, hoping it was her, fearing the more likely outcome: that it was Teacher, calling to tell him the next move he had planned – the next move Montano knew he would make, whether he tried to stop it or not.

"Yeah, it's me," she said, and Montano's heart rose a bit. Maybe, he thought, just maybe, this was a small hole in everything Teacher – Thomas Easterly, he had to remind himself – had done. "I –"

"Are you still at Tac-Com?" he asked.

***

I wasn't. I'd been escorted out as soon as Montano left and Agents Ryker and Heigl realized I hadn't followed him. Since then I'd been skulking around inside the police staging area, mostly managing to stay on the RHS grounds by staying in squad cars of cops I knew and who had benefited from knowing me enough that they were willing to turn a blind eye. That enabled me to listen in on the police radios (not much there, since everyone was worried about "Teacher" overhearing), and to pay attention to the ebb and flow of movement behind the police lines. Which was how I knew what I said after filling Montano in on my location:

"Montano, they're going in."

Montano's voice grew heavy with stress. "When?"

"As soon as they can."

"Oh shit. He knows."

"He knows what?"

"Thomas. Teacher. The guy." Montano was almost babbling, fear and stress perforating his typically cool demeanor. "He's been listening to us. Turned our phones into bugs, so he knows it all. Everything they're planning. You gotta tell them."

"Why not you?"

"We've been trying, but Teacher's blocking our outgoing calls." I heard a screeching sound and then he said. "Connie, they're headed into a trap."

***

The screeching sound was Montano taking a turn fast enough for two wheels to cease contact with the pavement.

"Who is this guy?" I whispered.

Montano either didn't hear me or just ignored me. "Connie, how did you get into the school?"

Normally, I wouldn't have revealed what I'd done – better to keep it secret, so if I got chucked out on my ear I'd be able to sneak right back in again. But normal had, like Elvis, left the building. Still, I didn't want to get shut out of the story, either. So I didn't tell him details, just, "There's a big hedge west of the gate, near the wall. Meet me there."

Another screech as Montano slid across asphalt. "This isn't the time to play ace reporter, Connie."

I gritted my teeth. I'd heard that kind of statement many times in my career. Interestingly, it was never a woman who said it. I reacted with my kneejerk response, though if I'd thought about it I'd likely have said the same thing: "Who's playing? I *am* an ace reporter."

***

Montano hung up, and looked in his rearview mirror. Almost to the school, and he thought he'd take another shot at something that had, until now, born little fruit.

He looked at the backseat, where Xavier Delroy was sitting. He and Eberhardt had picked up the guy as soon as they could after finishing their last talk with Thomas Easterly.

Neither he nor Eberhardt even suggested going to Delroy's home. They could have gotten the address, but somehow they both knew that the fat, oily man would be at Entercom, sitting in his office and either watching the RHS situation unfold or speaking again to the men who had been at his office.

They had thought originally that Delroy was involved simply because his daughter was at the school. Their suspicions that he was more integrally involved with whatever was now happening had grown through the night, and the fact that Thomas Easterly had told them to look him up while, for all he knew, his dead wife's corpse cooled in the room… that sealed it. They would have followed up with him regardless, but Easterly's instruction to bring him to the school had bumped him to the #1 Person of Interest slot.

They also expected Delroy wouldn't respond well – either to their barging into his office (for the second time, for Eberhardt), or to their demand that he accompany them to RHS. They were correct on both counts. He shouted. He accused them of harassment. He threatened to sue.

He also said he was going to phone "A United States Senator friend of mine" to make sure they were fired and then rendered unhireable by any law enforcement agency in the nation.

Eberhardt and Montano shared a glance at that.

"I'll bet you a hundred he's talking about Leigh," said Eberhardt. "Ten to one odds."

"No way I'm betting against that," Montano said back.

Delroy was still shouting, the shouts turning louder and more shrill. His secretary, Lenore Peabody, was in the room, wringing her hands, adding her own shouts.

"Do you know a man named Thomas Easterly?" asked Montano.

Delroy continued shrieking, though he shifted momentarily from "Get the hell out!" to "Why the hell would I?"

Eberhardt stepped forward and bellowed, "You better come with us, or what happens in Novi won't stay in Novi."

Delroy's screams cut off so quickly, and his face went so

white, that Montano thought for a moment the guy must have shrieked himself into a massive heart attack. Delroy looked at his secretary. "Get my car ready," he said.

"We'll take ours," Montano answered.

***

While Montano drove, both he and Eberhardt asked the squat, frog-faced entertainment mogul about Novi. What did the word mean? Was it a location, as Teacher made it sound? What happened there?

The man in the back was silent.

Now, driving up to the school, Montano tried once more. "You ready to tell us what Novi is?"

Nothing.

Montano turned off the road, following a side street. They were almost to the school, and he knew that if they went much farther they'd be stopped by the police or – worse – the reporters outside the barricades.

He drove a bit farther, then stopped the car.

"What's happening?" asked Delroy. He wasn't screaming anymore. He didn't sound sad, or happy, or even resigned. He sounded...

Dead.

That was the word that popped into Montano's mind. He hoped it wasn't an omen.

Teacher had beaten people to death. Had shot them in the head. He had turned a man's genitals to hash, and had killed a kid by force-feeding and sodomizing him with electronics.

And yet the detective suspected that the worst was yet to come. Thomas Easterly wasn't finished yet. *Teacher* hadn't finished his lesson.

***

The Science Building. This was the place that Winona "Win" Jackson and Beatriz Alcivar – the Computer GurlZ of RHS – had been working when Teacher and The Lady appeared.

This was the place half of the Colors had entered at the same time the other half went to the main office.

This was the place where Thomas Easterly neé Teacher had shot and killed Nicholas Vachnarian and Raymond Gunne, blowing their heads off for the video that would play in a continuous loop on certain of the police computers. The two men had been moved, but their brains and bone chips and blood still painted the walls.

This was the place that Dapper Dan had focused, since it was the nerve center for the school's electronics, including most of the logs of websites visited, computers used, and emails sent; and which also housed the controls and recordings for the CCTV video the police were monitoring.

Near that same Science Building, the police – now under federal command – continued monitoring the CCTV feeds. They watched as Teacher and the Colors wandered between the rows of students. Red pushed one of the cheerleaders – the one with the shortest skirt, and a tube top that covered less flesh than many swimsuits – with his foot, and she quivered in obvious terror.

Students on the floor. Students in front of the doors. A terrible setup.

And yet preparations were now underway for a tactical breach.

***

Vickers put on riot gear in the Tac-Com. Just outside, sheltered from view of anyone in the gym, C-unit was checking their gear, their minds going a thousand miles an hour as they went over the plans to breach, each replaying their parts mentally.

Agents Ryker and Heigl would watch from Tac-Com as

Vickers and C-unit went in. The agents knew that, if this went down wrong, their careers would be over. People didn't become United States senators without a ruthless streak and an ability to inflict revenge. They had to get in and grab Daxton Leigh before he died of his wounds.

The agents, Vickers, and C-unit knew that it was likely the boy was already dead, whether his body had realized it or not. Stomach wounds had to be treated quickly, or the perforated stomach and/or bowels would leak. Sepsis would result, continuing until the wound was shut, the body cleansed of the rotten matter, the body sealed and antibiotics administered.

Students on the floor. Students in front of the door. The key student dying or dead. Armed men walking between and among them.

A terrible situation.

And about to get much worse.

The cops considered themselves experts, and by and large that was true. They considered themselves well-prepared, and for the most part that was the case.

The police believed they would go in and save the day.

But belief and fact are sometimes opposed. In the end, fact always wins out, and here the facts were simply these:

Teacher was ready. He was waiting. He had begun to teach his lesson, but the class was not yet over. The conclusion had not yet been reached.

CHAPTER 27
Intended Response

Montano, Eberhardt, and Delroy skulked through the trees, all of them looking for the hedge that I had described to them. They found it... but also found one officer Jay Plannings, who was taking a cigarette break right in front of them.

Eberhardt grunted in disgust. "Plannings. That lazy shit."

"Not lazy," said Montano. "Just trying to stay out of the line of fire when things get dicey."

Actually, they were both right. Plannings had a ten-year career distinguished only by his ability to stay away from anything more dangerous than jaywalking grannies. Normally that isn't something a good reporter would say, but I feel free to do so in this case. First, because he was getting in the way of people who needed to get into RHS. Second, because he was let go from the force a month before the writing of this book, and the words I've used are nearly verbatim from his termination report.

But lazy or not, he was in the way. Eberhardt and Montano dragged Xavier Delroy with them as they backed up. Eberhardt almost screamed when they pulled back around a tree and found me already hunkered down behind it. He managed to quiet himself, but let out a mouse-squeak of fright.

"Damn, Connie. You should warn a man," said Eberhardt.

"If I see one, I'll keep that in mind."

Montano pointed toward the wall. "Is he supposed to be part of this?" he asked.

I shook my head. "That guy wasn't here last time I was. He looks like he's just on a smoke break, though, so we can just –"

"No time," said Montano. He looked at Eberhardt, and a silent communication passed between them. Eberhardt nodded. "When you're done," said Montano, "get to the hospital. Talk to Elise

Easterly as soon as she wakes up."

Eberhardt moved around the tree, heading toward the wall. "Pretty quiet for an old guy," I said.

"He's a geriatric ninja," Montano agreed, his head poked slightly into view, watching his partner.

I was about to ask what Xavier Delroy was doing here. Unlike most people, I knew who he was and how powerful a force he was in the shadows. But for the life of me I couldn't figure out what he was doing here.

Montano guessed my thoughts: "He's –"

Before Montano could finish, we all heard Eberhardt scream, "Help! Help, dammit, help!"

I chanced leaning out and saw Eberhardt on the ground fifty feet to the left of us, rocking back and forth and cradling his ankle. I also saw Plannings, visibly considering whether to go find out what was happening or pretend he hadn't heard. He heaved a sigh, pitched his cigarette, and ambled toward the still-shouting Detective Eberhardt.

"Okay," Montano said, "how do we get inside?"

"I'll show you."

"No, you'll *tell* me, then stay here."

I put my hands on my hips and, a bit louder (though not quite loud enough for Plannings to hear, I hoped) said, "I bet if I started screaming, too, it'd attract a lot of attention."

Xavier Delroy finally spoke up. "Shut up, both of you. Let's just get this over with."

His voice shook, and when I looked at him I saw perspiration beading his forehead.

Montano stared at the man. "Why did you agree to come? You know the man who's taken your daughter probably plans to kill you, right?"

Delroy hesitated. He opened his mouth, closed it, then opened it again to say, "There are things worse than death, Detective."

***

We had underestimated Eberhardt's speed and vocal capacity. He had already made it close to a hundred yards at this point, and was now sitting down on the ground, holding his shin as he caterwauled.

Plannings hove into view of the detective, who shouted: "Plannings! I banged my leg!"

Plannings, predictably, smirked. "You need an ambulance? Or just a *waaa*-mbulance?"

"Screw you, Plannings."

Eberhardt motioned for the other man to help him and, after a moment, Plannings did. He grabbed Eberhardt's hand and heaved.

Eberhardt heaved harder, and instead of him rising to his feet, he brought Plannings tumbling into the dirt beside him. "Sorry."

***

I led Montano and Delroy through the hedge to a spot on the wall. I pulled bricks aside, exposing a hole. Small, but big enough to crawl through, and the number of tossed cigarettes at the base of that spot in the wall showed it was a long-used location for student escapes from RHS.

"How'd you find this?" Montano asked.

"Ace reporter. Which is why I'm smart enough to ask what Xavier Delroy is doing here."

"You know him?"

I did, and cast a sideways glance at Delroy before crawling through the hole. "I've been digging around his business for years."

Montano's mouth firmed, and I could tell he was thinking

that I didn't waste my time on a story for days, let alone years. *So what*, the detective was musing, *could occupy Connie Kendall, ace reporter and destined for a Pulitzer, for years?*

***

The new day had arrived in full. Montano, Delroy, and I moved through the school's outskirts, darting between buildings. No police were really in this part of the school – everything was in a cluster around Tac-Com, all eyes on the gym at this point. But no sense taking chances.

***

That was apparently Eberhardt's logic, too… which explained why Plannings now had his arms extended, embracing a tree, his wrists cuffed together. Eberhardt had taken the guy's phone and radio. He had taken the man's keys as well, figuring – rightly – that Plannings was too lazy to have walked this far.

A moment later, Eberhardt was in the other man's car, driving quickly through the trees.

***

Things were starting to come together. All of us told ourselves that they were coming together in a way we had more or less planned. All of us knew that we were lying to ourselves.

Thomas Easterly had planned all this to the minute. He was in control. But knowing it didn't mean we could stop it. And at least a few of us were starting to wonder if we should even try. I, for one, had done enough digging on Xavier Delroy through the years to figure that whatever Easterly wanted with the man, it wouldn't be good. And that was fine with me. Better than fine, actually, since it looked like I was on my way to a front-row seat.

Had I only known, I would have backed out. Ace reporter or no, some stories were not the kind you should ever look forward to.

Yeah, everything was starting to come together.

***

We drew in sight of the empty space between the cops and the gym. We could see C-unit prepping to go, and everyone else had settled into that quiet, tense, expectant state that cops entered into before something major – and majorly dangerous – was about to occur.

To me, Montano said, "Time for you to do something for me."

"I already showed you –"

"I need another diversion for me and Delroy to get through."

I resisted the urge to stamp my feet and throw a business-casual tantrum. "No way. I'm coming in. I –"

Montano's next words shut me up. Fast. "Connie, the whole place – the whole school – is wired to blow."

That gave me pause. I knew Montano wasn't above lying, but I didn't get that vibe now. "How do you know that?"

"Teacher told me. And I believe him. He wants to see me…" and he pointed at Delroy, "… and him. That's it."

I shook my head. Bomb or no bomb, I'd come this far. I wasn't sitting it out now. "You think I –"

"Connie, listen. I need you to get to Tac-Com and let them know. Tell Vickers that I sent you, and that if they move, Teacher's going to blow everything."

Still I hesitated. What can I say? The reporter part of me had grown over the years, crowding out more and more of the human part of me. Occupational hazard that few of us speak of, but it's real, and it can be both wonderful and horrid.

Softly, Montano said, "Connie, this is not a story. This is our lives, yours included."

He was right. And I was going to do what he asked, no matter what. But I didn't have to tell him that.

"I want an exclusive."

"I already told you –"

"Not on the situation, Montano. I want an exclusive on *you*. Assuming you actually make it out alive, you don't talk to anyone but me."

Montano nodded again.

***

Reporters really aren't supposed to insert themselves in the stories. But when Montano nodded, I suddenly understood that he was going to do whatever it took to end this. He was trying to save as many lives as he could, and didn't care about status or promotions or anything but stopping Thomas Easterly and getting the kids and staff back alive.

So I darted forward and kissed him. And yes, we had history. And yes, in that moment there was something undeniably appealing about a man who was willing to lay down a lifetime of toil for a moment of redemption.

Should I have done it?

At this point… sure. In for a penny, in for a pound.

Besides, I was pretty sure I'd never see Montano again.

And again, I didn't have to let him know that. So as I kissed him, I whispered, "Don't die. My story won't be as good without you."

Then I pushed him away. Montano led Delroy to the safe shadows of a building. As soon as I saw they had hidden themselves, I turned toward the mass of police and started running.

***

I made it much farther than I expected. I guess no one was really ready for a woman in high heels to run full speed into their midst, shouting at the top of her lungs. I got all the way to C-unit, shouting, "Don't tell me to leave! I'm the press! The voice of the people! I have a message for the angry chick in the uniform and the two feds with their heads up their asses! Take me to your leader!"

PC? No. But I was going for attention, not political correctness. Besides, all that was totally correct, so I felt okay shouting it. It's not libel if it's true.

***

While I screamed and shouted and made myself into an unignorable nuisance, flailing about so hard it literally took all of C-unit to subdue me, Montano dragged Delroy into the no-man's land between police lines and gym.

The C-unit commander spotted them halfway through their run. "Stop them!"

People moved, and I could tell Montano and Delroy weren't going to make it. So I started shrieking. Again, I relied on the secret weapon of journalism: the truth.

"Stop! Don't! You move in, this whole school will blow!"

Whether C-unit believed me or not, the rest of the cops heard the news. Murmurs erupted immediately: "You hear that?" "The whole school?" "No way." "But what if…"

C-unit's attentions were suddenly split between dealing with a possible uprising, and trying to stop Montano and his (to them) unknown fellow in flight.

The moment of indecision had the intended effect. Everyone paused long enough to let Montano and Delroy get to the gym. A door opened as they approached, and they disappeared into the place Thomas Easterly had directed.

Into Teacher's realm.

CHAPTER 28
Intended Response

Montano and Delroy were disoriented for a moment as they ran into the gym. Part of that was the shift from sunlight light to the dimmer space indoors. Part of it was simply the change from outside safety, to a place where all illusions of self-control fell away.

As a result, Montano didn't see much. Just a flurry of motion as various men with brightly-colored armbands hustled them through the doors at gunpoint, into the gym proper.

This was the first time Montano had seen it. His first response was one of quiet shock – both in himself and exhibited all around him. The kids lay on the floor, heads covered. Some sobbed quietly. Others lay so still it was only their shallow breathing that showed them to be alive. They looked worn and filthy to a point that shocked him, with almost all of them wearing clothing that had been soiled beyond what he would have thought could be accomplished in a single day.

His hatred for Teacher exploded, and he could no longer think of him as Thomas Easterly. There was no grieving father here, there was just a sort of terrorist who had put children – and, he saw, a few surviving members of the staff, also hooded, also filthy – through a living hell.

He also saw Daxton Leigh off to the side. The boy was curled into a fetal position. One hand lay on the floor, the other had somehow wedged under his shirt, holding his innards together as he tried to keep himself from bleeding out.

It hadn't worked. The boy's eyes were blank and glassy, pointed at Montano but seeing nothing. He was dead.

Montano's rage grew a bit more.

And, oddly, in that moment, he also hated Xavier Delroy. Not for whatever part in all this he was playing, but for the fact that the man had looked all around. Had seen the students, including the hooded girls in cheerleader's uniforms off to one side.

And had not rushed toward the outfit that obviously marked his daughter. Had not even said a word about her.

Xavier Delroy, in the final analysis, was concerned only about himself.

And, Montano thought, whatever *Novi* was.

***

Montano's second realization: that the bleachers were gone. Or rather, transformed. The thick wood and heavy support struts had been taken apart, then re-constructed into thick, wheeled barricades that rested to the sides of the doors.

As though waiting for him to see, Colors now rushed forward. They pushed on the barricades, shoving them in front of the doors that Montano knew C-unit would try to come through.

He also knew enough about police tactics to know what C-unit would do, and what effect those barricades would have.

It was all going to blow up – literally – in their faces.

***

Delroy apparently noticed Teacher staring at him, and decided it would be in his best interests to at least pretend to care about his daughter. He took a step in that direction, but a gun butt knocked him to his knees. Teacher loomed over him.

"All in due time, Xavier."

***

By this point, C-unit had managed (more or less) to subdue me and, like good military bureaucrats, decided quickly to do the smart thing and pass the buck. So a few seconds later they dragged one kicking, screaming ace reporter into the mobile command center.

Agents Ryker and Heigl looked up, with surprise, and Vickers headed toward me so fast it was almost like she had been expecting something like this.

"What the hell is she doing –"

Greenie, the C-unit commander, didn't waste time, "She said she's got inside info that the school is wired."

Vickers stared at me, and I could tell that she was already half-convinced.

Agent Ryker spoke up. The man has a shrill voice, guaranteed to produce migraines at fifty feet and able to paralyze squirrels at seventy-five. "How do you know that?"

***

Inside Tac-Com, I was answering questions.

Outside, regular cops and support began pulling back. C-unit had dumped outside, deciding on their own that they were going to start an evacuation, discovering that the troops had already made that decision at the same time.

But C-unit remained. Greenie and his team were professionals. And, as I have stated repeatedly both in my articles and during several of the post-disaster trials and hearings, none of what came next was their fault.

They were excellent officers. They were well-trained, and highly motivated by duty and a sincere desire to protect and serve.

It wasn't their fault, what happened.

It wasn't their fault, what had already been set in place.

It wasn't their fault, what was, at this point, inevitable.

CHAPTER 29
Intended Response

Montano looked at Teacher. "Still need the mask?" he asked. He allowed scorn into his voice as he gestured at Xavier Delroy and said, "Worried he'll recognize you?"

Teacher laughed and took off his mask, revealing Thomas Easterly. He looked just like the pictures in his house, save this: his eyes, once alive and youthful and warm, had grown old and tired and cold.

Easterly shook his head as he turned toward Delroy, who still lay on the floor where Easterly had knocked him down. "No. He doesn't recognize me at all." He leaned in close to the man and said, "Do you?" Delroy didn't answer, and Easterly said, "In fact, I'll let everyone go right now – throw open the doors, let the hostages go, and surrender to C-unit if the man can tell you anything about me."

Montano was struck, again, by the fact that he believed Easterly. And was completely unsurprised that the man knew C-unit was coming in. "Well, Xavier?" said Easterly.

Delroy flinched. "What do you want from me?"

Thomas looked back at Montano. "Don't you find that interesting? Surrounded by all this, with his daughter under a funeral shroud just ten feet away, and he asks, not, 'How can I save her,' or even, 'What do you want?'"

Easterly nudged the man with his toe, and Xavier cried out as though he had been kicked full-force. Fear lends pain to any situation. Montano felt rage again, and disgust at Xavier Delroy's cowardice, and (above all) concern at the fact that Paige Delroy, lying so close, had not cried out herself. She must have heard his voice, but she had not shouted for help. She had not yelled to ask how her father was doing. She had not screamed at the sound of her powerful daddy, brought low by a monster greater than him.

Montano glanced at the cheerleaders, strung out in a row.

None of them looked harmed – filthy, terrified, but otherwise unblemished, as far as he could see. But he couldn't see their faces. They could have been beaten into comas for all he could tell.

Thomas Easterly didn't notice or care about Montano's observations of the daughter. All his attention was still on the father as he said, "No. Xavier Delroy wouldn't ask about someone else. He just says, 'What do you want from *me*?' Because it's all about you, Xavier. Isn't it?"

***

A pile of cell phones sat on the ground outside of Tac-Com. Vickers had insisted. No telling how many of them were bugged and, she reasoned, no sense chancing telling Teacher what they were planning.

***

Inside Tac-Com, Vickers sat beside Oberczofski. On the whole, Vickers thought Oberczofski was a bit soft at this point. She didn't notice that at the rare moments he spoke, he always had something important to say. Nor did she recognize the fact that there was value in the negotiator remaining on-duty but, for the most part, out of the way. He had the wisdom to know when he wasn't needed, but she had been, overall (as reported post-incident) disappointed in his contributions to this point.

For his part, Oberczofski thought that the woman beside him was a bit too ready to go in guns-a-blazin'. She was more likely to get people killed than not, and that terrified him. But he was also a team player and, more than that, wise enough to recognize that with someone like Vickers it was better to remain quiet and at least be heard than it was to scream and shout and be ejected. He thought she was a competent cop overall, despite her failings – just not the ideal candidate for this situation.

But, their personal animosities aside, both were united in this moment in their horror at what was being planned.

I sat beside them in the Tac-Com. I wasn't sure whether I'd

been allowed to remain as a courtesy or (more likely) under the "enemies closer" part of the old adage. Either way, I was there, and I couldn't help but say, "Don't do this. He knows you're coming."

Agent Heigl at least had the grace to try and sound like she was explaining to me. The effect was marred, though, by the fact that she spoke with the same tones one would use for a child who had been dropped on their head as an infant as she said, "Which is why we got rid of the phones."

Agent Ryker, ten times more direct, said, "And maybe he knows we're coming, but he doesn't know *how*." Then, a *thousand* times more callous, he added, "Either way, we're doing this."

Turning away Ryker jabbed his finger at a set of gym blueprints that had been spread out. "We go in here. Only one hostage in front of this door. We cut the power in case they've got any explosives wired into the building. C-unit uses det-cord for an explosive breach, goes through the door and hits the student with bean bag rounds. Then –"

"What if the student is too close and gets hit with the explosion? Or takes a round to the face?" Vickers asked.

A *million* times more heartless: Ryker's face showed how little he cared about either of those very real possibilities.

Oberczofski crossed himself. He started mumbling, and I was pretty sure he was praying.

Toss a few up there for me as well, Oberczofski, I thought.

I didn't know then and I still don't know now if there is a god. But I do know that I didn't believe any prayers would work at this point.

In God we might trust, but by now I recognized that it was Teacher who pulled the strings.

***

In the gym, Montano had shifted slightly, which brought a half-dozen guns to bear in his direction. Thomas Easterly didn't move, though. He just kept staring at the man curled up on the floor at his feet.

Montano put up his hands for a moment, then shrugged and put them down again. Whatever happened now, it was going to happen because Easterly wanted it to happen, and it wouldn't matter if Montano's hands were raised or not.

Might as well go out looking brave.

He didn't feel brave. He felt afraid, sure. But also confused and, above all, still angry. "What do you want, Easterly?"

Easterly didn't so much as glance in his direction. "I already told you what I wanted, Detective Montano."

"No, you blew smoke up my ass and –"

Easterly wheeled on him and – with so much violence that the teachers and staff screamed in fear in their dark prisons, and Montano stepped back in sudden terror – shrieked, "*NO!*" He closed his eyes, getting himself under control before finishing, "I never blew smoke up your ass. Not even once."

"Then stop playing games."

"I've never done that, either."

With that, Easterly turned back to Xavier Delroy and methodically, calmly, carefully began pistol-whipping the man.

***

Montano moved to intercede and got slammed to the ground for his troubles. Easterly stopped beating Delroy, now curled in on himself in a strange imitation of the dead Daxton Leigh, and gestured for the Colors to stand down. He looked at Montano

"I said I wanted an end to villainy," Easterly said. "An end to children forced to lay on the floor with guns to their heads."

Montano almost started laughing. He looked at Thomas Easterly. At Delroy. The Colors, with guns pointed at children and adults alike.

He probably *would* have started laughing, too, but didn't want to push Easterly over whatever edge he teetered on. He heard Oberczofski in his head, the negotiator's calm voice telling him what to say. "He was involved in the cover-up. It was your daughter that was raped, and he –"

Unlike Montano, Easterly did start laughing. He laughed loud, hard, long. It bordered on hysterical, and Montano's body started to tremble in fear.

"No," said Easterly. "No, it was another man's daughter who was raped. Another mother that saw her daughter changed in an instant, the light taken from her child's soul. But I found out. While I was preparing for all… this. It couldn't be borne."

Montano was reeling. He had been so sure that Thomas and Elise Easterly had been the parents of the girl who was raped. It was the only thing that fit.

But Easterly wasn't lying. He could tell, and would have bet his life on that conviction.

"Then why? Why beat Delroy? Why kill –" He swallowed. "Why kill Daxton?"

"Because it was *what that little shit deserved*," Easterly snarled. "*They* couldn't do it, so I gave that girl's parents what they couldn't take for themselves: justice. I killed Zane Kennedy quickly: he was a stupid boy, a moron who was in thrall to Daxton Leigh and would have done anything for him. But no matter what his state of mind was, he *watched*. He watched it happen, and he watched out to make sure they weren't interrupted."

Easterly looked around, surveying the students. "I had a worse end in store for Konstantin Tarov, because I thought it appropriate that he know how it feel to have something shoved into you, hurting you, tearing you apart. It wasn't enough, nothing could ever be *enough*, but appropriate would have to do."

He swiveled to look at Daxton, a bloodless gray ball, a pill bug curled in on itself in death. "And the worst, longest pain was reserved for the son of a powerful man, who raped a fourteen-year-old and never saw the inside of a prison or even a courthouse. Who never suffered, because his father was powerful, and the other father was not."

Montano gestured at the rest of the kids, some crying, most silent. "Then why are you doing all this? Those boys are dead, and even if they weren't, you yourself just said it. It wasn't *your* daughter they hurt."

Something in Easterly's face changed. The sad, angry man who had been Thomas Easterly drained away from him. This was again – and would remain, now and forever – only the man known as Teacher.

Detective Montano had thought school was in session. He had thought the lesson already well underway. But now he realized that this hadn't only been a lesson. Teacher had been handing out tests for a long time.

Now, the grades were being announced.

***

Teacher shook his head and, again looking into the empty nothing-spaces where he did not and never would see his daughter again, he said, "No. These boys didn't rape her."

He turned to Montano. Stepped toward him and actually put his hands on the detective's shoulders, like a friend sharing a grief.

Teacher had insisted he told the truth through all this. But he didn't have to insist this time. Montano could tell that here, now, the truest thing Teacher had yet said was about to be uttered:

"I only wish my daughter had been raped by a trio of evil boys. That she had been left for dead at my door, and spiraled into a depression that led her to take her own life three months later. I wish that she had been... so... *lucky*."

PART FOUR:
IN MY OWN FLESH

When I heard the cannon of the war, I listened with my own ears to my own destruction.
When I saw the torn dead, I knew it was my own torn dead body.
It was all me, I had done it all in my own flesh.

- D.H. Lawrence
  "New Heaven and Earth"

CHAPTER 30
Teachable Moments

Montano's confusion remained, and deepened. But fear seeped into his mind as well, and that fear deepened to horror as Teacher and the Colors yanked the surviving adult hostages to their feet. They shoved them forward until they stood in a line, all of them facing Montano.

One by one, the Colors yanked the hoods off the teachers and staff. They forced them to their knees. Montano, suspecting what was about to happen, stepped forward.

Teacher had expected this, too. No sooner had Montano done it than something hard slammed into the back of his right knee. His leg buckled automatically, and he found himself down as well. Not on both knees, but on one. A supplicant, though perhaps not quite so low as the men who stared at him in terror.

Now Montano understood why no one had called out for help; why Paige had not shouted for her daddy to save her when she heard Xavier Delroy's voice. Beneath the hoods, all the adults were gagged – and so, he figured, were the students. Some of the men's gags appeared only loosely tied. Others had been yanked so tightly against the captives' mouths that they had torn open the corners of their lips, creating faces that grinned in horror, dried blood caking their cheeks and chins in a scabrous mask.

Montano took them all in. Placed faces and names to the files he had memorized in the last twenty-four-plus hours.

Isaiah Mulcahey and Jonas Chambers: the two surviving teachers. And, thanks to Dapper Dan, Montano also knew that Mulcahey was one of those who received strange deposits in his bank, while Jonas had not. Those facts were undoubtedly connected to their gags: Mulcahey's was one of those that had torn him wide at the cheeks, while Jonas' seemed tied on so loosely it likely served as a gentle reminder not to speak more than any serious impediment should he wish to do so

Beside them: Holden Wright, secretary. Like Jonas Chambers, he had not received anonymous deposits to his bank account. As with Jonas Chambers, Holden's gag was loosely tied. The secretary saw Jonas, and his eyes widened. He started to shuffle sideways, terror for the other man obvious in his eyes.

Colors pushed him back into place. But gently, Montano noted. Firmly, but carefully.

What's going on?

What's about to happen?

***

Teacher nodded to Red, who unholstered a gun.

At first Montano almost laughed. Nerves, he knew, but there was no denying that Red had drawn a gun that looked more like a toy than a weapon. Smaller than many children's cap guns, the tiny semi-automatic almost disappeared in the man's hand. Montano guessed (correctly) that it was some kind of .25 ACP shooter – basically a modernized version of the old derringer many a TV viewer has seen up the sleeves of Old West card sharks.

The urge to laugh disappeared, though, when Red kicked Isaiah Mulcahey to the floor.

"Why bring me here if you're just going to kill them all?" Montano asked. He all but shouted the words, as though volume alone might be enough to turn Teacher from his course.

"I'm not going to kill them all, detective. Just the ones who deserve it. And you're here to bear witness. To see, and to speak."

He nodded at Red, who aimed the tiny semi-automatic and began to pull the trigger.

Small or not, the sound was still loud in the gym. No matter how terrified or tired the students were, they knew the sounds meant everything had gone from bad to worse (or from horrific to whatever lay beyond that point), and they began to scream around the sounds of the tiny semi-automatic going off over and over and over.

Red fired a total of nine times. Then he popped a small clip out of the gun, reloaded, and fired another nine.

Mulcahey screamed during the first seven. He writhed for another five. He was silent and still for the last six.

***

Montano figured Mulcahey was dead by then. Later examination showed otherwise. Nothing Teacher did was left to chance, and that extended to everything done by the Colors.

The gun used on Isaiah Mulcahey turned out to be a Beretta 950 Jetfire. As Montano guessed, it was loaded with .25 ACP rounds: something easily purchased all over the world or from the comfort of your own home with the click of a button. These, however, had been modified so as to actually *reduce* the already-low stopping power of the original rounds.

Teacher wanted Mulcahey dead, no doubt about it. But first, he wanted him to hurt. Whether this was because he personally judged Mulcahey more culpable than those who had already been killed is up for dispute. I, personally, believe that Thomas Easterly would have preferred to draw out all the victims' pain for longer (at least, the adult ones), and the only reason he killed any of them with merciful quickness – as with the quickly-murdered school IT pros, Ray Gunne and Nicholas Vachnarian – was so the police and media would immediately both pay attention and take him seriously.

Whatever his reasoning for choosing Mulcahey at this moment, the bullets did not immediately kill the teacher.

The first shot went into Mulcahey's pelvis, battering through one of the body's largest nerve clusters before lodging agonizingly in the man's hip. Mulcahey screamed, though the screams were cut short when the next shot perforated his left lung.

The next carefully-aimed shots shattered his ribs, but did not penetrate farther into the body where major arteries lay. At this point, given that Mulcahey was no longer moving, it was easy for

Red to take careful aim and shoot off the man's outer ears and nose without risking damage to the skull or brain.

Red then stretched out Mulcahey's hands on the floor and shot off the thumbs and fingers of the man's hands, leaving only the pinky fingers.

Finally, he hammered the butt of his now-empty gun on Mulcahey's face: two quick strikes that shattered the other man's cheeks and sent shards of bone into his eyes.

Isaiah Mulcahey survived almost three weeks. During that time, he was deaf and blind, lame, could not hold anything, and had to evacuate his bladder and bowels via tubes. Almost the only part of him that remained as what most of us would think of as human was his tongue. Teacher had left that untouched, though Mulcahey did not speak a word during those weeks.

He simply screamed.

***

Outside the gym, the shots could be heard – but only barely. The concrete walls and the carefully modified bullets meant that only a series of light, high *pop*s could be heard.

Enough to worry.

Enough to make everyone move a little faster.

But that was as Teacher wished, too. He wanted them moving quickly. If they had gone slower, they might not have walked so easily into his trap.

***

As Mulcahey was literally being shot to pieces, Montano screamed right along with the students and staff. The RHS shouts were wordless; his were not:

"No! Stop! No, no, no, stop, please, no, no…!" and on and on in a merry-go-round of useless repetition.

Teacher looked at the now-motionless form of Isaiah

Mulcahey, then switched his attention to Xavier Delroy. The squat man had pushed to his knees. He coughed twice, and flecks of blood speckled a suit, shirt, and tie worth more than Montano made in three months.

One of the Colors made as if to shove Delroy back to the floor, but Teacher motioned for him to stay his hand. He squatted in front of Delroy.

He stared at the man until the screams lessened, then said, "I'll make you a deal: I'll let everyone in here go right now, you included, if you tell Detective Montano what I meant when I referred to Novi."

Delroy looked at Montano. At the kids and the few surviving staff members.

"For God's sake, Delroy," said Montano.

Delroy spit in Teacher's face.

Teacher wiped the spittle away, his expression never shifting. "I thought so," he said, then stood and went back to stand in front of Montano. "You've been asking yourself all the wrong questions, detective. So I'll ask the right ones, starting with this: What's the connection between school staff members who get deposits to secret accounts the day before away games, a school with unfiltered internet, boys who sext girls and then rape them, and a huge entertainment machine?"

He turned his back on Montano, and pointed at the exhausted, filthy students. "Why are these *particular* students here?"

Montano said nothing. He wasn't playing mind games. He just didn't know the answers. He had suspicions, but too few to make any concrete statements. Teacher had the only answer key.

"No? Well, I'll let you stew on it for a bit. You'll get it."

***

Life and death in the gym. The sounds of screams and cries and whimpers of pain and terror.

There were similar sounds playing out in the ER of the closest hospital. Some were the normal type: broken bones; a few hacking coughs; and one person who had somehow accidentally been stripping paint with a razor, slipped, and the razor had ended up almost completely buried in the palm of his hand.

The hospital was not a particularly busy one, usually. On any normal day, all of these people would have been seen.

Today, they were triaged and then sent back out to the waiting room, because the ER staff and many of the available surgeons were dealing with wounds and maimings on a level none of them had ever seen: those sent home early from Teacher's lesson.

One of the sheltered nooks of the ER was silent, though, save the slow, steady beep of an EKG and the slow, steady breathing of a man wishing he was home with his wife.

Detective Eberhardt knew he couldn't help Montano on the scene. Not only that, but it was entirely possible that if he had remained at RHS he would have been arrested on an obstruction charge. Maybe fired, maybe lose his pension and benefits. He would have stayed just the same, if he thought it could help Montano or the people at RHS. But he doubted it. So after leaving Plannings shackled to a tree he had driven here as fast as he could.

Now he waited. Beside him, Elise Easterly lay unconscious on a bed. In front of him, her personal effects lay on a tray nearby: a lipstick, a small brush, and a set of keys had been found in her pockets. The keys didn't go to the house, and he wondered what part of all this they would end up playing, not doubting for a moment that they had *some* part to play.

Eberhardt pushed the keys and toiletries aside. He watched the woman on the bed. He prayed that she would wake, and tell him something he could use to save Montano and the rest of the people under Teacher's thumb.

Not much hope, but it was something. It was all he had.

Elise slumbered on.

CHAPTER 31
Teachable Moments

Montano had once stepped barefoot in an enormous pile of dog crap, and he suspected he hadn't looked half as revolted as Teacher now did, staring at Delroy Xavier.

"One more chance, Xavier," said Teacher. "Novi?" Delroy just stared at him. "How about if I make it even easier? Tell us where Entercom gets most of its off-the-books income. You can even pretend you just found out about it and –"

Delroy finally lost control. "I don't know! I –"

Red hammered his rifle down on the back of Delroy's leg, high up on his hamstring. Delroy shrieked as the simultaneous crack of a broken bone sounded. The students and staff jerked in place, but perhaps they were all screamed out – Montano didn't hear any of them shout along with the rich man brought low.

Teacher went to the hooded cheerleader with the tiniest outfit and grimiest body. Perhaps she had been beautiful before this began – Montano suspected she was, given the outfit. But now she sagged on the floor, her body looking soft and waxy as death stood above her.

"What kind of man would sacrifice his own daughter?" Teacher said. Then, shifting his gaze to Montano, he added, "And if he could sacrifice his own child, what would he be willing to do to the children of other people? People he didn't even know?"

Montano looked at Delroy. The man's screams had ceased suddenly. "Delroy? What is he talking abou –"

"This madman's got a gun to my daughter's head – to all these students' heads – and you're asking me what *I've* done wrong?"

Teacher cocked his gun. Shoved it against Paige's head. She whimpered inside her hood.

Delroy said nothing.

Teacher nodded at a Color: Yellow, who took a tablet from one of his pockets and entered something on it.

***

At the station, Reggie Meikle was witnessing something that, to his knowledge, had never been seen before:

Dapper Dan looked almost beaten.

He refused to give up, though. He kept working, kept carving his way into whatever crack in Teacher's electronic defenses that he could find. When Reggie and the others took short naps – not much, just a half-hour to stave off dropping completely – Dan worked on. He was a machine, Reggie thought. A machine pitting his will against other machines and, for the first time in his life, unable to beat them into submission.

That was the moment when, at RHS, Yellow tapped a button.

Dan's computer beeped. The screen he'd been working on flickered, and his email inbox pushed itself into its place. A blank email opened. The cursor arrow tracked to the attachment.

Clicked.

Dapper Dan read it.

His eyes, dull and exhausted only a moment before, lit up.

***

Montano's phone chimed, alerting him of an incoming text. When he didn't move, Teacher said, "You should get that."

Montano opened the message. It was a list: twelve dates. After every other date, a name appeared. The dates blended together, and Montano spared a tiny shred of his brain to think how exhausted he was before he focused on the six names listed:

Ariel Zaharian. Clarice Keppler. Emily Yamada. Madison Licausi. Olivia Trachte. Briana Stahl.

"What is…" The question fizzled to silence. Montano forced himself to look closer at the dates. Looking up at Teacher, he said, "Six of these are the dates when the dead faculty got payments in their bank."

Teacher nodded. "Each one the day before an away game. But you knew that, didn't you?"

"What about the other dates? And the names?" Montano squinted at his phone. "The other dates are each the day after the away games."

Teacher's eyes went to that faraway place. "The date a girl would go missing."

Montano frowned. "You're saying the teachers were paid to kidnap these girls? That doesn't make any sense."

Teacher shifted his gaze to Delroy. "It would be ridiculous – and risky – to steal too many girls away from near your home, wouldn't it, Mr. Delroy. But what if you had a daughter? What if she was a cheerleader, and you – the doting father – went to her games. Just the away games, though. And not even all of them, for that matter. Just, say… the girls' athletics events. Who would you see there?"

Montano didn't want to answer. Teacher spared him the trouble: "You'd see all those girls on the other team. Young, athletic, pretty girls, just the kind who will fetch top dollar. No one questions your presence – or, if need be, other people in your employ. You all have children at the school, don't you? But no one who lives there will know who you or your people are. No one will remember *you* when their children go missing."

Montano was finally starting to see where Teacher was going. He had been praying for Vickers to somehow convince the federal agents not to breach. They wouldn't be ready for what Teacher had done, and more people might very well die.

But that, he was starting to suspect, would be infinitely preferable to what Teacher was planning.

***

Teacher looked at Mulcahey, motionless and – to Montano's eye – dead on the floor. "But though the other team's parents don't notice, what if the RHS teachers do? Especially if you and your people are the type who barely notice their own kids, and who don't look at them once during the games – just the other teams' girls? What if they notice that you only go to away games? To *girls'* athletics? What if a few of them figure out – or perhaps just luck into – the fact that girls are going missing whenever you show up at a game? Not everyone at RHS, mind you. Just a secretary and a vice-principal. A few gym teachers. So you pay them off. It's easy to pay them off before they even suspect what's really going on, in fact. To them, you're paying for discretion: no one's getting hurt, are they? It's just a few slightly perverted older men who like to stare at the girls on the other team, or at their cheerleaders. And really…" He nudged Mulcahey with his toe, and his face twisted as he finished, "What red-blooded male these days could be blamed for that?"

Montano flashed, for some reason, to his screensaver. To his mini-conversation with Eberhardt in the moments before this nightmare began.

"That's not boobs, you dirty old man. That's ambience. And I'll have you know she's an award winner."

"Of what?"

"Sports Illustrated's Swimsuit Model of the Year, 2019."

Teacher was still talking, giving his final lecture: "But better safe than sorry. The head coach, a few assistants. The principal finds out, too – even figures out what's *really* happening – and since he's a powerful man in his little pond, he gets even more money. Oh, and let's not forget the school's IT professionals, two men who notice some strange correspondence logs, go to the teachers to ask about them, but instead of turning anyone in, they end up getting extra paychecks of their own."

Montano felt like he was trying to catch up to a runaway

train while chained to a treadmill. He was behind the curve, always had been, and couldn't keep up even now. "Why go to such trouble and expense –"

Teacher wasn't interested in the lecture becoming a discussion. Not yet. "Did you know that one of the most-searched terms on the internet, is 'teen girl sex' or 'teen cheerleader sex'? Did you know that you can sell an innocent, beautiful girl to the right party for a hundred thousand dollars or more? If she's young enough, if she's pretty enough, if she's a virgin... the sky's the limit."

Montano couldn't help it. He looked at his phone. The lists. The names of the girls that hung there in digital form.

Teacher leaned in close to him, speaking low so only Montano heard. "It was risky, to take the girls. But worth it. Besides, the people behind it were careful. They never poached their own territory, but it went even beyond that. They used different methods to kidnap the girls. They even used different 'contractors' each time a girl was taken. Six girls, six different kidnappers."

Montano's reality crumbled. He'd been wrong about everything. Not just about who was in charge, but about why, and who else was here.

Everything.

Everything.

***

"Why?" Montano asked. "Why tell me like this? Why do *any* of this?"

Teacher shook his head. "We're almost done, Detective Montano. You've almost figured it out. So I just have one thing left to do."

He made a circling motion with his hand.

The Colors moved to the end of the gym. Standing twenty feet away from the students who lined the floor, they aimed their guns as one.

***

Teacher watched. The Colors held their position, obviously waiting for the command to kill anyone and everyone but Teacher and, perhaps, Montano.

Teacher waited. Waited.

The moment stretched out. Montano felt like he could hear the creak of tendons as the Colors held their triggers at the last possible millimeter before gunfire began.

Teacher pulled a small device from a pocket. It looked to Montano like a simple garage door opener.

Teacher smiled, and looked strangely alive. He hummed a few bars of a song. Winked as Montano realized what it was, and where he'd heard it.

Teacher pressed the button.

***

It was worse than Montano could have imagined. The sound of gunfire louder than anything he'd ever heard, the screaming a frenzied maelstrom that threatened to sweep him off his feet. He smelled the tang of gunpowder, the coppery scent of blood misting in the air.

He screamed, too.

And only slowly realized that what he had taken for gunpowder was not. That the gunfire was not. That the blood was not... at least, not in the way he thought.

He looked around.

The students screamed, but not in pain. Not in the throes of agonizing death. It was fear as they heard the *cr-cr-cr-cr-cr-crack* of the explosions, terror as they felt blood and flesh rain down on them.

Teacher had been humming a song from *The Wizard of Oz*: "Somewhere Over the Rainbow."

Red, Orange, Yellow, Green, Blue, Violet.

Teacher had told them they were not to speak, but that they each had assigned jobs. That, he had told them, was what the armbands were for: so that each could known where their coworkers were, and that the job each Color was assigned had been taken care of. And all that was true enough.

What was also true, but which Teacher had not told them, was that the armbands each held small but extremely powerful explosives similar to the det-cord C-unit planned to use to blow open the gym doors.

The charges had ripped the Colors in half.

Red, Orange, Yellow, Green, Blue, Violet.

"Six colors. Twelve dates," Montano mumbled, but didn't hear the words. All he heard was ringing, and all he felt was numbness and wet as he absently wiped smears of blood and streamers of flesh from his face.

CHAPTER 32
Intended Response

Vickers heard the explosion and barked into a walkie-talkie she was already holding. "Avril, cut the power! C-unit, go. Repeat, go for breach."

I was still at Tac-Com, too. Watching it all, knowing that everything was going wrong, and about to go worse. The monitors still showed the image of the gym, but no one was watching them. Everyone was watching the gym itself, or watching C-unit as they ran forward.

That was why I was the only one who saw what was happening, and what *wasn't*. I leaped toward Vickers, screaming, "Tell them to stop. Tell them –"

Vickers nodded to one of the techs, who tried to usher me out. He failed, and ended up on the floor, holding tightly to the bruised testicles sending fire into his belly.

Before Vickers could react, I pointed at the monitors and screamed, "No one triggered an explosion!"

Vickers turned to look at the monitors. "What?"

I jabbed my finger at the images. "No one even moved!" The Colors were doing what they'd been doing since I got into Tac-Com: some were walking up and down between the rows of students, a few sat on the bleachers. I hadn't seen Teacher, Montano, or Delroy, but then I hadn't expected to. I figured they were out of range of the cameras, having whatever heart-to-heart they were involved in.

But that wasn't it at all. I didn't see them because they weren't on the feed, and never would be.

Oberczofski was the next one to realize it: "It's a recorded loop!" He looked at Vickers. "Get C-unit back here, *now* – they're heading into a trap!"

CHAPTER 33
Teachable Moments

Montano looked at the dead Colors, ripped in half. Ears still ringing, he said, "Six different girls, taken by six different men."

Beside him, Teacher said, "Men willing to do anything for the right price."

"Which one took your girl?"

"Actually, none of them."

Even as he said it, Montano realized there was a small math problem: six girls taken, six Colors – the men who had kidnapped them, now blown apart.

But there was a seventh girl, who had not been named: "Bella Easterly."

He swiveled to see that Teacher was standing over Xavier Delroy, who was now holding very, very still. Montano doubted it was shock – the man just understood how close to death he was.

Though death, of course, was the least of his worries.

"I never found out why," Teacher said, his eyes never leaving Delroy's face, "but Bella got special treatment. Would you like to explain what it is you saw in her, Xavier? Why you came down from your palace built on the bones of children, and took… my… *girl?*" By the end of the question, Teacher's words came out almost painfully, cutting their way through his suffocating grief.

Delroy said nothing, did nothing. He did not even look away.

"I thought not," Teacher said.

He turned away, moving so fast Montano could barely track him as he yanked Paige Delroy to her feet and threw her at the detective. Montano caught her automatically as she stumbled toward him.

Arms full, he couldn't do anything to stop Teacher from pulling Delroy to his feet as well, placing a gun against his neck as he opened his mouth to speak…

***

… at the same time as C-unit triggered the strip of det-cord they'd wrapped around the lock and hinges of one of the gym doors.

Vickers' voice came over the radio as Greenie's thumb pressed down: "Abort! Abort! They know you're –"

The rest was lost in the explosion as the door blew in.

C-unit, hunching around the side of the wall a few feet beyond the door, didn't see that, though the door had blown off its hinges, there was still a pile of wood and metal beyond: the barricade Teacher had had his Colors create.

Smoke covered the barricade a moment later. No one would see it until they'd committed to the next step in their planned breach.

***

Inside, Montano had the delicious sensation of seeing Teacher caught offguard. The rage the man must have been feeling, to hold the man who had taken his daughter, must have clouded his otherwise pristine focus on the timing of his plan. So when the det-cord detonated, even louder than the series of explosions that had torn the Colors apart, Teacher's focus wavered.

Montano had been in a daze nearly every second he had spent in the gym. Now, though, his training and instincts took over. He drew and fired. Teacher screamed and fell back as he was hit.

Delroy, still standing – though lopsidedly, trying to keep his weight off his injured leg – fingered his coat. There was a hole in the side panel; Montano's shot had gone that close.

"You almost shot me, you –"

Xavier Delroy's next words were lost as Montano punched him out of the way. "Check on your daughter, you piece of human garbage."

Montano turned his back on the man and went to Teacher. Blood was wetting the man's side, turning his already dark clothing to a deeper shade of black. Still, Teacher smiled as Montano patted him down and stripped him of everything in his pockets or on his person.

"Why?" Montano muttered. "Why the game? Why the circus?" He shook his head. "It doesn't matter. It's over. It's –"

Behind him, Delroy had finally gone to his daughter. He took the hood off her head. And screamed.

Montano looked, and as he did, he heard Teacher start to laugh.

***

Outside the gym, C-unit tossed a concussion grenade through the smoke-shrouded gym doorway.

They weren't counting on the barricade.

The grenade hit it, bounced back, exploded.

C-unit was down, and Teacher hadn't had to lift a finger to do it. They did it to themselves – which was part of the lesson

***

Montano didn't notice the noise. He was too busy looking at Paige Delroy. She was gagged, dazed, staring at her father. She wasn't hurt that Montano could see, but she didn't seem to recognize the man who held her and screamed.

And it was then that Montano realized that she *wouldn't* recognize him. Because it wasn't her father. The girl in Xavier Delroy's arms wasn't Paige at all.

***

Montano finally did what he had neglected to do when he entered. He turned, another memory surfacing as he started counting:

"Tell me how many hostages I have, Montano. You have fifteen seconds."

"You started out with 10 faculty and staff and 24 students."

"And how many are left?"

"Three faculty, twenty-three students."

Montano finished counting and, horror in his eyes, turned back to Teacher. "Where are they? There are six kids missing. *Where are those kids?*"

Teacher just kept laughing.

***

Montano's fists balled up at his sides, and he almost punched Teacher. But he didn't, and was glad – if he'd started, he suspected he wouldn't have been able to stop.

"Where are they?" he said again.

Teacher's laughter subsided. "Our friend Xavier knows."

A few more pieces fell into place in Montano's mind: Xavier Delroy, owner of Entercom, which held a massive stake in the adult entertainment giant, Bright Dreams. "He forced her to work in the sex industry. Trafficked her," said the detective.

Teacher laughed again. Quieter this time, as blood loss took its toll. "The sex industry starts with the porn. It's the beginning of a chain, you see. Curiosity leads to desire, and desire to need. A need to see, then to experience. So the need is filled. Girls are trafficked. For some reason, there are never quite enough of them, so more 'talent' is scouted by 'good, upstanding citizens.'"

His lip curled, and he gestured around, pointing at the teens still on the floor. "We called them all here, you know. They would have had detention, they always did… but my wife and I decided they'd come in on this day. On our day – on *her* day." He shuddered, grimaced, placed a hand on his side as he looked around at the kids still on the floor. "All of these kids are porn addicts, and most of them have child porn on their computers. To them, it's not evil... it's just out there. Easy." Another shudder shook his frame. "I thought they should see the end result. What they do to innocents." His eyes started to glaze. Suddenly far away, he said, "Our Bella. My beauty."

Delroy dropped the girl he'd been holding – proud member of the Computer GurlZ Winona "Win" Jackson – like a sack of garbage. She fell, totally unprepared, and lay there, stunned, in another girl's clothes.

Delroy rushed past Montano and grabbed Teacher.

"Where is she? Where's Paige?"

Teacher – Thomas Easterly – smiled at him. His teeth were slicked pink with blood that welled out as he said, "Beginning her journey." He laughed, a wet, drowning laugh. "On her way to Hungary with the rest of them. The ones whose parents work for you, Delroy."

"That's why you gave us two hours to get here: you used the time to get them out of here – to have the Colors finish your lesson."

The awful realization Montano had come to washed over him: he'd been a pawn throughout, and had been used in this final moment as nothing more than a stall to give Teacher the last bit of time he needed, to do unto others what had been done to him.

***

Montano rushed to the barricade and hammered his fists against it. "This is Montano! You hear me?"

He heard Greenie's voice, dazed and muffled but still understandable. "Montano? What the hell –"

"No time! Six girls who got out, taken by an unknown number of captors."

"How'd they –"

Again, Montano cut him off. "I don't know, but they thought

of everything, so they found a way to get out. Now move before they're gone forever."

He looked at Teacher, who stared at the ceiling. His lips moved, and Montano thought he was saying, "Bella, Bella, Bella," as he faded away.

CHAPTER 34
The Plan

There were six of them, shoved through the forest behind the school. Paige Delroy was one. There were also three other cheerleaders, including Danila Tarov, sister to the dead, red-headed Konstantin, daughter to one of the men in Xavier Delroy's employ. Three more girls – all, as Teacher had said, daughters of men or women employed by Entercom and/or Bright Dreams – brought the number to six.

All six were stumbling, nearly falling through the trees as they ran, pushed along from behind by people they couldn't quite see. It was the heroin that The Lady had given them. It had worn off enough that the girls were starting to feel the pain of the brands that had been burnt onto them, but still held them tightly enough to disorient, to make everything slick and dizzy beneath their feet.

None of them wore their own clothes. Teacher had had the Colors change them out for other students' – just a bit of insurance that he counted on (correctly) to cloud the issue of who was there and who was not.

Besides, he had intended from the beginning to be there when Xavier Delroy realized his daughter, far from being where she should be, was gone from his arms, from his power, from his world.

That was what Thomas Easterly had felt. So that was the pain Teacher had decided Xavier Delroy should suffer as well.

CHAPTER 35
Intended Response

Outside, Vickers was coordinating the search. Men and women had abandoned any caution about traps Teacher might have set. They just ran through the forest, following the trail of the girls whom Teacher had spirited away.

"The bastard probably did it while we were pulling back so C-unit could go in. Not long ago, but that doesn't mean we can afford to do this slow," Vickers was hollering to anyone who would listen. "Move, move, move!"

Then she was alone in the mobile command unit. Everyone had started searching, no one was to remain behind. Seconds counted, and every eye was needed.

A moment after realizing she was alone, she sighed and ran out the door as well. Sometimes the commander stayed behind. Sometimes the commander just did the same grunt work everyone else was doing.

CHAPTER 36
Teachable Moments

Montano was trying to pull the barricade back. His back was turned to Delroy, so he didn't see the squat man pick up Teacher's gun from the floor where Montano had thrown it a moment before.

Montano turned around when he heard the hammer pulled back. He saw Delroy, gun pointed at Teacher, saying, "You bastard," over and over.

Teacher's gaze swam toward the present again, but even when he fully recognized the threat staring him in the face, he didn't seem frightened. He just smiled. "You already killed my wife and me years ago. And now you'll know." He coughed. Blood spattered the floor beside him. "You won't find her, until it's too late and you finally see her violated, torn body in the dirt. Actually, you probably won't even see that, since by then you'll have lost everything." He coughed again, but this time sent the upwelling of blood at Delroy as he spat in his enemy's face.

Delroy wheeled back, pawing at the blood and saliva, trying to clean his face with hands he didn't realize were already spattered with blood. All he did was wipe his own filth on himself.

"You sonofa –"

Teacher seemed to will himself to strength, to push his voice above and over Delroy's. "Files have been sent to police and reporters, detailing Entercom's involvement in human trafficking." He let out another wheezing, drowning laugh. "It's over. *You're* over. You're a cancer, a malignant tumor just like everything you represent, and you're going to be cut out. You'll lose your business, your name, and all the while you'll know it's nothing compared to what's happening to your daughter." Another one of those awful laughs, and this time red froth bubbled out of Teacher's mouth with it.

"Teacher, I –" Montano began.

Teacher didn't hear him; didn't even seem to notice him at all. It was, in that moment, just the two men. Just the two fathers. "And then," Teacher continued, the blood now running freely from his mouth with every syllable, "when you've gone to jail, you'll find out how that feels yourself. You'll find out how prisoners treat cellmates who have kidnapped and tortured and molested children." He grinned, the first genuinely happy expression Montano had seen on the man's face. "You were right: there are worse things than death. And you're going to feel every single one of them."

Montano saw Delroy realize the gravity of what Teacher had done, just like he saw Delroy truly believe that Teacher would make it all happen, exactly like he said.

He still held Teacher's gun. Montano saw the man trying to decide if he should kill his enemy.

Instead, he put the gun to his own head, and pulled the trigger.

***

Montano was already moving. Running toward Delroy as the man pulled the trigger, tackling him, falling with him.

By the time he had done all that, he also realized that, though Delroy had pulled the trigger, no shot had been fired. Still laying on top of Delroy, Montano looked at Teacher.

Teacher shook his head. "You don't get off that easy," he said. "The tumor never ends itself. *We* have cut it to pieces and then burn it to dust. And sometimes..." He managed a weak, cold smile. "Sometimes it's a pleasure to do the cutting and burning."

"There's still time to fix this. To stop it," said Montano, even as he cuffed Delroy's hands behind him.

"I doubt it," said Thomas. His smile widened in a way Montano did not like at all. "You can't stop it, because... because..." His eyes fluttered. Closed.

***

In the forest, a group of six police hit the dirt as gunfire started sounding. They radioed for Vickers, for C-unit, for God Almighty to come for them.

The rest of the police closed in on the spot. Vickers, close to the rear but gaining fast, breathed, "We've got you, you bastards," and looked forward to seeing the look on Teacher's face when he realized that at least this small part of his plan hadn't come to fruition.

***

Teacher's eyes opened again. Not dead, as Montano feared, though the cop could tell that moment wasn't far. "You can't stop it because it's already done."

***

The cops burst into the clearing where they had heard the gunfire.

No one was there but a teen, setting off rolls of huge firecrackers. When he saw all the guns pointed at him, he nearly fainted. "I give up!" he shouted.

That was when Vickers caught up. She took it all in in an instant, and knew that this was Teacher's final statement to those of the police who were still looking for the girls: they weren't here.

And hadn't been for a while.

***

Montano sagged as Teacher spoke the next words: "The girls are gone. They've *been* gone for days."

Montano almost leaped to his feet. He spun in a circle, noticing anew what he had already seen: the students, hooded, laying on the floor. They looked horrible. Soiled, messy.

Too soiled. Too messy.

"This didn't start yesterday," Montano realized. And remembered Teacher on the phone the day before: *"We brought more than enough food and water of our own to last for days."*

Days, Montano thought.

Turning to Teacher, he said, "You altered the timestamp on the video. Showed it happening yesterday when it was really days ago." Bitterly, he added, "So much for not lying."

Teacher grinned. "I never lied, Montano."

"You said you took the school yesterday."

"Did I?" Teacher shook his head weakly. "I never said any such thing."

Montano looked around again. Had Teacher said he took the school the day before? Had he ever said that at all? Did it matter?

No.

All that mattered was what had happened: "They've been here since Saturday. That's why you needed food and water for them."

"And I knew you'd bug it," said Teacher, "and thought that feeding young Konstantin Tarov the electronics – and shoving them up his ass – would be a good lesson for him."

"What about the bombs?" Montano asked dully. "How do I defuse the bombs in the school."

Teacher chuckled. His eyes rolled back. "No... bombs," he whispered. "Guess I did... tell one... little... fib."

And he died.

CHAPTER 37
Understanding

It might have been tough for anyone to figure out exactly what Teacher and The Lady had done between the time they took over the school on Saturday and the time they finally let anyone know it had happened. But it was made considerably easier by the fact that they left behind an answer key in the form of journals the police found in their home… and the videos.

Some of the videos were found over time, at Thomas and Elise Easterly's home. They had hidden cameras throughout the school, from the teachers' lounge to the bathrooms, many of which ran through the entirety of the events at RHS, giving the police entirely new fields of view as to what happened at the school. Along with hard drives containing the video recordings Thomas and Elise had made of the school and its staff and student body, there were also diaries, logs, and other daily journals that provided insight in a situation where so many of those who remained behind were unable to speak of what they knew, for one reason or another.

But the most important things were those videos; and the most important of *them* were on a flash drive in Teacher's pocket: what came to be known as the Reina Recordings.

***

Montano had actually pulled the flash drive out of Teacher's pockets when he stripped him of weapons in the gym. He didn't see it immediately – he was too busy trying to get the barricade moved aside so he and the hostages could get out. But as soon as he managed that, he started moving the kids out the door, and that was when he saw the drive.

It was bright red, with a blinking blue light that caught his eye. No-brainer that Teacher wanted it found, and wanted Montano to watch it. Especially given the fact that the drive had Montano's name inscribed in vivid yellow on one side, and the words "Watch Now" on the other.

Montano stopped what he was doing. Other cops were filing in by then, so he wasn't as necessary. He went to Tac-Com and grabbed a laptop, then took it to a cruiser, plugged in the drive, and began to watch.

***

"Video01_Saturday_10.07_am.mp4"

The Colors silently herded the staff and students into the gym. They looked shattered, but Montano noted (and kicked himself mentally) how much better they looked than they had when he finally saw them two days later.

After the Colors, The Lady/Elise Easterly and Teacher/Thomas Easterly entered.

They stood to the side as the hostages were gagged, hooded, and forced to the floor.

***

"Video02_Saturday_10.32_am.mp4"

The students and staff had been laid out in lines on the floor. Some of the Colors walked up and down, some of them sat on the partially pulled-out bleachers.

It was the scene that I would later recognize as the one that had been looped and then played back during the time C-unit readied to breach the gym.

***

"Video03_Saturday_10.55_am.mp4"

The Lady hauled Paige to her feet and marched her to where Winona Jackson had been pulled – albeit more gently. "Swap clothes," said The Lady.

Paige looked like she was going to fight it – but only until The Lady pointed her rifle at the cheerleader. The two girls stripped down to their underwear, then changed clothes. Winona had obviously been chosen for this moment: she was the same approximate size as Paige, though not nearly as toned (and again, Montano cursed himself for not seeing what was there, hidden in plain sight).

The scene was repeated with the other cheerleaders. One changed with the second of the Computer Gurlz, Beatriz Alcivar. The Misfits had girls among them who swapped with the other cheerleaders, mixing up who went and who stayed.

Twelve girls, in all.

The groups were forced to lay down again, swapping even their placement in the gym. Again, the Colors walked up and down, up and down, up and down. More loops that would be shown to the police. The lighting didn't even need to be changed: the gym was so closed off that it was always the exact same time of day inside – fluorescent o'clock.

Up and down, up and down, up and down.

***

"Video04_Saturday_12.14_pm.mp4"

A new video feed, this one obviously shot from a webcam or handheld or perhaps one of the students' own phones.

The cheerleaders in their new clothes – outfits they never would have allowed in any other circumstances – were pressed against the wall in Coach Fertetti's office.

They were hooded. They were gagged.

Still, there were muffled cries as rubber tubing went around each arm; as heroin was injected into the crook of each elbow.

They were branded by The Lady. She wore goggles when she super-heated the metal loop that would serve as a brand, but no mask when she actually marked the girls, as though it was important for the universe to see and to witness that it was Elise Easterly who did this thing. In her eyes, Montano saw no empathy, no sympathy, no soul. To The Lady, these girls were cattle to be marked, objects to be used.

She pressed the red-hot circle against each girl. Some cried out, others barely noticed. But whether they knew it or not, they had begun their preparations for the journeys they would take.

***

Montano didn't open the next video right away. He called Eberhardt. "She awake yet?" he asked.

"No," said Eberhardt quietly. He seemed to intuit what Montano was going through, if not what he was actually doing. "You need me?"

"Not yet. But call me the second she wakes up."

"Will do."

Montano hung up the phone, realizing as he did that he had not worried for an instant about the possibility he might not be able to reach Eberhardt. Teacher was dead. The job was done. There was no need to hack or block or listen.

Montano had hung up, but he hadn't put the phone away. He looked at it. Swiped the screen to wake it. The screen background mirrored the one on his desktop at work: Sports Illustrated's Swimsuit Model of the Year, 2019.

He opened his email. Downloaded an image. Moved to his phone settings. When he went back to the home screen, the beautiful woman was gone. In her place: a thin, young arm, with a bracelet that marked her as beloved, and a brand that marked her forever as less than human.

Montano wept then, and could not stop for a long time.

CHAPTER 38
Understanding

"Video05_Saturday_1.50_pm.mp4"

Again the image was one taken on a camera or handheld recorder. It looked like some kind of bodycam setup. This time, the images showed Red and Purple and Orange shoving the six branded, hooded cheerleaders through the trees beyond the school.

Whoever wore the bodycam followed. Montano realized it was The Lady when he saw a hand go up, finger extended, and her voice said, "Over there."

Other than that, there was only silence and the quiet crying of some of the girls who had come out of their dazes enough to know that they were in pain, and falling over branches and brambles that they could not see in the dark world left to them after being gagged and hooded.

The school could be seen in a few flashes. Then the forest swallowed them.

***

"Video06_Saturday_2.07_pm.mp4"

The Colors and The Lady pushed the girls into the clearing that, later, the police would find manned by a boy with firecrackers.

Now there was no teen. There were, however, people waiting. A pair of businessmen in pricey suits – similar to the ones favored by Xavier Delroy, in fact – stood in the clearing. Beside them, a quartet of armed thugs waited, automatic weapons held at the ready.

A dark sedan idled in the clearing. Beyond it, a truck with a horse trailer attached.

One of the businessmen stepped forward, looking at the group of girls as they entered the scene. He was a slim man, with a disagreeable air and hair that was such a vivid shade of red it almost seemed unreal.

His eyes wandered over the girls' bodies. No lust, he was simply doing a quality check of the product about to change hands. "Who's in charge?" he asked.

The Lady motioned, and the Colors who had accompanied her shoved the girls toward the horse trailer. The businessman watched for a moment, a frown on his face, then turned back to her. "I'm uncomfortable buying them without seeing their faces."

The Lady laughed. "We both know that if you only sell them for organs, you'll at least quadruple your money."

The red-haired man sighed, then nodded at his compatriot. The second businessman gestured, and two of their armed bodyguards split off to help the Colors load the girls into the horse trailer. The thugs followed them in, and the second businessman got in the truck and drove the girls away.

The red-haired man watched them go.

"I don't like it," he said. The tone of his voice indicated he was talking mostly to himself. "They're probably scarred and disgusting…" A shrug. "But my boss makes the decisions."

Almost brightly, The Lady said, "You just carry them out, like a dog." Before the man with the bright red hair could do more than sputter a bit, she added, "You're Tarov, aren't you?"

The man with the red hair – unfortunately bright, or, as Daxton Leigh would have said, the same shade of Neon Carrot as his son, Konstantin, and his daughter, Danila – said, "How did you know that?"

The Lady didn't answer.

Tarov's eyes took on a dangerous sheen. "I think you had better explain –"

Still speaking with a strange happiness, The Lady said, "You want to see the girls' faces?"

She gestured to Red, who walked forward with a phone. He held up a picture, then scrolled to another. Another. Five of the six Reina girls. Tarov squinted. "These girls look..."

"Familiar?" said The Lady. "They should. All of them are children of your coworkers. On the team."

Something flickered in Aleksandar Tarov's eyes. Fear. "Team?"

"The cheerleading team. With your daughter."

Red, waiting for that, showed Tarov the last picture: a photo of Danila with her brother Konstantin's arm over her shoulder. The look in Tarov's eyes changed: understanding joined the deepening fear, the two combining to form a burgeoning horror.

He looked back at the departing truck. Flashes of it still visible as it bounced along a rutted deer track toward its next stop on the long trip. Tarov opened his mouth to scream for it, but Red shot him with a pistol and Tarov crumpled.

Still alive, though. Gasping as The Lady leaned in close and his face and gasping mouth filled the video.

"You're just the second level of scum," she said. "But high enough I wanted you to know. To know that you've just sold your own daughter into sexual slavery, and that by the end of the day she'll be beyond anyone's grasp. Well, not anyone, I suppose." She laughed. It was an ugly, angry sound. "She'll be well within the grasp of whatever animal buys her. And I know, I know – you're worried about your son. What will poor Konstantin do without his playmate?" That laugh sounded again. "Don't worry. He'll be dead in two days."

She straightened and, obviously speaking to the Colors, said, "Now."

They took off their masks, revealing the faces of hardened, heartless men. Tarov's mouth sagged open in shock. "Garrett? Kopelson? What's going –"

The Lady cut him off with a snort. "You recognized the hired help faster than the girls you just sent away, the friends of your own children." A sigh. "But the problem with hired help is they won't always stay with you. Not if the right deal comes along." Again, she leaned in close to Tarov. She spoke quietly this time: words for Aleksandar Tarov alone. "Don't worry, though: all the men you've hired to steal our children will be dead soon, too."

Tarov turned his face toward Red. "Kopelson, you don't know –"

Moving with an effortless economy that showed she'd been waiting for Tarov to try this, The Lady put her gun against his cheek and fired. The bullet plowed through cheek, mouth, tongue, then out the other cheek. Not fatal, but Tarov was done talking.

She straightened, the man at her feet no longer a consideration. Turning to the Colors who were already donning their masks once more, she said, "Any of you having a problem with this?"

The Colors laughed, as Purple said, "With the money you're paying, you can kill my mother and I'll just ask you where I should put the body."

The others murmured their assent.

Elise winked humorlessly at Tarov, then shot him in the knees and elbows and took his phone from his coat. Two of the Colors dragged him into the forest as he screamed through a ruined mouth.

***

"Video07_Saturday_2.57_pm.mp4"

The same forest. The same bodycam. The same Colors.

The three men who had accompanied The Lady to this place had taken out small collapsible shovels and were scooping dirt over Tarov's still-living form. He managed to slur out a single, twisted question.

"Who… you?"

The Lady leaned down. Her hands entered the frame, tracing lazy circles in the dirt beside Tarov's head.

"Just one more person whose daughter you helped to sell."

Tarov hacked out blood. Several teeth could be seen in his mouth, blasted loose of their moorings, floating in the gore that remained. Maybe he was trying to speak, maybe not. The Lady yanked what remained of his jawbones apart and shoved dirt into his mouth, then stood back and watched silently as the Colors buried him alive.

"Okay let's get back and get moving. There's a lot to do before Monday. After all, we want everyone to have a nice Memorial Day."

CHAPTER 39
Understanding

I was standing near the gym when Montano exited. I watched as students filed past. Watched as body bags were carried out.

Vickers saw me. Under any other circumstances, she would have tossed me outside the police lines with all the dignity of a sack of rotten potatoes.

On this day, she just nodded. I think she could tell that I wasn't going to act like a hated reporter. I was watching, the same way they all were. Later? Later I would tell the stories. But for now I was one of many witnesses. I think she felt, as I did, that there could never be enough people seeing this. Not the horror, perhaps – people should be spared seeing the things I saw that day – but the aftermath. The moment where kids and a few teachers were ushered out of Hell and into the light.

After everyone had gone, I stayed. The gym was empty, though I knew I had only minutes before forensics teams began swarming, trying to glean any missed facts, any dangers unseen.

Again, on any other day I probably would have tried to see what was inside. It was all part of the story, wasn't it? And my job was to see, to remember, to tell.

But today, I wouldn't do that. I would stay outside the gym, because it was a place somehow both hallowed and horrible.

***

My phone rang. I didn't know it when I picked up, but Montano had just finished watching the videos Teacher and The Lady had prepared.

"I haven't forgotten my promise."

I was numb from it all, and couldn't think what in the world Montano was talking about.

Even though I said nothing, Montano knew. "The exclusive. I'll tell you everything, and speak only to you. I wanted you to know that."

"Thanks."

"But Connie?"

"Yeah?"

"I don't want you to tell the story – I want you to scream it. Shout it. People have to know."

"Most of them already do."

Montano knew what I was saying. No one outside the police on the scene and a few back at the station would know what had happened *here*. But everyone knew that, somehow, we had slipped into a world where human life was no longer the crown jewel of divine intervention or evolution or whatever other process you preferred.

It was just a product. Just another thing to be sold. To be put on a pedestal for some, to be broken in pieces for the joy of it by others.

"Maybe you're right," said Montano. He sounded dejected. More than that, there was a hopelessness in his voice that dragged a bit of the color out of my life.

"But Montano?"

"Yeah?"

"I won't just make them know. I'll make them understand."

He was silent, then said. "Good. And then do your best to make them care."

It was a tall order. I would do what I could. I'm still doing what I can.

PART FIVE:
SUFFICIENCY

AT last came death, sufficiency of death,
and that at last relieved me, I died.
I buried my beloved; it was good, I buried myself and was
gone.

- D.H. Lawrence
    "New Heaven and Earth"

CHAPTER 40
Teachable Moments

Montano sat on the chair beside Elise Easterly. He held her balaclava in his hands and turned it over and over as he waited, as though he might be able to see behind it and in so doing see behind the thoughts of the woman who had worn it.

He had waited here, like this, neither sleeping nor eating, for a night and a day and another night. Nothing but the nurses who came in and out, adjusting machines and making notes and pretending they were able to influence the fate of the woman in the bed.

In that second night, something changed. It wasn't a sound, just a feeling. He looked over and saw Elise staring back at him.

"It is finished."

Montano waited, unsure of how to respond to Elise's pronouncement. Finally, he managed to say the word that had turned over and over in his mind as he turned the mask over and over in his hands:

"Why?"

Elise, pale, weak, wan, managed a smile. "Why you? Why what we did? Why stretch it out so long?"

Montano nodded. "Sure. Let's start with those."

***

Elise stared at the ceiling as she spoke. "None of this mattered if we weren't heard or believed. We had to have a good cop who would be listened to, after it was all over. We had to have a long standoff, so the media would eat it up and everyone would be listening. So they would ask, 'Why would they do this?' and then the real story could be told: the end result of a society that teaches us to look at a person and see a plaything."

Montano stared at the ceiling as well. He had looked up the

files of the girls whose names Teacher had sent him, and suspected that Elise was seeing them in the nothing above her eyes, just as he was:

Ariel Zaharian. A girl with a smile that lit the world. She played the flute well, the oboe better. She struggled in history, but loved math.

Clarice Keppler. The one all her friends went to after a breakup, because they knew that even the infinite pain of teenage heartache could be salved by her presence.

Emily Yamada. Madison Licausi. Olivia Trachte. Briana Stahl. They weren't just files or photos, they were people.

And they, like Bella Easterly, like the six girls from Reina High School, were gone and never to be found.

***

"You helped send those girls away," Montano finally said. "And you did it in a way that guaranteed we'd never find them, so you're just as guilty."

He looked down, back at the mask. He didn't want to see the woman beside him. He needed answers, but he was damned if he'd look at her.

Elise surprised him by saying, "No, we *want* you to find them." And now Montano did look at her. He searched her face for the joke, the trick, and failed to find either.

"I don't underst –"

"We want you to find them all, Detective Montano. But for that to happen, the world has to change. And what if people listen? To a good cop? To his honest partner? To a respected computer expert and a few journalists who already knew that we're encouraging people to send our children off to be enslaved every time we put money in a pornographer's pocket."

Again, Montano had nothing to say to that. Elise smiled a too-bright smile. "Cheer up, Detective. 3,287 children are kidnapped each day. That's 136 an hour. You only lost eleven over several days. And I only lost one." A tear glistened in her eye. She blinked it back. "So we're the lucky ones, right?"

Montano looked away again. "Tell me how to find the girls. Help me –"

"I think I'm done talking now."

Montano tried. He cajoled, he whined, he wheedled. Elise said nothing else until her court-appointed lawyer showed up. And then she said nothing else at all, because the court-appointed lawyer allowed her to freshen up.

Three swipes with the brush that Eberhardt had found on her person.

One flick of her wrist to paint her lips with the lipstick: a bright, garish color better suited to a teen who hasn't quite learned how to match her makeup.

The lawyer told Elise Easterly the usual: I'm here to help, it's best to be honest, etc. etc. All the usual platitudes and lies that existed in a system that pretends to fairness.

Elise Easterly finished freshening up. She blotted her lips. Then she carefully bit off the rest of the lipstick and swallowed it.

***

They told Montano first. Everyone knew who he was. Everyone knew what he had done, and the part he had played in the Easterlys' plans. He was in the hospital cafeteria, drinking coffee, thinking of what he could or should do next, when they found and told him.

For someone who orchestrated the takeover of a high school, the murder of students and staff, and the sale of the children of several high-profile industry giants, burying a bit of poison in a tube of lipstick was child's play.

They brought Montano into her room, where she still stared at the empty space above her, though now with eyes that could see nothing at all.

"Some kind of neurotoxin," said the doctor with *just* the right amount of soothing, professionally-honed grief. "We did what we could, but…"

Elise Easterly's body was alive. But everything else – everything that had once made her not merely an organism, but a living soul – was gone.

Montano watched the doctors take away her empty shell. "And we're the lucky ones," he said.

CHAPTER 41
Homework

Contrary to the popular adage, time does not heal all wounds. Some remain open forever. But time does allow us to view them with less pain. And it allows for some things to balance those pains.

Montano sat at his desk several months after seeing Elise Easterly. The reports were done, the paperwork filed. There were still investigations, and hearings, and the media was still afire with what had happened. No one had forgotten. Not yet.

Montano stared at his computer monitor. Like his phone, the background was a picture of Bella. Her hand, thin and loose. Her arm, branded as a sign that she was less person than possession.

Her bracelet, which she had somehow kept with her. Montano hoped that bracelet had given her some small measure of light in that dark prison.

Eberhardt came into the bullpen. Sat down across from his partner. "You hear about Delroy?"

Xavier Delroy had already been sent to two different prisons. Word was that no matter where he went, there were plenty of men eager to show him what it felt like to be a punching bag, a plaything, a possession.

The day before, Montano had gotten a call from a friend who worked the prison Xavier had last been stationed at. So he knew what Eberhardt was talking about. "'Accident' in the laundry room," he said.

Eberhardt nodded. "Paralyzed from the neck down. And it couldn't have happened to a nicer person."

"No, it couldn't," said Montano.

It wasn't a joke, so no one laughed.

And it didn't change any of what had happened, so no one

smiled, either.

"I still don't understand why he wouldn't just talk," said Eberhardt. "Just tell Teacher what was up with Novi, and Teacher would have let him go."

Montano nodded. "I keep going back to what he told us about there being worse things than death. I think as bad as he's had it since everything blew up, there are men out there – his business partners – who will make it even worse on him if he betrays them."

"They'd have to be seriously bad, and seriously powerful," said Eberhardt.

"Just the kinds of people you'd want working with teens," agreed Montano.

***

The bullpen had several TVs running off to the side. One of them was airing a report, and when Montano saw who it was, he got up and walked over to the TV.

"She's good," said Eberhardt as they listened to the report – the tease story for a series of exposés that earned or were at least shortlisted for just about every major award that year:

"... still no leads as to where the girls have been taken, though with every day that passes, new revelations come to light regarding the men who assisted Thomas and Elise Easterly with their plans to take Reina High School hostage. The hostage-takers all had ties to Entercom, and police have named them as persons of interest in various missing persons cases: all girls, some as young as thirteen.

"As for the six Reina High School students who are still missing, police have no leads as to their whereabouts. I'll be airing a three-part exclusive interview with Detective Rick Montano, who was the lead on the Reina case and who has recently assumed command of the Trafficking Department. We'll be talking about how this tragedy could have been averted, as well as the links we're uncovering between 'adult' entertainment, the sex trade, and human trafficking."

The reporter paused, then said, "I hope you'll tune in this evening at six o'clock. Until then, this is Connie Kendall, Channel Nine."

The shot cut back to the studio. To the other news crowding for the day's attention. Montano and Eberhardt went back to their desks.

There was work to do.

AUTHOR'S NOTE

Michaelbrent here. Connie Kendall – as smart and snarky and witty as I hope you found her – has done her job, and has gone the way of all my literary creations: back into a well-appointed, if cluttered, room in my mind; and perhaps (if I did my job well) in yours, too. She's not locked up, just resting – waiting to come out and play again, should the story permit, or the audience demand.

But for now, it is just me – though because Connie and I share some traits, you might see her peeking out occasionally as I write my Author's Note. Like when I mimic her enjoyment of a good section break.

**

Here are some things I believe:

I believe that some things in this world are good.

I believe that some of them are evil.

I believe that not everyone who does a good thing is a good person at heart; and I believe that some evil things are done by good people who either knew no better or had no other choice.

The last two – when good people do bad, and when bad people do good – are the "gray areas" that define each of us: not just the moment where we fall into something that may be against our nature, but the *following* moment… where we choose to climb into the light, or allow ourselves to tumble into and become one with the dark.

**

Here's another thing I believe: *pornography is bad* and *it hurts the world*.

The more I researched this book, the more I found that the true horror wasn't the idea I started out with – a pair of angry parents who cooked up their best "let the punishment fit the crime" scenario

– but the way pornography has influenced humanity for the worse; the way that influence continues to grow, both in size and in depth of darkness.

There is a link between the huge (and I mean *huge*) porn industry, the sexualization and exploitation of teens and children (largely female), and the horrifying world of human trafficking. That should be obvious, but there are still a lot of naysayers.

I feel like we're watching a replay of the debate over tobacco as it was a hundred years ago – where on the one hand, people who tried to get the product restricted were labeled as crazies, religious fundamentalists, extremists, and so forth and so on; and on the other hand, you could find ad campaigns proclaiming, *"More doctors smoke Camels than any other cigarette!!"*[1]

Tobacco companies also went after people via their physicians this way: telling them, essentially, "Look, they're going to smoke regardless, so let's at least get them to smoke healthier brands."

Eventually, the evidence that tobacco was kinda, you know, *killing* people became incontrovertible. At which point, the tobacco companies quickly repented of their ways, gave up lying, and switched over to growing wholesome products.

I'm kidding – they just doubled down in other countries where they're still allowed to target kids with cartoon ads and lie through their (cigarette-stained) teeth about how Awesome Cigarettes Are!

***

So far as I can see, pornography is following similar trends: tell everyone it's good for you (e.g., watching it as a couple can be a good, romantic adventure that gets the engines revving at home); or that it's natural, no harm done (we're just made this way!); or at least

---

[1] This was an actual ad, for those who aren't aware. Interestingly, the ad didn't mention that the "study" methodology went like this: 1) Give a physician a free box of Camel cigarettes. 2) Ask which brand they smoke.

that it's better than the alternative (wouldn't want those horny teens out Raping and Whatnot!).

And, when/if one country closes up shop for pornographers, they move on to the next country, or double down in their already-profitable regions… and just hope, hope, *hope* that no one finds any big smoking guns, like:

… the mental health problems that seem far more prevalent in the porn industry than in other professions; or

… the risk of life-changing health problems (like STDs) that keep having "outbreaks" no matter how many safety precautions are (claimed to be) instituted; or

… the fact that so much of the porn industry involves getting the "talent" hooked on drugs; or

… that porn viewing teaches people to look at other humans not as valuable people, full of experiences and skills and great, wonderful ideas, but simply as *things*; or

… the statistical certainty that if a person watches enough porn, they will have watched at least some *involving minor children* in other countries; or

… all the teens that are kidnapped to feed sex trafficking needs; or

… that so much of porn involves depictions of one person hurting the other.[2]

---

[2] There are people who argue that this is because porn includes BDSM depictions, which on its face seems at least a passably rational argument. It loses a lot of weight, however, given that most people looking at such depiction didn't get there by searching for "A reasonable depiction of BDSM interactions" and then letting the internet do its magic. They were looking for "teen sex" or one of the other big searches that runs the world wide web, and ended up seeing something that depicts one person being graphically tortured. This is especially harmful when you're talking

***

I'm not urging a return to the good ol' days, where sex was done in a windowless room, on the longest night of the year, for breeding purposes only – and even then only with both parties closing their eyes and praying to deity to forgive them for their Lustful Antics. Partly because that was never actually a thing, but also because it sounds terrible and marginalizes what can and should be a marvelous, healthy, good part of human existence.

But pornography is not a marvelous, healthy, or good thing. Pornography doesn't teach humans how to make connections with other humans, it teaches us that the person we look at – or, perhaps, have sex with IRL – is there solely for our amusement. That when we're done, we should be able to discard, to move on, and to forget what damage may be left behind.

I'm also not going to say we need to run around covering up every iteration of the human form – like crafting marble lederhosen for the David (a masterpiece of art), or drawing an Olde Tyme striped bathing suit over Botticelli's rendition of Venus. But there's a pretty clear difference between those and some of the most popular websites that exist primarily in short snippets of people having sex and nothing more.

I'm a big believer in art. But I also believe that artists have a responsibility to the consumers, to the audience, to the world. And saying, "But it's my *art!*" shouldn't give me or anyone else a license

---

about kids stumbling onto these sites – either purposefully or accidentally – and whose first sexual experience is thus linked to concepts of domination and violence that may not reflect the rest of the world's hopes or desires when they think of sexual interactions.

Besides that, one of the best ways to counter an argument is to get someone to argue about something else – and arguments over whether it's BDSM or "violent porn" seems likely to do exactly that, rather than focus first on the basic question: does this stuff hurt people? To which the answer seems to be a resounding *yes*.

to act like a sociopath, or to function as an all-purpose defense to any accusation that I'm being a moral sinkhole so that I can make a buck.

Are there some situations where figuring out if something is "pornography" or "art" will be hard? Sure. But again, those gray areas are where we define (or lose) our humanity. And just ignoring the question because it's hard, isn't really ignoring it at all... it's just choosing one side by default: in this case, the side that depends on a steady influx of not-necessarily-willing flesh to survive.

***

I feel compelled here to say that, though I believe pornography is an absolute blight, I don't believe everyone involved in that industry is evil. Some might be making a bad choice out of ignorance (and I, at least, find it hard to point a finger at someone who genuinely doesn't know any better). Some may have no choice at all, as in the people who are trafficked into the business of sex.

But that's a question of intent. Intent is notoriously hard to judge, since it involves people's most private feelings, and can be lied about fairly easily.

So I'll avoid the question of evil people, and urge readers of this note to do the same.

But pornography isn't a person, it's just a thing. An act, an action, a business. And those statistics quoted by Teacher and The Lady? They're true. Again, pornography – as a practice, as a business – is a bad thing, and we need to talk to our kids about that, and focus on how to get rid of it.

***

Another thing I believe: I believe that horror is – or at least, can be – the best and brightest and most redemptive of genres. It is the one that takes its protagonists, hacks away anything not truly *them*, and then tosses them into a deep, dark pit where the monsters dwell.

Then, with luck or courage or friendship or grace, those hapless souls may climb out of the darkness and into the light. They may survive, and in so doing they may show the readers that survival is possible; that it is never too dark to find hope and salvation – be it physical, emotional, or spiritual.

But sometimes, the monsters win. And sometimes, I think, they *need* to win – at least in the story. Especially when the story is about a thing that is really happening in today's world.

Malignant isn't a true story, in the sense that the events depicted actually occurred. But it's truth in the sense that the horror at the heart of the book is still alive and strong, and waiting for the right moments of darkness to consume our children.

So, in *Malignant*, there are no happy endings. Because the monster is alive in the real world, and so it cannot and must not die in the story. That would make the story not just a fiction, but a lie – which is something no story should ever be.

***

Malignant is a horror story, in its purest sense – or at least, I hope it is. The things that happen in this story are horrific, and should cause readers to shudder and squirm. And, worst of all, they are representatives of real things that happen to real people.

Teacher and The Lady are not based on actual people, of course – in that there have never been (so far as I can discover) a pair of tech-minded criminal masterminds willing to go to any length to exact revenge on those who hurt their daughter.

But there *are* parents whose children have been taken.

There *are* people who prey on innocence, and people who drive that predatory practice with their own need and desire.

Do I think everyone who looks at a "naughty picture" on the internet is evil? Of course not.

But will I call an industry evil if it traffics in images and acts marketed as healthy representations of human interaction when in fact they deny the depth and breadth of all that makes us human? Yes I do, and yes I will.

And, having called it evil, I must let others know the same, and encourage them to think before clicking that link, to talk to their kids about the difference between loving someone and using them, to look at their own lovers as receptacles for joy rather than just objects to be used.

We are more than possessions.

Or at least, we can be.

And, to be sure, we should be.

- Michaelbrent Collings

GET A FREE BOOK!

Sign up for Michaelbrent's newsletter and you'll get a free book (or maybe a few!) with nothing ever to do or buy. Just go to bit.ly/mbcfree to sign up for your freebie, and you're good to go! You can also visit his website at WrittenInsomnia.com.

A REQUEST FROM THE AUTHOR:

If you loved this book, I would really appreciate a short review on Amazon (or anywhere else you'd like to post it).

Don't worry about anything fancy – just a single sentence is *beyond* wonderful. Even, "This book good. Me like this book. This book a booky book of bookness!" is fantastic.

And dropping a review really makes a difference, because the more reviews there are, the more likely retailers are to show this book to others, which enables me to take care of my family, and to keep sharing stories with the world.

Thanks again!

- MbC

Acknowledgments

No book exists in a bubble – they are born slowly, often painfully, in a world that involves a host of other concerns. Paying the bills, medical issues, and just figuring out day to day life are all vying for the same brain space that I use for stories, and so I thank sincerely everyone who took a bit of their time to free up a bit of mine.

Thanks to my parents and to my wife's – you're all my moms and dads, and in this extraordinarily trying time, it's been good to know that I have people like you looking out for me.

Thanks to the Collings Cult, for supporting this book when it first went out to the world. Special thanks to those who (as always) found errors and so kept me from looking dumber than absolutely necessary. Folks like Julie Balla, Priscilla Bettis, Bonnie Burskey, Doreen Fernandes, Sean Flanagan, Emily Haynes, Trevor Holyoak, Logan Kearsley, Jeff Lanham, Jeffrey McMillan, Victoria Morton, John O'Regan, Jen Potcher, Christina Smith, Dennis Smith, Cher Spradlin, B. Jayne Stenstrom, Barb Stoner, and everyone else who took a moment to point out a mistake – thank you all!

And thank you most especially to my kids and my wife. "I couldn't do this without you" is something I hear artists say – and it's true enough in this case. But more than that, without you all… I wouldn't even want to.

FOLLOW MbC

Twitter: twitter.com/mbcollingsv
Facebook: facebook.com/MichaelbrentCollings
YouTube: youtube.com/michaelbrentcollingsauthor
Patreon: patreon.com/michaelbrentcollings
Amazon: amazon.com/author/michaelbrentcollings

*

SUPPORT MbC ON PATREON

Sign up for MbC's Patreon page and get EXCLUSIVE merchandise, free short stories, and chances at cool prizes like one-of-a-kind collectors editions and more! Just go to http://patreon.com/michaelbrentcollings and sign up!

*

GET MbC MERCH

Want to grab merch and swag? Check out MbC's merch page at http://teespring.com/stores/michaelbrent-collings, and grab tees, sweaters, mugs, and more fun than you can shake a stick at!

*

FOR WRITERS:

Michaelbrent has helped hundreds of people write, publish, and market their books through articles, audio, video, and online courses. For his online courses, check out http://michaelbrentcollings.thinkific.com

*

ABOUT THE AUTHOR

Michaelbrent is an internationally-bestselling author, produced screenwriter, and member of the Writers Guild of America, but his greatest jobs are being a husband and father. See a complete list of Michaelbrent's books at writteninsomnia.com.

NOVELS BY MICHAELBRENT COLLINGS

SYNCHRONICITY
THE FOREST
STRANGER STILL
SCAVENGER HUNT
TERMINAL
DARKLING SMILES
PREDATORS
THE DARKLIGHTS
THE LONGEST CON
THE HOUSE THAT DEATH BUILT
THE DEEP
TWISTED
THIS DARKNESS LIGHT
CRIME SEEN
STRANGERS
DARKBOUND
BLOOD RELATIONS:
    A GOOD MORMON GIRL MYSTERY
THE HAUNTED
APPARITION
THE LOON
MR. GRAY (aka THE MERIDIANS)
RUN
RISING FEARS

THE COLONY SAGA:
THE COLONY: GENESIS (THE COLONY, Vol. 1)
THE COLONY: RENEGADES (THE COLONY, Vol. 2)
THE COLONY: DESCENT (THE COLONY, VOL. 3)
THE COLONY: VELOCITY (THE COLONY, VOL. 4)
THE COLONY: SHIFT (THE COLONY, VOL. 5)
THE COLONY: BURIED (THE COLONY, VOL. 6)
THE COLONY: RECKONING (THE COLONY, VOL. 7)
THE COLONY OMNIBUS
THE COLONY OMNIBUS II

THE COMPLETE COLONY SAGA BOX SET

**YOUNG ADULT AND
MIDDLE GRADE FICTION:**

THE SWORD CHRONICLES
THE SWORD CHRONICLES: CHILD OF THE EMPIRE
THE SWORD CHRONICLES: CHILD OF SORROWS
THE SWORD CHRONICLES: CHILD OF ASH

THE RIDEALONG
PETER & WENDY: A TALE OF THE LOST
　(aka HOOKED: A TRUE FAERIE TALE)
KILLING TIME

THE BILLY SAGA:
BILLY: MESSENGER OF POWERS (BOOK 1)
BILLY: SEEKER OF POWERS (BOOK 2)
BILLY: DESTROYER OF POWERS (BOOK 3)
THE COMPLETE BILLY SAGA (BOOKS 1-3)

Copyright © 2021 by Michaelbrent Collings
All rights reserved.
No part of this book may be reproduced or transmitted in any form or by any means, electronic or mechanical, including photocopying, recording, or by any information storage and retrieval system, without written permission from the author. For information send request to info@writteninsomnia.com.
NOTE: This is a work of fiction. Names, characters, places, and incidents either are the product of the author's imagination or are used fictitiously, and any resemblance to actual persons, living or dead, business establishments, events, or locales is entirely coincidental. The scanning, uploading, and distribution of this book via the internet or via any other means without the permission of the author is illegal and punishable by law. Please purchase only authorized electronic editions, and do not participate in or encourage electronic piracy of copyrighted materials.
Your support of the author's rights is appreciated.
Cover image elements by zieusin under license by Shutterstock
And by sframe and kasezo2 under license from Depositphotos.com.
Cover design by Michaelbrent Collings.

website: http://writteninsomnia.com
email: info@writteninsomnia.com

For more information on Michaelbrent's books, including specials and sales; and for info about
signings, appearances, and media,
check out his webpage,
Like his Facebook fan page,
follow him on Twitter,
or
subscribe to his YouTube channel.